Praise for the works of Rebecca K. Jones

Stemming the Tide

An excellent legal thriller by a strong writer who has developed a main character who we can root for. The book will be enjoyed by readers who like strong characters, complex plotting, a few angst filled moments and a satisfying ending.

-*The Lesbian Review*

Stemming the Tide by Rebecca K. Jones is an exciting and action-filled mystery and intrigue novel. Those of you who love immersive crime novels filled with twists, turns, angst and thrills should definitely get this novel.

-Betty H., *NetGalley*

Steadying the Ark

Steadying the Ark is a fantastic debut—I cannot wait to read more from Rebecca K. Jones in the future.

-Natalie T., *NetGalley*

Hard to believe this story came from someone who has never had a book published, it's that good. If this is a sample of Ms. Jones's skills as an author, I look forward to reading her next book because I'm sure there will be others. Very enjoyable read.

-Bonnie S., *NetGalley*

After reading *Steadying the Ark* by Rebecca K. Jones, I must tell you how impressed I am with this book and the author. This is the debut novel for Ms. Jones, and honestly, I'm having a really hard time finding anything to criticize. The story is practically flawless and very entertaining. I can't wait to read more from this author. If you love a courtroom drama filled with excitement, suspense, and thrills, then this is the book for you.

-Betty H., *NetGalley*

STAYING THE COURSE

COURSE

REBECCA K. JONES

Other Bella Books by Rebecca K. Jones

Steadying the Ark
Stemming the Tide

About the Author

Criminal appeals attorney by day and crime writer by night, Rebecca K. Jones lives with her two chihuahuas in the Phoenix area. Her short stories and translations have been published in *Ellery Queen's Mystery Magazine*, *Sherlock Holmes Mystery Magazine*, and a number of anthologies. This is the third book in the Mackenzie Wilson series.

STAYING THE COURSE

REBECCA K. JONES

BELLA
BOOKS

2024

Bella Books, Inc.
P.O. Box 10543
Tallahassee, FL 32302

First Edition - 2024

Editor: Heather Flournoy
Cover Designer: Kayla Mancuso

ISBN: 978-1-64247-594-4

PUBLISHER'S NOTE

Dedication

To Elizabeth Reamer, who is a fierce ally, a formidable foe, and has probably never dated a serial killer. Everyone should be so lucky as to have a Jess on their side.

PROLOGUE

She threw the phone across the room and watched it bounce. She knew she should check the screen for damage but didn't bother to get up from the couch. She was just so *tired* lately. She barely had the energy to get through the workday. She certainly didn't have the energy for the conversation she was about to be forced into. *If* he actually showed up. He never had been great with follow-through.

She looked around her living room and considered what she'd have to change. The coffee table was glass-topped marble, all sharp corners and hard edges. The television stand could tip over. The afghan her mother had knitted for her was probably a choking hazard. Everything in her life was about to change, but the truth was she liked her life as it was. She liked being in charge of her time. She liked kickball and late nights with friends and the routine she'd built for herself.

The doorbell rang, and she reluctantly went to the front door. She glanced out the window, and there he was, smiling behind a bouquet of daisies. That smile that still made her feel like the prettiest girl in the world, though she was on the wrong side of thirty. She hadn't been able to believe that someone as handsome and worldly as he would be interested in a nobody like her. He'd brought daisies to their first date, too, and by the time they left the restaurant, the flowers were too wilted to save. So he threw them away and went into the grocery store next door, came out with a fresh batch, smiling that smile, and it had been all over for her from there. She hadn't even told her mom, knowing that she would only find reasons to criticize. He was too encumbered, too unsettled, too…whatever. All the things she liked best about him, her mother would hate.

Even now, despite the arguments they'd had over the last week, the back-and-forth and round-and-round that never seemed to lead anywhere, she felt a brief surge of pleasure and relief when she saw him. If anyone could help her find a path through the darkness that was closing in on her, it was him.

He handed her the flowers and bent down to take his boots off. The hunting knife he wore strapped to his ankle glinted in the overhead light. "You look terrible, Pooh-bear."

She deflated. She knew she didn't look her best lately, what with one thing and another. She was bloated and couldn't bear the idea of the gym. But still…what a thing to say. When they'd first started seeing each other, he constantly praised her looks, her intelligence, even her clothes. As the months passed, though, the compliments had faded into memory. She couldn't remember the last time she'd received one of those precious gifts.

"I didn't think I'd see you tonight."

"Yeah, well, I didn't think you'd keep me out." She could smell the alcohol on his breath. She shouldn't have let him in. She should have made it clearer over the phone that he wasn't welcome in her house. Not anymore. Not after the terrible things he'd said.

She took the flowers into the kitchen and busied herself finding a vase, trimming the stems, arranging them in ice water. Out of the corner of her eye, she saw him grab a beer out of her fridge without asking. Of course, that's why she had them, right? She'd paid attention that first night and kept her fridge stocked since.

"Is that a good idea?" she asked, trying to keep the judgment out of her voice. Whatever was coming, she knew she'd be better off if he was sober. Not that he'd been violent. Well, not *very*, at any rate. It's not like he hit her all the time or anything. He'd never broken a bone, never even bruised her face. Sometimes he just got carried away—and he certainly wasn't the only one. She'd known lots of men who were the same way. All things considered, he wasn't that bad. But she knew the conversation they were about to have was going to be emotional. Contentious, even. Sobriety seemed like a good starting place.

"Why not?" he asked and popped the cap off on the edge of the counter. He drank down half the bottle in one swallow, his Adam's apple bobbing up and down. She wondered how many he'd already had and wished that just once a DUI patrol would have pulled him over.

"I don't know what you think coming here is going to change," she said. She looked down at her pajamas. Black. Oversized. She crossed her arms over her chest to make herself look even less inviting.

He dropped onto a stool at the bar and set his bottle on the counter. "I just think we should talk about it. Face-to-face. I think we should talk like civilized people, where you listen to my opinion, for once, and then we make a decision together, instead of you going off on your own and doing whatever the hell you want."

She sighed. "You've made your opinion clear. I've listened to it. But this is my choice, not ours."

He studied the bottle in front of him, empty now. She looked at it, too, trying to figure out what was so interesting about it. Her head was killing her—the afternoon's tears coming back to bite her.

"That's the thing of it," he said. "I don't think you really *have* listened to my opinion. If you had, you'd see I'm right. You're just being an obstinate little bitch."

Suddenly, the bottle shattered. Her first instinct was to grab a broom and warn him not to get up—he'd cut his feet. But then she saw that he was gripping the neck of the bottle and pointing the broken edge at her.

When the screaming started, she wasn't sure at first if the noise was coming from his throat or her own.

CHAPTER ONE

Mackenzie Wilson yawned. The heat made her so sleepy. She pulled her sun hat lower over her eyes and contemplated the afternoon stretching before her. It couldn't be earlier than four, probably, so another two hours before they could reasonably head back to the room to shower and get ready for dinner. Their seating was at seven. She scratched her arm, skin dry from the salt water. Two hours would be enough time for four more piña coladas in their tiny plastic cups. Maybe more, if the waiter came by regularly, and he had so far. She had picked the resort, and the reviews of the service—especially the beach service—had been one of its big selling points.

Mack had never been a fan of "the beach." Between Ohio, New Hampshire, and Arizona, she'd never lived near an ocean, and she'd grown up afraid of the water. But when Beth Shankar, Mack's new—well, girlfriend was too strong of a word, but friend wasn't nearly strong enough—had found a flight deal to Cancun, Mack had for once agreed.

Mack had set up her out-of-office response, alerting those attempting to contact her at the Tucson District Attorney's Office that she was out of phone and email reach until Monday, and she had mostly resisted the urge to check, had just left her phone in the beach bag she and Beth shared. The piña coladas helped, as did Beth's delight at the chance to frolic in the gentle surf. The most helpful thing, though, was definitely the way Beth's dark skin looked in her bright-red bikini.

They hadn't been seeing each other long. After they'd met during the final days of an investigation into a serial killer the previous year and Beth had given Mack her number, Mack had resisted the urge to call for six weeks. It was Sergeant Dave Barton who finally convinced her.

"You only live once," he said over dinner one night. "Call the pretty girl. Take a chance, Mack."

Mack didn't know if it was the wine that made her vulnerable or the fact that Dave was talking to her like he would talk to a teenage daughter. Either way, she'd called the *very* pretty Beth the next morning. Hadn't even agonized about whether texting was the safer first move. Just picked up the phone and dialed, like she'd been doing it all her life. She still panicked when Beth answered, but she'd recovered and managed to ask her out to dinner.

Since then, six months had passed. They saw each other once or twice a week, usually, depending on their schedules. Mack was surprised at how easy it all was—Beth seemed to genuinely enjoy their time together but had never pushed for more. Sometimes, Mack wondered if Beth was seeing other people. She wouldn't always pick up her phone, not that Mack called her often, but sometimes it took a day or more to hear back from a text. When Beth did get back to her, however, she always seemed happy to talk, and they always had a good time together. Besides, Mack reminded herself, Beth had been the one to suggest the Cancun trip.

She finished her drink, which didn't have quite enough rum in it. Two more hours on the beach. She redid the math in her head. Maybe she could convince Beth to leave the water early, which would give them more time in the room before dinner. Heck, if they left the beach now, Mack was sure they could come up with other things to do for the entire rest of the weekend.

Drops of cool water falling on her bare stomach shook Mack out of her reverie. Beth was standing over her, fresh out of the Caribbean, laughing.

"Were you napping?"

Mack put her hand on Beth's thigh. "Maybe dozing a little," she admitted. "Your skin is so cold."

Beth shook her head, intentionally spraying Mack even more. "You're flushed," she said. "You've been up here on the sand too long. If you were in the water, you'd find it delightful."

She handed Mack a bottle of sunscreen, reached into their shared beach bag with one hand, and signaled to the waiter with the other. "Two more of these," she called out, holding up Mack's cup. She fished Mack's phone out of the beach bag and glanced at the screen. "You're blowing up in here."

Mack grudgingly looked at her notifications. Her mother, asking if there was any risk of hurricanes in Cancun. Her dentist, reminding her of her annual cleaning the following week. Jess Lafayette, her best friend and colleague, setting up lunch for Monday. Then seven texts all from Dave Barton. Mack sighed and tossed her phone back in the bag without reading Dave's messages. She'd respond when she got home, and until then she wasn't interested in anything he might have to say about the cartel wars raging outside the resort zone.

"Remember the cop who was with me when we met?" she asked.

"Mmm," Beth hummed. "Sorta. Bald, kind of short?"

"Yeah," Mack said. "Really good guy. Dedicated detective, always brings me solid cases, went out on a limb for me in that situation last year." She hated admitting that she had been the lead suspect in a series of murders that had actually been committed by Jess' fiancé, but Dave's role in that investigation had cemented their friendship. Mack had even started having dinner with Dave and his wife, Meredith, once a month. "Anyway, he's been on my ass about this trip ever since I told him we were coming to Mexico."

"Why?"

The waiter handed them their drinks, and they clicked cups before each taking a long swallow.

Mack flinched. "Brain freeze." She waited for the pain to pass. "He thinks it's super dangerous here. With the cartels and stuff. No matter how much I tell him that Cancun is safe, he doesn't believe me."

"He's a cop," Beth said. "Wouldn't he know more about that stuff than you? The violence, I mean?"

Mack shook her head. "He does sex crimes and domestic violence. Not drug cases. I have three drug rips gone wrong on my caseload right now, and I texted the case agents when you suggested coming down here. They all promised me it was safe—one of them is bringing his wife and kids next month."

"What's a drug rip?"

Mack was surprised. Normally, Beth avoided talking about Mack's work, and Mack was used to biting her tongue. Beth's life had been blessedly free from the terrible things that one person can do to another—except, of course, for the time she'd found a corpse in a plastic tub at a trailhead—and she liked keeping it that way. Mack had gotten used to not talking about crime outside the office and was pleased by how natural the change was becoming.

"It's when people meet up for a drug deal, but one really intends to rob the other." Mack paused to make sure she chose the least violent way to describe a crime she had seen far too much of already. "Someone often ends up dead—either the buyer or the seller, or sometimes even a third party who isn't a part of it."

Beth shuddered and finished her drink. "I'm sorry I asked."

Mack felt a momentary sting of rejection. She and her ex-girlfriend, Dr. Anna Lapin, might have talked too much about work, but at least Anna had understood where she was coming from. "Yeah. They can be…grim, I guess."

Beth held out her hand for Mack. "Let's go in the water," she said. "At least sharks only kill you when they're hungry."

Mack stood, stretching. She remembered a documentary she had recently watched late one night while waiting for a verdict, which claimed sharks had been observed killing for sport, and she considered bringing that up but thought better of it. "Actually," she said, fighting back her fear, "that sounds great."

CHAPTER TWO

"You're stupidly tan."

Mack looked up to see Jess leaning against her office doorframe, arms folded and a disdainful glare firmly in place. She gestured at the empty chair in front of her desk. "Good morning to you, too. It's nice to be back, yes, I missed you, too, and I had a very nice vacation, thank you so much."

Jess rolled her eyes and dropped into the chair. "Your refusal to wear sunscreen will never not shock me. It's like you want to be a withered old crone before you're forty."

Mack bit the inside of her cheek, resisting the urge to return the insult. She had applied sunscreen every two hours the whole weekend. She'd even bought a second bottle when the first ran out Sunday morning, worried that the four hours before their flight home would be too much for her naturally pale skin. Mack wasn't sure that Jess had any right to be handing out skincare advice—her friend's two-year assignment in Homicide had already aged her. Instead, she fished the souvenir parrot pen she'd bought at the Cancun airport out of her purse.

Jess smiled and tucked the pen into her bun. "I have to tell you the news."

"News?" Mack asked. "I missed one workday."

"All I have are rumors and innuendo, but it seems, based on her empty office this morning, that Theresa Henderson was boxed and walked."

"Really? Theresa? What happened?"

Jess shrugged. "They're saying she was having an inappropriate relationship with a detective that she didn't disclose, and Campbell can't risk the scandal—"

"Because it's an election year," Mack chimed in. It was a familiar refrain, used to justify all kinds of odd decisions over the previous five months. The office had become a game of musical chairs, with all the high-profile, low-productivity senior attorneys struggling to keep their places. "Still," she said, leaning back in her chair and rubbing her neck. "That should be easy to fix. Just disclose."

"Not so easy," Jess said. "Since she was specifically seeking out cases her boyfriend—her *married* boyfriend, I might add—worked on. Apparently, he had a habit of skimming from the drugs he collected during search warrants, and she was helping him cover it up."

Mack whistled. "Shit."

"Indeed," Jess said. She let a respectful moment pass in silence. "So, ready to get back to work? We're supposed to speak to the new-hire class after lunch."

Mack leaned forward and scrolled through her Outlook calendar with dismay. "I haven't forgotten. I'm slammed, though. Any chance you can do it by yourself?"

Jess shook her head and pushed herself out of the chair. "No chance," she said. "You made our slide show, and without you to play the straight man I'll have no one to make jokes to."

"Make jokes about, you mean."

"Shoe, fits, etcetera."

Mack put her earbuds in and worked through the morning without stopping, sorting emails and drafting two quick motions with the latest Thao and the Get Down Stay Down album on repeat. The only pressing thing she hadn't been able to take care of was a cryptic email from Nick Diaz, a defense attorney she'd become friendly with over the years. She mentally scanned her heavy caseload. Nothing with Nick, so why had he emailed her? It wasn't as if they'd ever socialized.

When she finally looked up, thirsty and aware of the beginnings of a headache gathering behind her eyes, it was already 12:15 and she was late to meet Jess for lunch at the sandwich shop down the street.

She grabbed her phone, noticing three missed texts from Jess.

12:05: *Where are you?*

12:10: *Are you ok?*

12:15: *I'm on my way back. I grabbed us salads. But not the one you like. Retribution.*

Mack smiled. *We all have to make a stand sometime*, she responded. She checked to see if Beth had texted or emailed. Nothing. Not that that meant anything. They'd just spent over three full days together, and Beth's job as an engineer for Raytheon in a secured facility in the northern part of town kept her busy during the workday. Mack wasn't even sure she was allowed to take her phone into her office with her. Still, she was unexpectedly stung by the lack of contact.

She opened their text thread. *Hey!* she typed and deleted. The exclamation point was too much. Reeked of desperation. *My desk is much less fun than the beach was*, she tried next. No, "desk" wasn't right. She looked at the message, trying to decide whether "office" or "job" worked better.

Jess cleared her throat, and Mack looked up.

"If you bailed on lunch to stare at your phone," Jess said, "I'll just take this extra salad home with me and have it for dinner."

Mack blushed and hit send. "Desk" would have to do.

"Sorry," she said, putting her phone in her purse and accepting the plastic container. "Thank you for this, even if it is"—she looked at the contents of the bowl—"egg salad and mixed greens?"

Jess shrugged and sat, spreading her own lunch out over the open files on Mack's desk. "I think I still owed you for something, anyway, and don't pretend you don't need the protein. That rabbit food you normally get isn't enough to get you through a teaching afternoon."

They ate quickly and reviewed the slide show on coping with evidentiary issues in trial that Mack had developed for the training they gave to every new-hire class. It was dry material but crucial for attorneys who wanted to be trial dogs, which most new hires usually did. People who didn't think they wanted to be in a courtroom didn't usually choose prosecution.

Jess glanced at her watch and took a final drink of her Diet Coke. "Let's go impart some wisdom."

The training room, covered with dreary gray government paint, was in the basement, cold even in the heat of a Tucson summer. With the exception of the district attorney's seal on one wall, there was nothing to distinguish it from any other drab training room in the county, even the classrooms at the jail. The level of training provided, however, was unparalleled. Mack was grateful every day for the weeks she herself had spent underground in that room as a new hire, learning from some of the best and most dedicated prosecutors in the country. A sense of awe surged through her that now she was one of the attorneys called on by the office to provide that kind of training. It was an honor every time.

She surveyed the class as Jess introduced herself. Six of them, four women and two men, none of whom looked older than twenty-five. They'd probably gone straight from undergrad to law school, and this was their first "real" job. They were dressed for the occasion—all in suits, although one of the men had his jacket over his chair and his tie loosened. This was the third week of their training and, in theory, they could have been in business-casual garb.

The presentation started smoothly, and the class seemed engaged and enthusiastic as they moved through the slide show's hypotheticals.

"Okay," Jess said, clicking to the next slide. "In this example, you are cross-examining the defendant in a drug-sale case when he says that a guy named Joe actually put the meth in his pocket right before the police rolled up. What do you do?"

Mack was distracted by a rustling noise and looked at the class. Five eager faces looked back at her. The man in the loosened tie, however, was looking into his silver hard-sided briefcase.

"Hey, there"—Mack glanced at the name tag in front of him—"Tyler, do you need something?"

The young man looked up and shook his head.

"Do you want to go ahead and make a suggestion for how to proceed?" Mack asked.

He shook his head again and looked back into his briefcase. Mack turned to Jess, unsure what to do. Jess widened her eyes comically, shrugged, and called on one of the young women.

Mack kept her eyes on Tyler, who continued rustling through his briefcase. She moved closer and saw what he was sorting through—small packages of snack food. Crackers, cookies, whatever the grocery store carried in single-serving packs, Tyler appeared to have at his fingertips.

"Did they keep you back from lunch today?" Mack asked, interrupting Jess' attempts to engage the other students.

The girl sitting next to Tyler shook her head.

"Did you get lunch really early?"

Again, no.

"So, we're your first class after lunch," Mack said, her voice quiet now and deadly serious. "And you need a snack so desperately that you're not able to focus on the material?"

Tyler looked at her, seemingly just now realizing that she was talking to him. He held a package of Goldfish Crackers aloft, tilted his head, looked at the crackers, and set them back in his briefcase.

"Thanks," Mack said.

Tyler didn't respond.

Mack turned back to Jess, who clicked forward to the next hypothetical. As two of the students started debating, Mack again heard a rustling behind her.

This time, Tyler held a snack-pack of Oreos, examining it closely.

"Are you diabetic, Tyler?" Mack asked. She was trying to think of any possible explanation for his behavior and coming up empty.

He shook his head, dark waves falling across his forehead.

"No snacks in class, then, okay? Let's focus on the material."

Tyler closed the briefcase, and Mack felt her jaw unclench. She walked to the front of the room and took the remote from Jess. "Let's move on," she said, clicking to the next slide. "In this situation, you are trying a domestic-violence case. John Doe is on trial for beating up his wife, Jane, and Jane is testifying. She says—and you didn't expect this—that John actually beat her up every Tuesday night for the last three years. What do you do?"

The girl in the front row—Jenny, according to her name tag—raised her hand enthusiastically, and Mack called on her. As Jenny was talking through her options, Mack heard a clicking noise and jerked her head toward Tyler. The briefcase was open again, and he was rustling through his snacks *again*. She checked her watch. They were forty-three minutes into the ninety-minute class, and she'd had enough.

"Hey, Tyler, you were warned, you were given an explanation, and nevertheless, you persisted. Why don't you go wait in the hall until this class is over? You can take your briefcase and rustle as much as you want."

He looked at her, dumbfounded. Mack folded her arms across her chest and held eye contact, waiting. He set his Nutter Butters down.

"You can't kick me out of class for having a snack," he said. His voice was higher than Mack had expected. Hints of California. Of course.

"Can," Mack said. "Did." She pointed at the door. "I'm sure your cohort will let you know when we're finished in here."

Tyler packed up his snack case and slunk out the door. Mack sighed.

Jess clapped once and the students looked at her, startled. Mack was startled, too.

"Show's over," Jess said. "Let's continue with Jenny's excellent insight into how to deal with Jane's sudden disclosure."

The rest of the time passed quickly, the students seeming eager to compensate for Tyler's bad behavior, and soon Mack and Jess were taking final questions. Jenny approached them as they were disconnecting the computer.

"Thank you," Jenny said. "He's been doing that every class the whole time we've been in training, and everyone else has just put up with it. It's infuriating. How did he even make it through law school?"

Jess laughed. "I guess everyone needs a nice cool place to eat their snacks."

Mack took a long drink from her water bottle.

"I appreciate you having my back," she said once the final student had left the room.

"No problem," Jess said, following Mack out the door. "But you need to relax, Wilson. Have you ever thought about going on vacation?"

CHAPTER THREE

Three days later, a new case hit Mack's desk, a binder full of reports and a summary written by Debbie Wood, a detective she hadn't thought about in a year or more. The last time Mack had heard from Debbie, she was calling to report that Benjamin Allen—the defendant who had attacked Mack in her home two years earlier—was dead. Mack had always respected Debbie for being a diligent, thorough investigator, but the lack of a phone call now was off-putting. Mack wondered if it meant that Debbie knew the case was unchargeable trash.

"Oh, well," she muttered. "No sense starting the case annoyed." She pulled a fresh notepad toward her and flipped open the binder to Debbie's summary.

The suspect, Liam Ferguson, had full custody of his daughter, Daisy. The girl's mom had left when Daisy was four and died, as far as Mack could tell, sometime later. That left Liam to raise Daisy on his own, however he saw fit. Child Protective Services had been involved on and off, but they never had quite enough to remove Daisy from the home—or homes, really, as Liam seemed to move around a lot. Daisy had never spent an entire year in a single school.

Daisy had suffered a miscarriage the day after her eighteenth birthday. Medical care was unavoidable—she couldn't stop bleeding and got scared. When the nurse at the ER asked if Daisy knew who the father was, something inside the girl snapped, and the whole story tumbled out of her in one long explanation. Liam had been sexually abusing her for years, almost exactly since her mother had left.

Mack's heart ached for the girl, but she couldn't figure out why *she* had been assigned the case. It seemed like a classic case for Sex Crimes, and there were plenty of capable prosecutors in that unit.

Frustrated, she picked up the phone. Debbie answered on the first ring, and they exchanged awkward pleasantries.

"It's been a long time," Mack said. "I'm not sure if I'm just reading your report wrong, but I wanted to check in about the Ferguson case. I don't see why you submitted it to Homicide."

"You just read the summary, huh?" Wood asked. "I didn't put the homicide facts in there. They're not as clear-cut."

Mack rubbed her eyes. Of course they weren't. "Why don't you give me a rundown?"

"So we had Nicole Rose do a forensic interview with Daisy. Even though she's an adult, the duration of the abuse is just so lengthy that it seemed cleaner. And she disclosed that she had actually given birth once before. She was thirteen. Same deal, dad's the father. But that time, it was a live birth and Ferguson was committed to keeping the baby. Well, time passes, the baby is like six months old, and Ferguson gets frustrated one too many times. Shakes him."

Mack gasped. "Did the baby make it?"

"No. So Ferguson buries the body, warns Daisy he'll do the same thing to her if she crosses him. That has the intended impact, and Daisy keeps quiet until that night in the ER, when it all comes out."

"Jesus," Mack said. "Okay, well, now I understand why you sent it to Homicide. How do we prove it, though?"

"I should've put this in the summary, but I didn't want it leaking. We have the body. Daisy told us where Ferguson buried it, and we have it."

"After six years in the ground? Was there any evidence of his having been shaken?"

"No," Wood said. "Unfortunately. But there is DNA proving that Ferguson and Daisy are the parents. We just got the results—that's why I didn't just go scoop him."

"So he's going to claim the baby died naturally," Mack said, thinking it through. "And he buried it to cover up the sex abuse? Or he'll have some explanation that omits the sex abuse entirely, I guess is more likely. We sure he doesn't have a twin brother?"

Wood laughed. "I'd forgotten you're funny."

"Thanks, I think."

"No sign of a twin. I really recommend you watch the forensic interview. If you come away from it less than convinced, then I'm fine if you just charge the sex counts. But I think you'll be exactly where I am, which is that this guy should hang from the rafters. I don't think there's enough for this to be a death case, but certainly first degree—premeditated and felony child abuse."

Mack looked at her watch. It wasn't even two o'clock, and she had dinner plans with Beth downtown at six. Plenty of time to check out the interview.

"It's a deal," she said. "I'll be in touch."

Wood had attached a flash drive to the front of the binder with a twisted paperclip. Mack plugged the drive into her computer and found the forensic interview.

She'd been to the child advocacy center a hundred times or more, but every time she watched the videotaped interviews it took a moment to orient herself to the soft rooms, so called because they were designed to accommodate child victims and witnesses to crimes. Instead of the stark industrial barrenness of a suspect interview room, these soft rooms had comfortable armchairs and art on the walls. They even had crayons and colored pencils for kids who might have an easier time expressing themselves without words.

The camera was situated in the upper corner of the room, so Mack had a bird's-eye view of a girl with her legs to her chest, curled into one corner of an armchair, when the interview began. She was so still, Mack wondered if the video had frozen, but then she looked up when forensic interviewer Nicole Rosc came into the room. Mack liked Nicole—they had worked together many times when Mack was still in Sex Crimes. She was glad they'd had someone so solid do the interview.

"Can I get you anything?" Nicole asked. "Water? Are you hungry? A blanket?"

Daisy shook her head but unfolded herself and sat up straight in the chair. She looked younger than eighteen. "I'm okay," she said, and her voice sounded younger than eighteen, too.

Nicole reviewed the rules of a forensic interview—tell the truth, correct the interviewer if she gets something wrong, and it's okay to say "I don't know"—and they got started.

Mack usually skipped the rapport-building section—hearing about a kid's day at school wasn't usually important for Mack's purposes—but she let this one play uninterrupted. As she listened to Daisy's slow, quiet words, she tried to picture how the girl would do on the witness stand. Confident witnesses were usually best, but not always. Too confident, and jurors would say that a victim was strident or had an agenda. No risk of that with Daisy. She even phrased what she'd had for lunch that day like a question. She sounded like a stereotypical victim.

Mack took sketchy notes as they moved into a discussion of the abuse. Daisy exhibited many of the signs of script memory—she couldn't parse out one incident from another.

"He would come in?" she said, the end of the thought lilting upward. "Like every night? And then? He would, you know, like, mess with me?"

"Okay," Nicole said empathetically. "And did this happen one time or more than one time?"

Mack smiled. Forensic interviewers were taught to use questions like that automatically, even if it was clear from the words being used that a victim was describing repetitive abuse. One of the goals of such an interview was that a defense attorney shouldn't be able to accuse the interviewer of influencing the victim into making false or excessive disclosures.

"More than one time?" Daisy said. "Like, every night from when I was five, maybe? Right up until I was in the hospital yesterday?"

"Okay, and can you describe everything that happened when he would 'mess with' you? Start at the very beginning and don't leave anything out."

Mack tuned out Daisy's response. If the baby's DNA really matched Ferguson, she didn't have a problem charging him with the sex counts, and Debbie could give her a rundown of the allegations. She didn't need to listen to the graphic details yet. Instead, she turned back to the flash drive's directory, looking for the reports from Daisy's trip to the ER. If police had been able to do a DNA test on the products of conception, that would be incredibly strong evidence that the abuse had lasted to the present day. She couldn't find documentation of that test, though, and made a note to ask Debbie.

On the screen, Nicole asked, "Was there ever a time when something different happened?"

"When I was pregnant?" Daisy said. "Not this time? Because we didn't know yet? But the first time?"

Mack could tell from the slight hesitation before Nicole's next question that the interviewer hadn't known about the prior pregnancy. She recovered quickly.

"Okay, tell me everything about when something different happened when you were pregnant the first time."

Mack watched another five minutes of the video, turning it off when Daisy started talking about her father shaking her baby to death. Debbie was right. There was no doubt in Mack's mind about the trauma Ferguson had inflicted on his daughter. Now she just had to prove it.

She opened a blank draft indictment form and got to work. If she was lucky, she could get the case in front of the grand jury the next week, and they could have Ferguson in custody soon after.

CHAPTER FOUR

Adam Bennett, Jess' serial-killer ex-fiancé, had hold of Jess. Mack knew it was up to her to save her best friend. There was no one to call, no one else who could do what needed to be done. She checked to make sure her handgun was loaded. Suddenly, out of nowhere, something dropped into her hand—a tooth. She probed her gums with her tongue, and two more fell out. She put the gun down. She had to stop the bleeding before she could help Jess.

Mack jolted awake with a gasp from the same nightmare she had been having for months. She groaned and checked her phone. Almost midnight. She knew she wouldn't sleep again, would have to get by the next day on the two hours she'd squeezed in before the dream took hold.

Intellectually, Mack knew she needed therapy. A five-minute phone call to Anna would result in a list of referrals and maybe even some ideas to try in the meantime, but she hadn't been able to bring herself to pick up the phone. Whatever was going on with Beth, whatever Anna's reasons had actually been for abandoning her during the police investigation the previous year, Mack wasn't ready to mend fences. Anna had kept her distance, too. It had been over six months since Mack had seen or heard from her.

In the absence of a therapist, Mack had increasingly turned to long runs and reality television saved on her DVR, but she'd already done five miles on her new treadmill before bed. She dragged herself to the couch.

The sound of her ringtone surprised her. As she answered, she saw that was almost three a.m.

"This is ADA Wilson," Mack said, trying to slow her racing heart.

"Mack, it's Dave Barton."

Mack smiled. "Little late for a social call, don't you think?" She could hear the murmur of voices surrounding Dave and knew what was coming before he responded. She stood and made her way to the walk-in closet, already trying to balance "crime-scene casual" with "might have to wear this into the office" if she was there for hours.

"It's a bad one," Dave said. "And the rare one where having a prosecutor on scene to start with might be useful. It may go capital, I think."

Mack shuddered. Only certain categories of particularly egregious murders were eligible for the death penalty. She had never tried a death case and didn't want to—the stakes were too high and the system too flawed. "You know if it goes death I'll lose it, right?"

"Yeah. But there's no one I'd rather have start on it."

Mack eyed the pink-striped Oxford shirt, dark-wash jeans, and black boots she'd chosen. They would have to do. That was the nicest outfit she was willing to sacrifice to a possibly gory crime scene.

The scene was less than a mile from Mack's house. She ran past the neighborhood sometimes, depending on her route. Too close for comfort.

She parked her old blue Saab down the street—given the cop cars, ambulance, and other emergency vehicles filling the block, she might as well have walked from home. She took a deep breath. Homicide scenes were never easy, but some were more horrifying than others.

Mack thought back to her first call out when she'd joined the Homicide unit only six months earlier. It was mid-afternoon on a warm day when she'd been summoned from her office to a trailer park on the edge of town. When she pulled up, officers in the portable command center—a kitted-out RV—had offered her pizza before showing her the body.

Mack had declined the pizza but dutifully followed them, stumbling in her heels over gravel, surprised when they led her past the row of trailers and out to the fence dividing the community from the desert. Her surprise increased when she saw that the dark lump on the ground was a person. There was no pristine white cloth covering the body like she'd expected from watching episodes of *CSI*. Instead, just a bloated corpse, turned purple in the sun, smelling like barbeque and urine. It was hard to tell the age or even the gender the person might have been.

"I don't see any injuries," Mack had finally said, stepping back from the body and swallowing hard against the rising bile in her throat. "You sure it's murder?"

The detective had nodded and pointed to a series of little yellow placards forming a trail Mack hadn't noticed back toward the homes. "Yep. Blood drops. The shots—four of 'em—are all in his back. No exit wounds. Plus, we have a witness."

The story was simple. "Creeper," the dead man, was a devoted member of his motorcycle club and an only slightly less devoted meth user. According to his wife, he owed some money to the wrong guys, other members of his club. Early that morning, they'd busted down his trailer door, found Creeper at his coffee maker, and shot him four times in the back. Adrenaline carried him out of the house, but the bleeding eventually took him down. They hadn't noticed his wife standing in the bedroom doorway. But she'd seen them, could identify the shooter, and the police had the whole thing wrapped up with a confession by dinner. Aside from the smell, it had been an easy introduction to homicide.

Mack shook her head. Whatever waited for her behind that crime-scene tape, it was bound to be worse than Creeper's invisible injuries under bright blue skies.

She flashed her badge at the patrol officer guarding the door. He handed her some paper booties to put over her shoes. The first person she saw inside was a crime-scene tech she recognized. JoAnn...something.

"Hey, there," she said, flashing a tight smile at the older woman.

JoAnn nodded. "Barton call you? Let me show you where he is."

Mack looked around as she followed JoAnn through the small ranch house to the main bedroom. From what she could see, it was simply but tastefully decorated in shades of gray and green. A woman's house. There were photographs and paintings on the walls, a full bookshelf in the living room, and a large decorative quilt hanging on the office wall.

Dave clapped her on the shoulder as she entered the bedroom. Three TPD floodlights illuminated a ghastly scene. Mack had never seen so much blood. Most of it was on the bed—the blanket and top sheet folded away from the crumpled heap in the middle, a pool of dark red spreading to the edge of the mattress. That wasn't all, though. Three large puddles on the carpet between the bed and the entrance to the en suite bathroom and spatter across the walls and floor.

The smell of rust was thick in the air. Mack cleared her throat and wished there was some airflow in the room. The overhead fan was turned off, and she knew that turning it on would risk destroying evidence.

"Tell me what we've got," she said, hating the way her voice shook.

"Victim is believed to be Amanda Wagner," Dave said. "It's hard to tell from her face, but that's the homeowner, and we think age and basics line up. We think whatever happened started in the bathroom, based on the blood. No sign of a weapon, but we have some guesses. We'll know more post-autopsy, of course, but we think he hit her with something by the sink, then they either fought to the bed or he moved her there. But, from the big puddles, we think she went down fighting. Then we think he moved on to either stabbing or shooting—it's impossible to say right now, although my guess is stabbing. We think he may have been angry about something."

"Yeah, right," Mack said. "You said 'he.' Do we have a suspect?"

"Not exactly," Dave said. "But stay with me, I'll get there."

There was a framed photograph on Amanda's dresser. The same young woman Mack had seen in other photos through the house, with a similarly aged man. Their arms were around each other. She pointed to him. "She got a boyfriend?"

"Not sure yet."

Mack was getting frustrated at the lack of answers. "Keep going. There must be a reason you called me out here. What else do you know?"

"Whatever happened in here was loud. You probably didn't notice when you walked in, but it's a zero-lot-line property. This wall here"—Dave gestured behind the headboard—"is about three feet from the neighbor's bedroom. Neighbor gets woken up by the ruckus, bitches and moans to his wife for a while, then she convinces him to check it out. They knock on the door, ring the bell, and when there's no response, they call for a welfare check."

Mack whistled. "That's the kind of neighbor everyone needs."

"When patrol gets here, they notice a smear—probably but not definitely, at this point, blood—on the handle of the front door. When they get no response to the bell, they decide they have PC to break in."

Mack gestured at the heap on the bed. "And find this."

Dave ran a hand over his shaved head, a tell that he was stressed or upset. "She was, amazingly, still breathing when patrol found her, but she was gone when the EMTs got here. They tried to get her back, but no luck."

Mack took in the space where this poor young woman—regardless of whether she was in fact Amanda Wagner—had taken her last breaths. "This is horrific, Dave, but I'm still not sure I understand why I'm here. There are horrible murders in this city every day, and ADAs don't get called to the scene. What am I missing? Why would this go capital?"

Dave hesitated. "When the EMTs were working on her, they attached some kind of monitor. You'll have to ask the medical examiner for the specifics, because I don't really understand it. But she was pregnant. Early in her pregnancy. The baby"—he cleared his throat—"the baby didn't make it, either."

CHAPTER FIVE

By the time Dave finished showing Mack around the house, it was five. The street was mostly empty as he walked her back to her car.

"I know this is really close to your place," Dave said. "But there's no reason to think you're in any danger."

She laughed nervously. Her head was pounding, and her throat was raw. "If you'd had the last two years I've had, you'd have a hard time believing that, too." She leaned into the hug Dave offered. She was comforted by the soft cotton of his polo shirt against her cheek and the familiar scent of his cologne.

"Okay," she said, reluctantly pulling away. "I've got to head home. I need to shower and get ready to head into work. You'll keep me posted as things develop?"

"Of course," Dave said. His phone vibrated in the holster at his waist. "Autopsy will be sometime this week. You want to be there?"

Mack flinched. She couldn't think of anything she wanted less than attending the joint autopsy of a young woman and her unborn child. "I'll have to check my calendar," she said, but Dave was already heading back into the house.

Mack was early to court, covering a sentencing hearing for Jess, who was busy in another division. She unbuttoned her jacket, settled herself at the prosecution table, and flipped open the file. Jess had prepared a sentencing memorandum for the judge, laying out the facts of the case to support her recommendation under the plea agreement: twenty years in prison with no possibility of early release.

It was a harsh plea. Mack glanced at the defendant's date of birth. Pedro Martinez had only been nineteen years old when he murdered his girlfriend's father. Depending on the circumstances, some murderers wound up doing as little as seven years. Pedro would spend more time in prison than he had spent on the planet before committing the murder. It was a *very* harsh plea. Pedro ran with an offshoot of the Barrio Centro gang—a Norteños set. His girlfriend, Silvia, was unaffiliated, but her dad, Alejandro, was hooked up with 13th Avenue Sur Trece, a Sureños set and the natural enemies of Norteños. Mack wondered if Pedro and Silvia had met in high school—there weren't many places where kids with such different affiliations could become close.

However Pedro had met Silvia, he and Alejandro had sniped at each other at a series of family gatherings, culminating the night of Alejandro's death at Silvia's cousin's quinceañera. Witnesses disagreed about what exactly set Pedro off, but he shot Alejandro twice in the back right in the middle of the dance floor. Alejandro's gun never even left his waistband.

Mack shook her head, disgusted by the casual violence that plagued her city, but was brought back to the courtroom by the sights and sounds of people getting to their feet—the judge was taking the bench. She hastily stood and pushed her hair behind her ears.

"Good morning, Your Honor," she said. "Mackenzie Wilson for the State on behalf of Jessica Lafayette."

Judge Kerchansky—a middle-aged white man who Mack couldn't even picture clearly if she wasn't right in front of him, so bland were his features—nodded at her without smiling.

"Nick Diaz, Judge, for my client Pedro Martinez, here in custody and ready to proceed to sentencing."

Mack hadn't noticed Nick come in and hadn't realized he was the defense attorney. She still hadn't returned his email. She gave him a tight-lipped smile. His client looked younger than his twenty-one years. Two jailhouse birthdays had left him with sallow skin and dark circles under his eyes, and he was dwarfed by his baggy orange jumpsuit. Civilians talked about the right to a speedy trial, but they didn't understand the system. Two years from arrest to sentencing meant Pedro's case had moved at a good clip.

Judge Kerchansky gestured the defendant and Nick to the podium and cleared his throat. "We are here today for sentencing, based on the defendant's plea of guilty to First Degree Murder. Is everyone ready to proceed?" He paused briefly, but no one spoke. "Hearing no objections, we will proceed. Ms. Wilson, I have reviewed Ms. Lafayette's sentencing memorandum. I also conducted the settlement conference in this case and heard from the victim's wife and daughter at that hearing. Is there anyone else you want me to hear from?"

Mack turned to scan the gallery. Jason McCormick, the office's youngest victim advocate, was sitting next to a crying middle-aged woman wearing an obviously custom-made T-shirt with a photograph of a smiling man on it. "RIP Alejandro," the shirt proclaimed below the photo. Jason nodded to Mack, who turned back to Judge Kerchansky.

"Yes, Judge," she said.

Jason took the woman's arm and helped her to stand, leading her through the swinging gate that divided the gallery from the well of the courtroom. Mack could see the back of her shirt as they approached the podium. "Por siempre en nuestros corazones." *Forever in our hearts.* Mack sighed.

Judge Kerchansky pursed his lips slightly as Jason and the victim's wife stood before him. "Hello, ma'am. We met at the settlement conference, and at that time you expressed your feelings about the plea agreement being too lenient. What additional information do you want me to have at this time? And can you please start with your name, just for the court reporter."

"Lupe Vega," the woman said, her voice shaky. "I am Alejandro's wife. And I just want to say—I mean—I want to tell you, and everyone, and this defendant, a few things."

Judge Kerchansky looked sour. "Ma'am, I'm going to ask you to refrain from addressing Mr. Martinez. The only person you should be talking to right now is me. Can you do that?"

Lupe wiped her eyes with the tissue she carried in the hand that wasn't clutching Jason's arm. Mack's heart ached for her.

"Yes, sir," Lupe said. "I just want to thank Ms. Lafayette, who isn't here today, and I want to thank Jason, who has helped my family through this nightmare. And I want to thank you, because you have a hard job, and I want to tell you how much I miss my husband, Alejandro. He was a good man—always helping his family or spending time with his mother and his nieces and nephews. That's what he was doing when this man killed him in cold blood. I've been knowing him since we were both fifteen years old, and he was always been a hard worker and a good man. A good father. He helped his family. He always worked hard for us, and now this man took him away from us."

Mack thought back to Alejandro's extensive criminal history, documented in the file she'd gotten from Jess. Delinquency adjudications for drugs and alcohol, a juvenile history of running guns for older gang members, and then he'd graduated to adult crimes. More drugs, more guns. Street-level stuff, nothing big. No prison time, but plenty of trips to county lockup. Lupe's husband had been far from a saint, but that never mattered to a wife in pain. She would always look at his potential, his future lost, rather than his past ill-spent.

"He loved his daughter, Silvia. Her whole life she had her papi wrapped around her little finger, and she's who brought this man into our home."

Mack heard a loud sob behind her and turned, looking for Silvia. She saw a dark-haired young woman wearing the same shirt as Lupe but sitting on the defendant's side of the courtroom. An older woman—Pedro's mom, Mack guessed—had her head on Silvia's shoulder, and they were both weeping, their hands entwined.

"We accepted that man into our home," Lupe continued. "Alejandro and me, because Silvia loved him. Even though we knew he ran with a bad crowd, I treated him like my own hijo. He spent the night with us, he bought us groceries, he helped my younger kids with their homework. So of course he came to the party. He even brought a present for my niece. But he was drinking, and I think maybe he had used the blues or something."

"Blues" were counterfeit M30 pain pills—fentanyl. If Pedro was high at the time of the murder, the judge would need to make a finding that he remembered shooting Alejandro and was able to legally enter the plea agreement. Without that finding, Pedro had a built-in ground for post-conviction relief, with a court overturning the plea and throwing everyone back into preparing for trial. She made a note on her legal pad to raise the issue with Kerchansky. Jess had told her that any warm body could handle the sentencing. She should have known better—Jess had been doing these cases too long to not see Lupe's grenade coming.

"...and the next thing I knew, Alejandro was on the ground and there was so much blood. I held him and kept saying 'Hold on, mi amor, just stay here with me.' But nothing I said made any difference. By the time the ambulance came, he was gone." Lupe took a deep breath. She was crying harder than she had been when she first started speaking. "So, anyway, I just want you to know that that man didn't just kill my husband. He killed me, and my relationship with my daughter, and my whole family. And there is no time that man can spend in prison that will bring Alejandro back, or me back, or my family back, or will give me my daughter back. But at least if he's in prison he can't kill anyone else, and that will have to be enough for me. Gracias, Judge."

Judge Kerchansky did not speak until Lupe had returned to her seat. "Anyone else?" he asked Mack. "Actually, before you answer that, I do want to note that I find no basis to believe that the defendant was impaired at the time of the offense to such a degree that he might not remember the events. He has knowingly and voluntarily pled guilty, and I have accepted that plea. The victim's wife's statement does not influence that decision. Okay, now you, Ms. Wilson."

Mack looked at Jason, who shook his head. "Nothing else, Judge. The state will rest on Ms. Lafayette's written recommendation and ask you to follow the plea."

She sat down, fuming. Jess should never have asked her to cover this. It didn't matter that the prison term was stipulated, or that Judge Kerchansky wasn't the sort of judge who would turn away a plea agreement. His reputation as having one foot already in retirement made him a popular choice when prosecutors and defense attorneys had agreed on an outcome and needed a judge to rubber-stamp it.

Judge Kerchansky turned to Nick. "Mr. Diaz? Anyone you want me to hear from?"

Nick looked to Silvia and his client's mother, both of whom shook their heads. He whispered to Pedro, who seemed even smaller and younger after Lupe's harsh words. "No, Judge," he said. "We'd just ask you to follow the plea."

Judge Kerchansky turned to face Pedro head-on, but the boy kept his head down, avoiding his eyes. "Mr. Martinez, you have the absolute right to address me before I impose sentence. Now, we talked some at your settlement conference, but if there's anything else you want to say to me, now is the time."

The defendant shook his head.

Judge Kerchansky stared at the boy in front of him for a long moment.

"Okay," he said at last. "Then let me tell you some things. I told Ms. Vega that she couldn't talk to you, just to me. But I'm the judge, and I can talk to you as much as I want."

Pedro looked up, and Mack could see the questions on his face.

"This whole crime was stupid," Judge Kerchansky said. "And it's stupid that you're here before me today." Mack tried to keep her face neutral but couldn't help herself. This was weird.

Nick looked at her, his face asking if he should intervene. Mack shrugged. She, for one, wanted to know what Judge Kerchansky was about to say.

"That's right," the judge continued. "I said it was stupid. And probably none of you are used to a judge saying a crime was stupid, but that's what it was. Boys argue. Especially over girls, especially with the fathers of girls. I argued with the fathers of the girls I dated, and, as a father, I argued with the boys my three daughters brought home when they were teenagers. But no one ever wound up dead from those arguments, and do you know why, Mr. Martinez? Because none of us were stupid enough to be carrying around guns."

Now Nick tried to interrupt, but Judge Kerchansky held up a hand.

"Enough, Counsel," he said. "I know where the lines are, and I will obey them. I just want your client, and everyone else in the room, actually, to realize that carrying a gun to a birthday party has never made anything or anyone safer. Men—let alone teenage boys—who carry guns aren't keeping themselves safe, and they aren't keeping their families safe. They're setting themselves up to get involved in stupid, childish *nonsense* and then the winner winds up in my courtroom." He took a deep breath and ran his hand over his thinning brown hair. "If there is one thing I have learned in my time as a judge, it's that guns make everything worse. So I want to make sure that your client hears me—no more guns. You come out of prison in twenty years. You'll still be a young man, with a whole lot of life to live. You'll be fifteen years younger than I am now. That entire rest of your life? No. More. Guns."

The defendant nodded, his thin shoulders shaking with his tears. Mack couldn't be sure if he'd learned his lesson, but Judge Kerchansky's speech would be hard to ignore. She wondered if the judge had lost someone close to him from gun violence, or whether the horrors that people inflicted on each other had just gotten to him over the years. Either way, Mack knew she had a new favorite division for her homicide cases.

CHAPTER SIX

Nick approached her as she was packing her tote bag to walk back to her office.

"Hey," Mack said. "Sorry I haven't returned your email. I don't have a good excuse, it's just been a busy couple weeks."

Nick smiled, his teeth bright white against his dark skin and stubble. When she wasn't looking right at him, Mack always forgot how handsome he was. "No problem. I know they keep you chained to your cases."

"Would you believe I found a jury summons in my mailbox this morning?"

Nick laughed. "You'd be a natural, if only there was an attorney in town who would let you serve. I didn't expect to run into you this morning, but Ms. Lafayette's absence turns out to be my good fortune. Do you have time for a quick cup of coffee?"

Mack thought through her schedule. Continuing to prepare the Ferguson case for grand jury. Checking in with Dave on the previous night's homicide. Nothing that wouldn't keep.

Nick led her to a café almost a mile from the court complex, off the beaten path and on the edge of downtown. They chatted during the walk, neither saying much of any import.

"Okay," Mack said as they settled at a table, a skinny vanilla latte in front of her. "What's this all about? It feels very secretive."

Nick took a deep breath. "I have a somewhat unusual job offer I want to discuss with you. But before I do, can I have your word that you'll be discreet about this conversation?"

Mack searched his face for some sign that he was kidding but found only sincerity. "I can't make any promises without knowing what the subject is, but I'll hear you out and, if I can ethically stay quiet, I will."

Nick laughed. "Oh, no," he said. "Nothing so exciting as a crime or an ethical breach. You know Melissa O'Connor, right?"

Mack did. She was the Democrat running against Peter Campbell in the upcoming district attorney election. An anti-death-penalty advocate, she had intrigued Mack until Mack heard her other ideas about the criminal-justice system. No cash bail, no prosecution for assaulting police officers absent serious injury, no prison on drug-sales cases—these were political maneuvers that Mack knew would make the community less safe, not more.

"We've never met," she said. "But I've certainly been aware of her campaign. We don't see eye to eye on much."

"Good," Nick said. "I thought you might not. Melissa is looking for—how should I put this?—friendly forces inside Campbell's administration. Not people who agree with everything she's campaigning on—although, between you and me, a lot of that is just posturing. She can't get rid of cash bail! There'd be murderers roaming free, and the electorate would riot."

"In other words, she's just another politician."

"Not at all. She really believes that Campbell targets Black and brown folks, especially men, and he's so focused on that he isn't keeping the community safe."

Suddenly, Mack found Nick a whole lot less attractive than she had moments earlier. "This is starting to feel like an attack,

Nick," she said, trying to keep her tone even. "I've worked for Campbell his whole administration. Is Melissa saying—or are you saying, for that matter—that I'm a racist prosecutor? I don't choose the murderers who come across my desk. I don't force them to kill, and I don't decide which cases PD can solve."

He placed a hand on Mack's forearm, and she resisted the urge to shake him off. He didn't know her well enough for that. "Of course not. Melissa's problem is with Campbell and his administration. She has no quarrel with line prosecutors. She knows you're just working in the system as it's currently structured. She's trying to bring Campbell down, to let the public know about the shady deals he makes."

That was enough. Mack pulled her arm away from Nick's hand.

"Let me explain why I wanted to meet with you," Nick went on. "Melissa's polling really well. She has a better than even chance of beating Campbell, but she's going to need a structure in place so she can hit the ground running. She's putting together a transition team—people she trusts, people who can help make decisions about staffing, reorganization, and so on. She brought me on to head that team and asked me to recruit not just from the community but from within the office. I've talked to a couple prosecutors so far, and they suggested you might be an ally."

Mack rolled her eyes. "Let me know who, and I'll send thank-you cards. Not to put too fine a point on it, Nick, but what does Melissa want from me?"

"I know and respect your work, Mack. You're one of the good guys. And with your experience, your reputation in the legal community...I was thinking you could run serious crimes. I'm going to be the head of criminal. You'd be my direct report. Third in line for the throne, as it were."

Mack laughed. "Get real. I've never supervised anyone a day in my life, and you want to put me in charge of fifty prosecutors, half of whom have more experience than I do? You've never even been a prosecutor. And Melissa, by all accounts, was a pretty awful prosecutor for less than a year twenty years ago and three thousand miles from here. This would be a disaster for the office, Nick. No, a disaster for the community."

Nick folded his arms on the table and leaned toward her. "Can you honestly say you agree with all of Campbell's decisions? What about how he treated you last year? From what I hear, he would have fired you in a heartbeat and slept just fine, if that's what the public wanted, but Melissa believes in loyalty. In rewarding people who work hard and get the job done. She wants young blood in leadership positions because she's tired of prosecution being dominated by old white men."

Nick paused for breath then launched right back into his speech.

"You don't know how to supervise? Okay, find a management seminar—any program you choose—and we'll send you there. I don't know how to prosecute? Teach me. Help me build the office you want to work in for the next twenty years. Keep your community safe. Safer than it will be if Campbell gets four more years."

Mack stared down into her cup. For the first time, doubt began to creep in.

Nick stood. "Think about it," he said and left the café.

"You owe me," Mack said, tossing the file onto Jess' already crowded desk. "Big time."

Jess looked up from her computer screen. "Was it bad? It couldn't be that bad, it was a stipulated sentence."

"Mm-hmm, mm-hmm, mm-hmm, I can see why you'd think that. But life, uh, finds a way. I won't bore you with the details, but you might want to call your victim's wife. She was not pleased with the sentencing, which I'm sure comes as no surprise to you, but she could probably use some hand-holding after today."

"Of course she could," Jess said. "She needed her hand held all the way through. She refused to believe that her banger husband might have said something to provoke her banger daughter's banger boyfriend."

"Careful, friendo. That sounds an awful lot like victim blaming."

Jess ran her hands through her long dark hair. "Alejandro didn't deserve to die. Of course he didn't. Even assholes have the right to live. But it was hard to keep a straight face when she kept telling me how great he was, despite all evidence to the contrary."

"He didn't sound so bad…worked hard to support his family?"

Jess laughed. "Is that what she said? Oh, well, I guess she gets to remember him how she wants to. Ese mostly worked slinging dope."

"That makes more sense," Mack said. She was uneasy with the relief she felt. Maybe Alejandro wasn't a great guy. Maybe he was even a bad guy. That shouldn't give his killer a free pass, though. Right? She rubbed her eyes.

"You going soft on me?" Jess asked.

"Just lack of sleep, I think." The tag of her blouse was scratching the back of her neck, and one of her dress socks had slipped lower than the other. In a perfect world, it would be time for a nap and a drink. Not necessarily in that order.

"The nightmare, still?"

She had told Jess about the nightmare when it started— when Jess had been having bad dreams of her own thanks to her homicidal fiancé. But Jess' had stopped months earlier and Mack's just kept on coming.

"I got called out last night. Well, this morning, I guess. Brutal scene right in that little pocket neighborhood around the corner from me."

"Whoa," Jess said.

"Yeah."

"Do you want to talk about it?"

"Not right now, thanks." She needed another cup of coffee if she was going to make it through the rest of the day. Between the murder and the sentencing, she felt fragile. She couldn't take another bump in the road. Maybe if she could hide in her office for a while, she'd rally.

"Beth texted me," Jess said.

Mack stopped in the doorway, curious.

"She suggested getting together this weekend."

"Am I invited?"

"No, I'm just telling you what you're missing out on. Duh, you're invited. I really like her, but it's not like we're hanging out without you. Yet."

"Oh," Mack said. "Okay. Well, I think my schedule's clear, so one of you can just let me know the plan."

This was what she wanted, wasn't it? Wasn't she tired of mediating between Jess and Anna, who had never really gotten along? The tension between them had made her sick to her stomach. And here was Beth, beautiful, funny, easygoing Beth, who had apparently formed an independent connection with Mack's best friend. Why did that make her so uneasy?

CHAPTER SEVEN

Although she would have preferred to skip it, Mack knew that her presence was expected at the autopsy of the murdered Jane Doe. She watched the clock on her computer with an increasing sense of dread. She hated autopsies. Jess had warned her when she'd come to Homicide that the first couple would be rough and then they would get easier. She would get used to them. Desensitized. But Mack's reaction had been the opposite. Each of the dozen she had attended had been harder than the last. The Tucson medical examiners showed nothing but respect for the bodies on their tables, but Mack couldn't escape her disgust. Being laid bare on a steel table was a devastating loss of dignity. Naked under fluorescent lights, victims' bodies were treated like crime scenes. Swabbed, measured, and photographed. They were searched for evidence before being cleared and released to their families, if they had them. Then, those left behind continued the terrible process of mourning their loved one. Unclaimed bodies had it even worse. They were cremated or buried, and any loved ones they might have would never know the fate that had befallen them.

Mack looked down at the old jeans and District Attorney's Office polo shirt she had changed into after morning court. The ME's office smelled like chemicals on the best of days—and more often like blood and decay. Mack hated ruining suits that couldn't be washed. She hadn't made that mistake twice.

At 1:30, she sighed and pushed herself out of her desk chair. At least it would be a nice walk through the court complex. She knew Dave would happily give her a ride back to her car if the autopsy went long and she didn't want to walk back in the late afternoon. Maybe they'd even be there until the end of the day and he'd be down for a drink at the bar across the street.

The receptionist recognized her and buzzed her through the secure door with no delays. Dave was waiting for her in the hallway outside the observation room.

"Wasn't sure you'd make it," he said.

"Do you not need me?" Mack asked. "Because"—she turned to go—"it's not too late for me to just—"

She was stopped by Dave's hand on her elbow.

"Let's head in, and I'll bring you up to speed."

They went into the dimly lit observation room. The far wall was taken up by a large window that looked into the exam room where the autopsy would be conducted. An intercom allowed them to communicate with the assistant medical examiner, who would give them preliminary results as the examination proceeded.

"Who'd we get?" Mack asked. The examination room was prepared, a white sheet showing the outline of a body on the steel table.

"Dr. Lee."

"Perfect," Mack said. Mina Lee was her favorite AME. Thorough, precise, and a great witness—a rare combination. "What about ID? Have you gotten anywhere with that?"

"It's confirmed. The homeowner, Amanda Wagner. We found her driver license in the search, and then her mom was able to make the final."

Mack clicked her tongue. "Poor mom. She local? Did she know she was going to be a gramma?"

"No," Dave said, "to both, but she's in town now to take care of things. And let me tell you, informing her was the worst thing I've had to do in a long time. Amanda was an only child, so... well, that was her shot. She thinks Amanda must not have known she was expecting. They talked the afternoon she was killed, and she didn't say anything. Mom says they were close enough that Amanda would've told her. In fact, mom says Amanda wasn't seeing anyone, hadn't been seeing anyone for a year or more."

"Maybe," Mack said, "but let's not take that for granted. Do we know who the guy in the photo was? From her bedroom?"

"That's the college boyfriend, per mom."

"Well, Amanda could have had lots of reasons not to say anything about the pregnancy. Do we know how far along she was?"

"We'll get that from the autopsy. And the forensics guys have her phone and laptop. She was an Apple user, unfortunately, but they think they can crack it. Hopefully, there'll be something in her texts or emails. Hell, I'd settle for a Google search history at this point. It's been three days since she was murdered, and we're no closer to a suspect now than we were on scene."

Dr. Lee entered the examination room and waved to them through the glass. Her green scrub hat and medical mask obscured most of her face, but Mack could tell she was smiling. Actually, Mack didn't think she'd ever seen her without a smile on her face. Her unflagging cheerfulness in the face of the horrors she observed every day was truly remarkable. Mack wondered what her secret was.

"Welcome, Sergeant Barton. Always nice to see you, Ms. Wilson. Let's get started." Dr. Lee busied herself preparing her workspace. Dave clicked the button turning off the microphone in the observation room so they could continue to talk without disturbing Dr. Lee.

"Let's think this through," Mack said. "We've got to assume the father of the baby is our main suspect, right?"

"Sure," Dave said. "Main, but certainly not only. Could have been a home invader, first date, neighbor, rapist—anyone."

"Of course. But what's the most recent stat? Over thirty percent of female murder victims are killed by an intimate partner."

"Something like that. Okay, fine, father is the most logical suspect. We can start there. Except, of course, that we don't know who the father is yet."

Mack paced in the small room. She thought better when she was moving.

"But we can assume," Dave continued, "that if daddy dearest is the doer, then he knew about her pregnancy."

"So hopefully there's some evidence of that on the phone."

Dr. Lee cleared her throat. "I'm ready if you are," she called.

Dave gave her a thumbs-up. Dr. Lee flipped the switch on the audio recording device an assistant would later use to transcribe her spoken notes and turned back the sheet covering Amanda Wagner.

"On first impression," Dr. Lee said, "this is a young Caucasian female. I know from collateral records that she was thirty-two years old, and her physical presentation is consistent with that information. Additionally, I am led to understand from police that a fetal heart rate was initially detected when EMTs arrived on scene. Therefore, although the body does not exhibit external signs of pregnancy, I anticipate recovering a fetus during the procedure today."

Mack cringed. She knew how important professional distance was, but this seemed callous.

Dr. Lee turned Amanda's body over, and Mack saw the wounds on her back. The doctor continued dictating as she measured the entry wounds.

Dave pressed the button, enabling their microphone. "Can you tell if they're shots or stab wounds, Doctor?"

Dr. Lee looked up. "Not yet, Detective. There is some preliminary evidence to suggest that these are not gunshot wounds, but I will need to keep looking to be sure. Because there are no exit wounds, if these are bullet entry wounds the bullets will, in theory, still be inside. If I can recover them, or fragments of them, then that will be pretty conclusive. Otherwise, it's unfortunately hard to be sure when we're dealing with injuries of this magnitude."

Amanda's body was returned to its original position, and Dr. Lee made the Y-shaped incision that would give her access to the body cavity. Mack had had enough. "I'm going back to the office, Dave. I don't think we're going to get anything today. If you get into the phone, though, let me know. My gut tells me we'll get way more from her words than her body."

CHAPTER EIGHT

That Saturday night found Mack tucked into a booth next to Beth at a wine bar on the north side of town. Jess was late to meet them, which was unlike her, but Mack was grateful for the chance to catch up with Beth.

"Did she show you the meme I sent her this morning?" Beth asked.

"Um," Mack said, trying to remember. "No. Wait, you're sending Jess memes now?"

Beth pulled out her phone and started scrolling. "Not often. We just send stuff that reminds us of you back and forth every once in a while. This one—I can't find it—but it was a woman face down on the ground and something about 'Be a runner, they said. You'll meet new people—like paramedics!' I thought it was really funny when it popped up on my feed."

"You're both just jealous," Mack said.

"Yeah, it seems like you've spent more quality time with your treadmill lately than with either of us." She leaned in to kiss the smile that had spread across Mack's face, but they were disrupted by a gagging noise.

"When did you get here?" Mack asked, looking up at Jess.

"Just now," Jess said. "Sorry for my tardiness. My prior engagement ran late."

"Prior engagement?" Beth asked. "Do tell. Also, do a little spin—I think I love that shirt, and I want to be sure."

Mack wolf-whistled as Jess gave a reluctant twirl. Beth was right; the black sequined tank top was adorable.

"Thanks," Jess said. "It's from my favorite Goodwill."

"I love Goodwill," Beth said. "Which one is your favorite?"

Mack stopped listening while they chatted enthusiastically. She couldn't get behind thrift shopping as an adult—she'd spent way too many hours as a teen sorting through racks and racks of donated clothes. After her dad had finally left for good, almost all her school clothes had come from local discount stores.

She finished her cider, and, since Beth was driving, gestured to the waitress for another.

"I'll have a vodka soda, extra lime," Jess said, when the waitress brought Mack's Angry Orchard.

"Now what was that about a prior engagement?" Beth urged.

"You know how I think I want to date a veterinarian?"

"Of course," Beth and Mack said in unison.

"Well, there's a new vet at the practice I go to. Tall, cute-ish in the face, yadda yadda, I don't really care about that. He's a vet, right? So Shirley had an appointment today to see if her allergy meds are working, and Annie, the vet I've been going to for years, came in. She's doing her exam, and the vet tech is there taking notes, and I start trying to feel Annie out about this new vet."

"The cute-ish one," Mack said.

"The ish is important," Beth added.

"Fine. Cute-ish vet. So I'm long past the point of subtlety and by now it's very clear that I am trying to find out if the new vet is open to dating a patient. Client? I mean me, not the dog. And Annie finally has had enough and tells me to ask the vet tech—the one who is currently in the room with us—because she's the new vet's wife."

Mack and Beth both hissed with secondhand embarrassment.

"Oh, that's got to hurt," Mack said. "What did the tech say?"

"She was *so* nice. Just *so* nice about it. She said he wasn't open to dating but it was nice to hear that other people found him good-looking. So anyway, I died. Right there in the exam room, just gave up the ghost and became deceased. It took me a while to scrape the battered remains of my dignity off the floor, which is why I am late."

Beth signaled to the waitress. "We are going to need two lemon-drop shots, please and thank you."

"You're not having one?" Jess asked.

"Oh, these are both for you," Beth said. "I mean, if Mack wants one we can get three, but you need two for yourself. I'll give you a ride home."

"Lemon drops?" Mack said. "Oh, I'm down."

The waitress seemed annoyed when Jess ordered more shots, but the three of them were too busy laughing to really care. Mack pulled Beth closer to her in the booth. This was exactly what she needed to get over the stress of the previous week: an easy night with her best friend and her, well, whatever.

CHAPTER NINE

"You look miserable," Jess said from the door of Mack's office.

"I am miserable. I'm trying to cut down on caffeine and it's not going well." Jess' casual clothes—jeans and a Lynyrd Skynyrd T-shirt—caught her attention. "You look super fun. Where are you going?"

Jess looked down and tugged on her shirt. "Thanks. I have a—well—I'm going on a first date today. So I changed after court."

Mack twirled her finger, and Jess obligingly turned around. "Cute," Mack ruled. "But some of your hair is caught in your collar. Is this another Hinge guy? Where are you guys going, and when?"

"Just dinner. I'll drop you a pin when we get there. Call me ninety minutes after you get the pin?"

Mack nodded. They had arranged the system in the aftermath of the Adam Bennett case, although Jess didn't always use it. It helped Jess feel more confident that her date couldn't get away with killing her and kept Mack from feeling like she was overstepping.

"Have fun," Mack said. "I got the Amanda Wagner autopsy report today, so I'll be digging into that this evening."

"No plans with Beth?" Jess checked her watch.

"She's busy," Mack said. "I really do think she's seeing someone, but I haven't had the balls to ask."

"Wouldn't it be better to know?" Jess asked.

"No. No, I don't think it's better to know. I think it's best to avoid knowing absolutely as long as possible."

Jess gave her a disbelieving look. "Healthy Coping Mechanisms, a new CLE taught by Mackenzie Wilson, coming soon to a law practice near you."

Mack laughed.

"Do you think it's possible," Jess began. "Just hear me out before you shriek at me—that part of Beth's appeal is her potential emotional unavailability?"

"What do you mean?"

"Well, if she's dating other people and you don't have her full attention, does that take some of the pressure off you?"

Mack rubbed the skin behind her left ear. "I can't possibly think about that."

"Do you want to try talking about it?" Jess asked. "Maybe? Just to see how it feels? I've got like ten minutes before I need to leave."

Mack looked at the stack of papers on her desk. Her to-do list topped the pile. She'd only accomplished one of the day's six tasks. "Maybe another time."

"Luckily, you know where to find me. At least forty hours a week, and usually more than that."

Mack hoped that her date went well. God knew Jess could use a nice guy in her life.

The autopsy report was thin—only ten pages. Mack knew from experience that these reports were written by clinicians for clinicians and included an exhaustive and often irrelevant survey of each of the victim's internal organs. She had yet to meet a case where the condition of the victim's thyroid made a big difference, but it would be pointless to argue. The reports were difficult even for lawyers to read and understand, and usually required a follow-up call to the medical examiner for clarification.

One thing to be grateful for was that the conclusions were in bold letters on the first page:

Cause of Death: Stab wounds to torso

Manner of Death: Homicide

How Injury Occurred: Stabbed by other(s)

Interesting. Mack would have bet money that they were gunshot wounds, but apparently not.

She flipped to the body map, where the injuries Amanda had suffered would be diagrammed and labeled for ease of reference. Dr. Lee had noted twenty-one stab wounds across Amanda's chest, stomach, and back. No defensive injuries to her hands—she hadn't fought back once the knife came out. The toxicology report showed the presence of alcohol in her system. Mack wondered if she'd been passed out in bed when she was attacked, but that wouldn't make sense, given the blood spatter or the screaming heard by the neighbors.

Mack turned to the Evidence of Injury section of the report. This was where Dr. Lee laid out the basis for her finding that Amanda hadn't been shot. Four penetrating wounds had resulted in significant internal bleeding. Dr. Lee couldn't say which of the wounds had been the cause of death—and would refuse to guess if asked—but all four were deep and did damage to organs or veins. No bullets recovered or other evidence of gunshots: no powder burns, no stippling on the skin, no fibers from Amanda's pajamas embedded in the wounds.

In other words, a whole lot of nothing. Mack tossed the report aside, frustrated.

Dave answered on the first ring.

"I reviewed the autopsy report," Mack said. "Thank you for sending it over. Not much there, though, huh?"

"No. I mean, the broken bottle is interesting."

"Broken bottle? What are you talking about?"

Dave laughed. "You have to look deep, but did you see what Lee pulled out of the wounds? Check out the long paragraph under Evidence of Injury."

Mack grabbed the report and found the relevant paragraph. The first time, she'd given up halfway through it, but now she read the whole paragraph. "Holy cow," she said. "There were shards of glass *in* the wounds?"

"Exactly. I called her to confirm—I was sure I was reading it wrong. She said that, in the photos, the wounds look like they're round—almost like bite marks. But the shards of glass and the depth mean teeth didn't cause them. She thinks it was a broken bottle. Green glass, like maybe Heineken."

"Did you guys find anything when you searched? Broken glass on the floor or in the trash or anything?"

"I don't think so. I think he did a pretty thorough job cleaning up."

"Another dead end. Perfect."

She heard a rustling on the other end of the call. "Hang on, Mack. I'm grabbing the search report and checking."

Mack reached for the Silly Putty she kept on her desk for circumstances just like this. Sometimes doing something with her hands kept her from pacing the room.

Dave whistled, and Mack pulled the phone away from her ear. "They found something?"

"Broken bottle in the trash. Near the top, partially covered. Looked like it had blood on it, so they bagged it. I think they assumed Amanda must have broken the bottle and cut herself cleaning up. Looks like no one submitted it for DNA testing or prints. Rookie mistake. I'll fix that in the morning."

"Yeah, well, who knows how long that will take. And at this point, it only helps us if there's something in CODIS. Hopefully we'll get a better lead from the phones." Mack thought through their next steps. "Can we do a call or meeting with mom? Maybe she can shed some light on things. I know she didn't know about the pregnancy, or a boyfriend, but you talked to her in the immediate aftermath. Maybe now that she's had some time, she'll have more."

"I think she's still in town," Dave said. "I can call her. Can we set it up for tomorrow, if she's available?"

Mack consulted her calendar. "Afternoon," she said. "I have grand jury in the morning, and it's likely to take a while. Really awful case with Wood."

"I like Debbie," Dave said. "She does good work."

"Oh, no," Mack said, worried she'd been misunderstood. "She did a great job. The facts are awful. The case itself is pretty solid."

"Phew. Okay, well, I'll loop back with you when I've talked to Lisa Wagner."

Mack looked up from the phone to see Sheila Erlich waiting patiently in her doorway.

"Hi, there," Mack said. "I thought I was the only one still here."

Sheila came in and dropped gracefully into one of Mack's guest chairs. Her shoulder-length blond hair and makeup were, as always, immaculate. She had been a prosecutor for over twenty-five years—homicides for almost twenty of them—and had led the Homicide unit for the last five. She had tried some of the biggest cases in Tucson's history and trained prosecutors across the country. Sheila's reputation was intimidating; she was known for her uncrackable professionalism. Her detractors referred to her as a frigid bitch. Mack had always admired her from afar and had jumped at the chance to work with her. Mack often found herself running toward intimidating women rather than away from them. Up close, Mack found Sheila to be a supportive and kind supervisor, eager to help young attorneys, especially women, reach their professional goals.

"I like working in the evenings," Sheila said. "It's quieter, and I can usually get more done without interruption."

"Same," Mack said, pleased by the common ground.

"When I saw your light was on, I just wanted to check in. How are you adjusting? We work at a different pace over here, and I realize that we really haven't talked much since you've been here."

Mack considered the question. She had been in the unit for over six months, and she thought things were going well. She had second-chaired three trials and had just hit the point of having a full caseload.

"Good, I think," she said eventually. "Things move slower here than in Sex Crimes, but much faster than the public-relations gig I had between the two trial assignments. I think I'm getting the hang of things."

"It's easy to let your personal life fall by the wayside," Sheila said. "Like in Sex Crimes—don't forget, I spent almost five years there, too. That was twenty years ago, but I don't get the impression things have changed that much."

Mack laughed.

"I know you've had a…difficult last few years."

They had never talked about Mack's life outside of work—never talked about anything beyond Mack's cases and an occasional quip about the heat—and Mack felt immediately on edge, worried about what was to come. She smiled nervously.

"It's been an unusual time," she admitted. "But nothing I haven't been able to handle. And, I hope you'll agree, nothing that has impacted my work performance."

Sheila pursed her lips and tilted her head. She examined Mack's diplomas hanging above her desk.

"Everything is fine, now," Mack continued. "I have my stats handy if you want to check. I have grand jury tomorrow and am resolving cases at or above the unit average, without sacrificing victim satisfaction or sentencing results."

"I'm not worried about the data," Sheila assured her. "But I am hearing some…rumors that concern me."

"What rumors?" Mack asked. "If you tell me what you're hearing, I can tell you what the truth is."

"There are things coming out of Melissa O'Connor's campaign, for one. But I also had lunch with Dr. Lapin not terribly long ago. I hadn't known about your relationship with her—or maybe I just hadn't put together that that was you."

Mack felt herself blushing. She couldn't imagine how her name had come up at lunch. She hadn't even known that Anna and Sheila knew each other. However it had come up, though, she didn't think Anna would have said anything to damage Sheila's opinion of Mack. At least, not on purpose. "Anna and I are no longer involved. As for the campaign, I don't know what you've heard, but I haven't made any deals or commitments to anyone—O'Connor or Campbell. I'm just a line prosecutor, and I have no intention of changing that."

Sheila waved her hand vaguely. "It's not necessary to get into specifics of the O'Connor issue. I trust that you'll let me know when and if it's something the office or I need to worry about. However, I am concerned about your past relationship with Dr. Lapin. That was disclosed, I assume? You know she often testifies for us, in the sexually motivated cases."

Mack's boss in Sex Crimes immediately came to mind. "James Harris knew about it," she said. "He looked at the policy with me and decided it didn't need to be disclosed in a formal memorandum. Whether or not Campbell knew about it, I can't say. Mike Brown did. But, like I said, the relationship has ended. Any conflict that might have existed certainly doesn't anymore. If I had a case where Anna's testimony was necessary, I wouldn't hesitate to call her, and we've always worked well together. I don't think she would tell you anything different."

Sheila leveled her gaze directly at Mack. "Did you know my first husband was a detective? Bernie Erlich."

Of course Mack knew. Everyone knew. Bernie was older than Sheila, and they'd met at the DA's office when he worked there as an investigator. Their arguments were explosive and public, often spilling over into the hallways where anyone could hear. There were betting pools on whether they'd settle for breaking up or one would eventually snap and kill the other, and those pools were only partially in jest.

"I've heard of him," Mack said. "But he was before my time."

Sheila smiled wryly. "A polite way of saying you know all the stories. Well, don't believe everything you hear. There was never any actual risk of violence. I bring him up now for one reason, which is to say that I know whereof I speak. Relationships with other ADAs, with cops, with…psychologists are dangerous. I advise you to avoid them, especially while working for me."

Mack nodded without speaking. She suspected "witnesses" would also feature on that list, but was Beth technically a witness? The case against Adam Bennett had never gone anywhere, since Dave shot him before charges could be brought.

"And if," Sheila continued, "you should find yourself in a situation where there's a potential conflict—either with an individual or with a case—I trust that you will inform me promptly. Right?"

Mack nodded again.

Sheila clapped her hands on the wooden arms of the chair, and Mack jumped at the noise. "Okay, then," her supervisor said, rising and moving toward the door. "I'm glad we had this opportunity to chat. Keep up the good work, Mackenzie."

Mack slumped back in her seat, exhausted. What had *that* been about?

CHAPTER TEN

The grand jury presentation on Ferguson went smoothly. The jurors had no questions, even on the issue of the death of the first baby. Mack was marginally surprised, though the bar of probable cause was a low one, since the evidence that he'd actually killed the baby, rather than just disposing of the body, was the weakest part of the case. Apparently, Daisy's disclosure had covered any gaps.

As she signed the indictments and chatted with the jurors after they returned the true bill, Mack surreptitiously checked her watch. She and Dave were set to meet with Lisa Wagner in fifteen minutes. It would be her interview—Dave would only be there in case Lisa said anything that might require a witness to testify. Mack excused herself and rushed back to her building. Dave was sitting in the lobby with a short, stout woman with tight red curls. Mack assumed this must be Amanda's mother.

"Mrs. Wagner," Mack said, catching her breath. "Come on up. I'm so sorry for your loss."

When they reached Mack's office, the woman sat on the very edge of the chair across from her desk, clearly uncomfortable. "You can call me Lisa. I remarried a few years ago, took my second husband's last name. So it's Linden now, not Wagner."

Mack made a note on her legal pad and shot a quick glance at Dave. He could have warned her. He widened his eyes. He hadn't been aware, either. So Lisa Linden wasn't necessarily the most forthcoming of interview subjects. Good to know.

Lisa turned to Dave. "Do you have any idea, Detective, who did this to my baby?"

"Not yet, ma'am."

"We're hopeful," Mack said, "that in talking to you today we can get some new directions to pursue. Why don't you tell us a little bit about your daughter?"

Lisa fumbled a tissue out of her sleeve. "Amanda is my only. But she grew up surrounded by family, lots of cousins on both sides. She was the heart of the group. Always organizing trips to Six Flags or the movies, making cookies at one of our houses. She loved going into downtown Chicago for theater or shopping or museums. She was a curious, high-energy child. Always busy with something."

"What brought Amanda out west?" Mack asked.

"School. She went to ASU, wanted to get out of our cold Midwestern winters."

Mack smiled. "That's what brought me out, too. I grew up in Cleveland."

Lisa didn't take the offered connection. "When she graduated, I thought she'd come back home, but her boyfriend at the time was from Tucson so they moved down here together, and she started working in real estate. She was a secretary at first, but she was good, a hard worker. She got her broker's license last year."

Real estate. That meant she was regularly in contact with strangers—lots of opportunities to attract a stalker. There had been a serial rapist in Phoenix several years ago who had been targeting agents. Maybe that was an avenue worth pursuing. Mack wasn't sure what had happened to that guy—whether he'd ever been caught—but she had friends in the Phoenix District Attorney's Office she could call and ask.

"What about outside of work?" Mack asked. "Did she have hobbies? Close friends here in town?"

"Oh, yes. She kept herself very active. She was in a kickball league, belonged to a gym and went every day, and was in a book club. She had a lot of friends from college still, and work. It was hard for her to find time to come visit, she was so busy here, but we talked every Wednesday and Sunday. I only knew some of her friends, but I'm sure you could find them on her Facebook."

Mack cringed. She didn't know anyone Amanda's age who still used Facebook for anything other than keeping in touch with elderly relatives. "Did she ever tell you about any problems she was having with anyone?"

"Never." Lisa sniffled into her tissue. "No one had problems with my Amanda. She was too sweet. Too gentle."

Mack hummed sympathetically. She thought about her own weekly phone calls with her mother. Even in the midst of the previous year's issues, she hadn't let on to her mom. What was the point of worrying her all the way in Cleveland? She wondered how much she and Amanda had in common in that regard.

"What about her dating life?" Dave asked. "You mentioned a boyfriend."

"William," Lisa said. "He was a nice boy, but they were never going to last. He didn't have the kind of ambition Amanda had. And, well, there was some tension toward the end, I guess."

"What kind of tension?" Dave asked.

Lisa looked down at the desk. "I don't want to—well, he was a nice boy, and I only know a little bit of what happened. But he—he had a temper, I guess. And finally Amanda had enough of it. She'd seen what it's like, being involved with a man with a temper. My ex-husband was the same way."

So he hit her. Mack wondered where William was now. Had he and Amanda remained in contact? Abusive ex-boyfriends were always a good lead, especially if their breakup hadn't been quite as definitive as Lisa thought it was.

"And since then?" Mack asked.

"No one serious," Lisa said. "Amanda was focused on other things. I wanted her to have kids, of course, but she always said 'Mom, I have plenty of time!' I didn't push her, because of course it was her decision. My mom pushed me, and I didn't want to do the same thing to my little girl."

"Sergeant Barton told you that Amanda was pregnant at the time of her death. She hadn't mentioned that to you?"

Lisa blew her nose. Mack handed her the tissue box she kept on her desk and waited for the sobs to abate.

"I know how hard it is to talk about these things," Mack said. "But we need a clear picture of what Amanda's life was like in order to figure out who did this and get justice for her."

"She would have told me," Lisa said through her tears. "She would have called me from the doctor's office, I know she would have."

Mack wished they had cracked Amanda's phone. She didn't want to push a grieving mother too hard, but maybe if they had something more concrete to show her, they'd start to get at the truth.

She checked her list of questions. They'd covered them all and gotten almost nothing to show for it.

The phone. That's where the answers would be.

CHAPTER ELEVEN

The email came in just at the point in the afternoon when Mack was most in need of a break. The sheer volume of reports already generated in the Ferguson case was intimidating. Police had interviewed family members, teachers, everyone who might have something that could corroborate Daisy's story.

Because Daisy had delayed reporting her father's abuse until that night in the hospital, organizing the material chronologically wouldn't work. Mack didn't want to start the jury off with the evidence of the murder, though. They had to believe Daisy before they heard about the baby—it was the only way Mack could be confident they'd convict absent evidence proving that shaking had been the cause of death. Mack made a note to ask someone in the Domestic Violence unit to refer her to an expert on shaken baby syndrome. She'd need someone to explain it to the jury.

She was considering whether she could get away with another cup of coffee without sacrificing any chance of sleep when her computer pinged.

It was Dave Barton, asking if she could come to the computer forensics lab. They'd finally managed to crack Amanda Wagner's phone and had found, as Mack predicted, useful information. Mack smiled for the first time that day and grabbed her purse. Finally!

She swung through a Starbucks drive-through on her way, and Dave gratefully accepted the venti black coffee she handed him when he greeted her in the lobby of the police building that housed the computer forensics team. Their work was split between examining digital evidence for detectives across the department—trying to crack a murder one day and an organized retail theft ring the next—and their own investigations into computer-based crime. Child pornography, hacking, cyber-terrorism, they saw a little of everything. Mack was always impressed by the level of knowledge the computer guys displayed. Her own expertise began and ended with, "Did you try turning it off and on again?"

Dave showed her into a spacious cubicle filled with a variety of unidentifiable equipment. The assigned forensics guy waved. "Drew," he said, reaching to shake Mack's hand.

"Show me what we've got, gentlemen."

Drew clicked through a series of screens on the middle monitor of his three-monitor display. Mack recognized the forensic extraction tool, which mirrored data from a phone and presented it in a user-friendly format.

"The most interesting stuff is in her texts," Dave said. "But let's go ahead and start with some of the smaller pieces. We've got her search history. Starting approximately two weeks before her death, she was looking for pregnancy information."

Mack watched Drew's cursor move across the screen. Amanda had been trying to figure out when she had gotten pregnant. She was also investigating termination options, from pills to local abortion providers.

"She was looking at abortion for two weeks but hadn't done anything?" Mack asked. "Doesn't that seem, I don't know, odd to you?"

Dave shrugged. "Can't say. But look at this. She starts searching on the thirteenth. We can assume, for now, that she took a test and it came out positive, because here she's looking for how reliable home pregnancy tests are. Then she starts figuring out the timeline. See? *How soon can an at-home test tell if you're pregnant.* Then immediately starts looking at termination—abortion pills first—but she must figure she was too far along. Then two days pass with nothing. That's Saturday and Sunday. Then Monday, she changes her tune. She's no longer looking at termination, now she's checking out single-parent blogs and stuff. That goes on for a couple of days."

Mack was getting a picture of Amanda: she was trying to figure out how to move forward under life-changing circumstances. She tried to imagine what she would do in the same situation. Well, it was different. If she got pregnant, it would either be intentional—and very expensive, from what she understood—or else a result of sexual assault, in which case she would terminate, no questions asked.

She thought back to the aftermath of Benjamin Allen's attack. She'd taken the Plan B pills she'd been offered and had waited anxiously for weeks until she was sure the emotional danger of an unwanted pregnancy had passed.

"So, what? She told the dad, and he wasn't into it? Decided to keep the kid anyway? Or did he want the kid and talk her into having it?"

"Maybe," Dave said. "Any of those are possible. But then—Drew, scroll down…there we go. On the twenty-fifth, she's looking at termination again. Not medication abortion. Abortion providers."

"It was too late for a chemical solution," Mack speculated. "But something changed her mind. And she was killed on the twenty-seventh?"

"Yes. Okay, let's switch to email briefly."

Mack zoned out as Drew clicked through a series of screens. What could have made Amanda go back to considering abortion? Had she found something on the blogs that convinced her she wasn't up for being a single parent?

"Okay," Dave said again. "Here's an email she received on the twenty-sixth."

Mack read through the short, auto-generated email confirming an appointment at Planned Parenthood for the thirtieth. "Can we find out what the appointment was for?" she asked without much hope.

"Probably not," Dave said. "I've got someone working on a search warrant for any notes or internal documents, including any forms she completed online, but HIPAA, you know?"

"Now texts?" Drew asked.

Dave nodded.

"There are two contacts in her texts that are potentially interesting," Dave said. "Unfortunately, both saved not under their real names. We've got 'Cesar Chavez – Tinder' and 'Billy Bumble.' Let's go with Cesar first."

Mack read the text thread as Drew scrolled through it in reverse chronological order. "This sure looks like a boyfriend," she said. "They're making repeated plans, and a lot of it seems pretty domestic. Dinners, she's offering to do his laundry, some sexy lingerie shots. That's not stuff you do for a casual Tinder encounter. But what's up with the fake name? Most people get rid of those once things get serious, right?"

Dave laughed. "Mack, I've been married since I had an AOL screen name. What do I know from Internet dating? But that sounds reasonable to me. Check out the timeframe, though. Everything is normal until two weeks before her death, then there's this big gap. Days go by with no texts, then it's intermittent up until she dies."

"She tells him she's pregnant and it's his, and he hits the brakes?"

"Seems reasonable, but now look at Billy."

A similar text thread. Domestic, repeated contact. Dinners at home. Then everything cooled off two weeks before Amanda's death.

"So she's what, like, polyamorous or something?" Mack asked. "And she hadn't told her mom? Not that anyone could blame her."

"Unclear," Dave said. "And since we don't have IDs on either of these guys, we have no one to ask."

"You working on identifying the phone numbers?" Mack asked.

"Actually," Drew said, "we've got that one covered. Subpoenas are already in. Should have subscriber info in a couple of days, assuming Verizon doesn't give us any trouble on Billy."

"Couple last things," Dave said. He pointed to the last texts between Amanda and Billy. "This is from the twenty-sixth. They make plans to meet that night, see?" He directed Mack to a second monitor displaying Amanda's call log. "Then an hour later there's a four-minute phone call, from him to her." He gestured back to the texts. "And they must have fought on that call, because it looks like Billy didn't show. Then we have four messages from Amanda in about twenty minutes, asking where he was and getting increasingly annoyed, and then this—"

"'Fuck you, then!'" Mack read aloud. "'I thought you were better than ghosting me, especially today of all days. But whatever, I guess you were just waiting to show who you really are. I'm done. Lose my number.'"

"So did he actually know about the pregnancy?" Dave asked. "Or did he get in a car accident and then get out of the hospital to find out his girlfriend lost her mind a little bit and dumped him? He calls her twice on the twenty-seventh but she doesn't pick up, and that's all we know. Except there's one more damning fact—but it cuts both ways. After his calls on the twenty-seventh, there's nothing. He never texts or calls again."

"Like he knows she's dead, so what's the point?"

"Yep," Dave said.

"And what about Señor Chavez?" Mack asked. "When's their last contact?"

"Great question," Dave said. "They've got a fifteen-minute phone call—her to him—on the twenty-seventh at seven thirty p.m."

"I wish we had that call," Mack said.

"Of course. But in the meantime, check out their final texts, after the call."

It took Mack a second to orient herself and adjust to reading from the bottom of the screen to the top.

Cesar: *Fuck you, I guess you just get to make this decision by yourself? Don't fucking do this to me.*

Amanda: *I am exactly the one who gets to make the decision. Fuck you right back. I don't need this shit*

Cesar: *Don't be like that. Look, I can be there in 15.*

Amanda: *I don't want you here. I won't let you in*

Cesar: *The fuck you won't.*

Then nothing. The last text was time-stamped 8:15, three hours before the neighbor heard Amanda fighting for her life.

"And then Cesar never tries again?" Mack asked.

"Right," Dave said. "Just like Billy. They both act like they know there's no point in trying to reach her. Which is…a strange coincidence, to say the least. Given what we have of the end of their communications, it seems weird that they would both just ghost her on the night she got killed."

Mack read the texts a second time. "So our theory is that Cesar showed up and Amanda did let him in? And then, what, he told Billy? Or that part was coincidence?"

"I'm not sure," Dave said. "But she sure had a pretty terrible two days, huh? I think that's what we have to assume at this point: she let Cesar in, he killed her, Billy is a coincidence. At least, there's nothing saying those two knew each other or were working together. I could go either way, Billy or Cesar. But, given the timing, I'm putting my money on Cesar."

"You'll investigate them both, though, right?" Mack asked.

"Of course," he said. "We always do."

CHAPTER TWELVE

The next morning, Mack walked into her office to find a thick pile of papers on her desk that hadn't been there the day before. A motion from Tom Colbey, Ferguson's newly appointed attorney. She'd worked with Tom before and, based on the results he got, always found his high opinion of his own lawyering skills to be unwarranted. He seemed to come from the school of "If you can't out-lawyer them, try to out-paper them."

Defendant's Motion to Dismiss Count 1 for Lack of Corpus Delicti. Seriously, a corpus motion? On the baby's death? The corpus rule dated back to English common law and was based on the premise that people shouldn't be convicted of crimes based solely on their own words. If delusional Joe wandered into a police station and claimed to have killed his wife, the police couldn't charge him based on that alone—they had to find the wife's body, or a big puddle of blood, or something else that corroborated Joe's words. Ferguson hadn't admitted to any of the charges against him, so there was no legal possibility for a corpus issue.

Mack skimmed through the document. Tom was arguing that, because there was no physical evidence to support homicide as the cause of the baby's death, all the police had to go on were Daisy's claims. No corroboration equaled no corpus.

Mack rolled her eyes. Under normal circumstances, this would be too stupid to worry about, but they were assigned to Judge Leyva, a former family-law attorney who had only represented fathers and was a member of a fathers'-rights organization. He was notoriously hard on the State—and weak on the law. In front of him, all bets were off.

* * *

"Have you ever responded to a corpus motion?" Mack asked as she approached the open door to Jess' office.

When she got there, she almost dropped the motion when she saw Dr. Anna Lapin sitting across the desk from Jess. She looked great in her summer-weight wool suit, immaculately tailored. Her hair was shorter than Mack remembered, with fresh, honey-colored highlights.

Jess glanced at her guiltily. "We're prepping for a hearing," she said. "Anna's testifying for me, and I wanted to go over some things in advance."

Anna smiled. "It's nice to see you, Mack."

Mack nodded, backing out of the doorway. "You, too," she said. "Okay, well, I'll let you guys keep at it. Good luck at your hearing. Jess, if you could stop by later?"

She slumped against the wall. Logically, she had known that she would eventually see Anna again. She could even, in theory, wrap her mind around their working together again—although that one was harder, and she had a long list of experts she'd try to call first, despite what she'd said to reassure Sheila. But she assumed she'd have time to prepare for a meeting, to fix her hair and be wearing her best outfit, not—she looked down at herself and groaned—old chinos and a DA's office polo. Of all the days to wear casual clothes.

To add insult to injury, Mack found a new email when she got back to her office. Judge Leyva's judicial assistant, Sarah, looking to set an evidentiary hearing on the corpus motion. What possible evidence could he want? The medical examiner testifying that the baby was dead? Daisy? Mack put her head down on the cool wood of her desk and closed her eyes.

She jumped up at the sound of her office door closing, and there was Anna, sitting across from her like the last year hadn't happened.

"It really is good to see you," Anna said. She ran a hand through her hair. Mack recognized the gesture. Anna was nervous.

"Shouldn't you be prepping for your hearing?" Mack asked. She could feel the thudding of her heartbeat.

Anna smiled. "It's all pretty clear. You know your friend Jess, she worries."

"She's thorough."

Anna dipped her head. "Yeah. Thorough. Anyway, I wanted to come say hi, even before you stopped by. Sheila told me you were in this unit now, and I was glad to hear it. They can use someone like you here."

"Thanks."

Anna sighed and repeated her nervous hair-combing. "I don't know why you're being so insistent on making things awkward, Mack."

"I don't know what you're talking about."

"I want to be friends again. I never wanted things to end up like this, where we can't even have a simple conversation. You were there for me last year, when I needed you most."

Mack looked away, staring at the framed photo of her and her mom at the Desert Museum. Her face was hot, and she could feel her eyes fill with tears. "I wish I could say the same." She cleared her throat. "Listen, I've really got to work on this motion. I'll call you, okay? We'll go to coffee or something."

"Okay, Mack." Anna stood and opened the door. "Okay. Whatever you say. I just...I want you to know, I'm trying, here. I'd like a chance to make things right. If you hang on to this pain forever, you'll be stuck. We've got too much history to just fall out of each other's lives. Okay?"

Mack focused on her breathing until the door closed behind Anna. In for five, hold for five, out for five. After several minutes, she felt her body return to normal, the tension releasing from her muscles, her heart rate slowing. She turned to the motion response in front of her and started writing.

CHAPTER THIRTEEN

The movie in the background was little more than a distraction as Beth and Mack cuddled on Mack's couch. Beth rubbed Mack's scalp with the deep pressure that helped Mack release the stress of a long week.

"Did you know I took a massage class in college?"

"Hmm?" Mack asked. It took her brain a second to catch up.

"I could help you loosen your shoulder muscles. You're so tense."

"That sounds great." Mack leaned into Beth's hands, strong thumbs now rubbing either side of her neck.

"You know what else would help? Getting out on the trail tomorrow morning. Jess and I are meeting at Tanque Verde."

Mack sat up. "Tanque Verde? You still go there? Even after last year?"

Beth shrugged. "Sure. I mean, it's my favorite trail for a reason, and that was…that was a fluke. Finding that girl's body like that. I don't like to go by myself, necessarily, but going with Jess will be okay."

"No, that's great. It's weird that she didn't mention it to me when we had lunch today, but it's great."

"You think it's weird?"

Mack paused. "I mean, don't you?"

"Not at all. I think it's normal for people to become friends when they have shared interests, and we both like hiking."

Mack let the misunderstanding slide. "Okay, I guess. I just don't think I'd be able to do it, if I were in your shoes. I'd let Bennett ruin things for me—like I always do."

Beth leaned back against the soft gray couch and gestured Mack to come closer.

Mack paused the movie. "Did I tell you about this conversation I had recently with a defense attorney—Nick Diaz?"

"I don't think so. What does this have to do with hiking tomorrow?"

"Nothing, I just can't stop thinking about it and want to talk to you about it, but then when I saw you earlier in your cute outfit and carrying a bottle of good wine, I got all distracted. But now I remembered."

She told Beth about her conversation with Nick and the job offer from Melissa.

"I just got this vibe from him, like maybe there's more to his mission against Campbell than he's letting on."

Beth took out her phone and checked the time. "Like what?" she asked. She sounded bored, but Mack needed to work through this. She stood and paced the living room.

"Like he mentioned the Petrou series last year—the one about me? And something about how he said it made it sound like, well, I know this sounds crazy, but I think he might have leaked stuff to Petrou."

"How would he have anything to leak?"

"I don't know. It's a small town, especially for lawyers. I don't know who his friends are. He said people in the office recommended me to him for this job with Melissa. Maybe they also let stuff slip last year. And he let it slip to Petrou."

"Could you ask him?"

"I'm not sure," Mack said. She poured herself another glass of the wine Beth had brought. "I'm not sure I can ask without putting the job offer at risk. And I'm not ready to do that yet, because this whole thing aside, he's right that I don't like or trust Campbell. I don't think he's good for the community, so if I can be convinced that Melissa is a safe bet, I think I'd probably want to sign up, right?"

"Don't ask me," Beth said. "I signed her petition to get on the ballot in the first place. I think she's great."

"Would you have signed the petition for any Democrat who asked?"

Beth smiled. "Any Democrat woman, you bet. And it doesn't hurt that she's cute."

Mack snorted. "Compared to Campbell, you'd think a female Crypt Keeper was cute."

"Well, if there's no way to know the deal with Petrou without blowing your chance at a promotion, then what's the point in speculating? Come on, let's finish watching Cate Blanchett seduce this girl and then go to bed. You can argue both sides of this debate tomorrow while we're on the trail. I bet Jess will even participate."

Mack reluctantly settled back on the couch, but she couldn't focus on the movie. She needed to move around, figure out how to ask Nick if he'd been the leak. She needed to get on the treadmill and run until she couldn't worry anymore.

The movie over, Beth stood and reached for Mack's hand. They walked into Mack's bedroom, but Mack still felt agitated, even when Beth told her to lie down and started kneading her shoulders.

An hour later, Beth had drifted off to sleep. Mack lay beside her, resisting the urge to get on the treadmill. If they were going hiking in the morning, she'd need a good night's sleep.

The doorbell rang.

CHAPTER FOURTEEN

"What are *you* doing here?" Mack asked.

The man on her doorstep was tall, with a deep tan and blond hair turned mostly to gray. Mack knew that many women would call him handsome, although she had never thought so. The features that meshed so well on Mack's face made him look too feminine.

"Aren't you going to invite me in?" Marcus Wilson—her father—asked.

Mack resisted the urge to slam the door in his face and go back to bed. "I haven't decided."

His smile widened. "Still the same old Mackenzie, huh? You don't pull any punches."

Mack remembered that smile. It was the smile he used to get women to do what he wanted. The smile he flashed at cops to get out of tickets. The smile he wore when he missed Mack's birthday, or her band concert, or didn't show up for visitation and left her standing outside school, watching the streetlights come on.

"I haven't seen you in like ten years," she said. "Mom said you were living in Oregon. What are you doing in Tucson? What are you doing at my house, at midnight? How did you even get my address?"

"I'll explain everything, kiddo. Just, you know, let me inside, huh? It's cold out here. I need to warm up these old bones."

She didn't want him in her house, and she definitely didn't want Beth to meet him. She stepped outside and pulled the door shut behind her. "It's almost eighty degrees, and your old bones are fine. We can sit outside, and you can say whatever it is you came here to say."

Mack thought back to the last time she'd seen her father, a professional union organizer who had spent her childhood moving from one beleaguered workplace to another, rarely paying attention to his daughter. Marcus had shown up on Mack's doorstep in Tempe early the morning of her law school graduation. She wasn't sure how he'd known about it—her mother, no doubt, keen to believe the best of her wayward ex-husband...

He sat at her kitchen bar that day—she didn't have a dining table and ate her meals on the couch or at her desk—and she leaned against the counter, sipping a tepid Gatorade in an attempt to tame her hangover.

"Knife, Knife, Knife," he said.

She flinched. "I've told you not to call me that."

He'd taken the nickname from an old Bobby Darin song, which he sang as a lullaby. Mack hadn't realized how intensely demented that was until she was in college and really listened to the lyrics.

"Old habits. So...this is a nice place you've got here."

"Thanks." Mack didn't mention the scholarships she'd earned, the loans she'd taken out, the jobs she'd worked, scrimping and saving for a place of her own. She knew better than to say too much. Anything she said could and would be used against her.

"Law school, huh? You really did it. I never thought you'd choose something so...I don't know. So corporate."

Mack shrugged.

"Do you know what you're going to do next? Your mom said something about the police, but that can't be right. The unions always need lawyers, you know, if you want to move back East, get out of this dirty desert. I've been doing some great things with a Teamsters local in North Carolina. I could get you hooked in with them, and I'm sure they'd be grateful for the help."

"That's a thoughtful offer, but I'll pass. I don't know anything about labor law. I actually have a job at the Tucson District Attorney's Office lined up, fortunately." Mack peeled the label off her bottle of Gatorade, unsure how much she wanted to reveal. "I have to take the bar exam this summer, but I'll be working as a law clerk until my results come in. If I pass, I'll be a prosecutor."

Marcus whistled, but his face was grim. "So your mom didn't get it completely wrong. I can't believe a daughter of mine would wind up working for the cops."

"I won't be working for the police, Dad. I'll be working for the district attorney. And I'm excited about it. I've wanted this job since college."

"Yeah, well, college students are still kids. I assumed you'd grow out of it. Heck, I wanted to be Batman when I was a kid."

"Yeah," Mack scoffed. She was close to losing her temper and struggling to get herself under control. Her dad had always seemed to enjoy provoking her. Staying calm was the key. "That sounds like exactly the same thing. What you wanted to do when you were seven and what I wanted to do at twenty. And besides, not everyone thinks the police are the bad guys. I don't think the cops are the enemy. Most parents don't teach their kids how to invoke before they teach them to tie their shoes."

"Most parents are sheep," Marcus said. "I taught you what you needed to know to get by in this world, and now here you are, pissing on everything I said. You know, I wouldn't be surprised if this whole law school thing was just your way of spiting me. How am I supposed to tell my friends, my *colleagues*, that my own daughter has joined up with the pigs? Some day, Knife, you're going to wake up and realize that you sacrificed your youth to get back at your old man. You give me a call when that day comes."

She hadn't responded, just watched him stomp out of her apartment and slam the door behind him. She hoped her mom, asleep in Mack's bedroom, hadn't heard the fight. Her parents had split up for good when Mack was seven or eight, but she knew her mom still loved the asshole, kept hoping he'd finally settle down and they could reunite.

When he didn't show up for graduation, Mack wasn't exactly surprised, but she half expected him to call, to apologize for accusing his only child of selling her soul. But as days turned to weeks turned to months, she realized that wasn't going to happen. He wasn't going to call. Eventually, she came to feel like she'd never had a father to begin with. When people asked about her family, she just talked about her mom, and most people never pushed for more.

Over the years, her mom had kept in touch with him. As far as Mack knew, she still didn't know about their argument the morning of Mack's graduation. Every once in a while, she'd mention Marcus in an email or during a phone call, but Mack never took the bait. She knew her mom couldn't help loving him, just like she couldn't help not. The only time she'd heard from him directly was via a bouquet of flowers he sent two years earlier, shortly after she was attacked by Benjamin Allen. She'd never even thanked him.

"So," she said when he was settled on the bench beside her front door—the first thing she bought when she'd moved into the house a year earlier. She leaned against the alcove wall. "Mom tell you where I was?"

"Nah," he said. "I was in Albuquerque a few years ago doing a thing with migrant workers, and when that wrapped up I came out here. Found you on the DA's website. Figured we'd run into each other at some point, but I guess we still move in different crowds, huh?"

"You've been in Tucson for *years*?" Mack asked.

"Yep. Turns out the desert air agrees with my eczema."

"And you never thought, 'Gosh, I should let my only child know I'm living in her city'?"

"Hey, I sent you flowers when that whole thing happened. The ball was in your court, Knife."

"Don't call me that," Mack said. That was just a reflex. In truth, she didn't care what he called her, not anymore. She hadn't cared for a long time. "Okay, then. Anyway, you've been living in Tucson for years and you just decided to come say hi tonight at midnight."

"Well, it's not exactly a social call, there, kiddo. I'm in a bit of a tight spot, and I hoped you might be able to help your old man out. For old time's sake."

Old time's sake. Right. Like when Mack was a kid and he'd raid her piggy bank, sometimes using her allowance for leaflets and poster board, but more often, she learned as she got older, for cheap beers after his protest du jour.

"Well, you see…I had…well, I had this girlfriend. Really nice lady, I think you'd've liked her a lot." He paused. Mack could see him struggling. "We had a…well, I guess you would call it a disagreement. Nothing serious. She didn't realize my age, is what happened. So when she did become aware of it, she decided she was a little young for me."

"How young is she?" Mack asked.

"Well, oh, I guess around thirty-two or so."

"Thirty-two? Jesus, she's almost six years younger than me! That is so inappropriate."

Marcus glared at her. "I'm not here for your judgment, thank you very much."

Mack rolled her eyes. Her father never had been willing to accept criticism.

"The thing of it is," Marcus said. "Well, the thing of it is that she…she went and got herself pregnant."

"You mean you got her pregnant? Gross."

He sent her another warning look. "Not necessarily. Ms. Mandy wasn't all that interested in monogamy, as a concept or as a practice. So I'm not sure to this day whether or not it was mine. But between me being a little older than she thought—"

Mack snorted.

"—and the baby, she broke things off with me."

"That must have been a relief," Mack said. "All things considered. I mean, you must have had a hard time keeping up with a woman half your age to begin with. Add a baby into the mix, and you must have been looking for the door."

"Things have changed since you were a kid, Mackenzie. Hell, *I've* changed. She was pretty sure the baby was mine, and I was ready to do the right thing. I told her I would stick around and raise the kid if a paternity test showed that I was the father."

"Touching, really. So when do I get to meet my new baby brother or sister?"

"Yeah, well, she didn't want the baby. I guess she took my initial response—"

"Which was what, you said it was somebody else's kid?"

"I might have suggested that," Marcus acknowledged. "Anyway, she'd made up her mind not to keep it, no matter what I said."

"Can't say I blame her," Mack said.

Her father looked up at her, his arms loosely folded around his knees. She felt a sudden stab of pity for the old man. Getting dumped hurt, no matter the circumstances.

Mack looked at her watch. "Get to the point, Dad. What tight spot are you in? Where do I come in to it?"

Marcus sighed. "I guess I should just come out with it. She's dead—murdered, I guess. The cops say there's no real doubt about that."

The hairs on Mack's arms stood up, and she was suddenly cold. "You called her Ms. Mandy," she said. "Your girlfriend was Amanda Wagner?"

"How do you know her last name?" Marcus asked.

"I was the prosecutor at the scene," Mack said. "I was there the night she was killed. You had a girlfriend who lived walking distance from my house, and you never showed up here until three weeks after she died?"

"I just got out of an interview with your friends the pigs. Thought it was time we talked."

Mack opened the door, her head swimming.

"You'd better come inside after all."

CHAPTER FIFTEEN

Mack brewed a pot of coffee as her father walked around her living room, pausing to examine a book here, a photograph there.

"I didn't make the cut, huh?" he asked.

Mack clenched her jaw. She wanted him out of her house. She didn't want to hear another word of his sad-sack, self-pitying bull. She really didn't want him to meet Beth. But her professional instincts had kicked in, and she needed to know what was going on.

Marcus sat at the dining table and accepted the mug Mack handed him.

"I have milk," Mack said. "Well, almond milk. And Splenda, I think."

He shook his head.

Mack drank from her mug. Adrenaline would keep her awake through the night, so the coffee was just to stave off a headache. "Okay," she said. "Why were you talking to the police?"

"I spent the evening with some friends. Went to dinner at a little Mexican place on the South Side. When I got home—I live in an apartment a few miles from here—there were two uniforms waiting for me."

"Did you get their names?"

"No. I didn't even realize they were there for me until they asked me to go with them to the station. I tried to say no, but they roughed me up a little bit and eventually I got in the car."

Mack doubted that was true. She could see no signs of a struggle and, if he wasn't under arrest, there wouldn't have been any reason for them to touch him. They would have let him drive his own car to the station...unless he was intoxicated.

"Have a few cervezas with dinner?"

He wagged his head from side to side. "Maybe. So we get downtown and they lead me into an interview room and leave me in there to stew a little bit. Then two suits come in. Burly guy, clearly the one in charge, and a woman. Classic good cop, bad cop."

"How about their names?" Mack asked.

"I didn't catch hers, but his was something with a B. Barber? Barnard?"

"Barton?" Mack asked, her throat tight.

Marcus slapped the table, and she jumped at the sound.

"Barton. Yeah, that was it."

"Okay," Mack said. She could feel herself begin to panic, memories of her own interview with Dave the year before flooding her mind. She needed time to think. She needed to get her father out of the house. Dave wouldn't go behind her back on purpose—she knew that—which meant he must not have put it together that Marcus Wilson and Mack Wilson were father and daughter. "Did you tell him about me?"

Marcus shook his head. "I didn't think that would help my case. They weren't really interested in getting to know me as a person, you know? They told me they had me figured for having killed Amanda, and the only thing they wanted to hear from me was a confession. Now mind you, I didn't even know she was dead until they told me. I just knew she'd dropped out of touch."

Amanda's murder had dominated the news cycle the day after she died. A pretty white woman killed by person or persons unknown, when she should have been safe in her home? The media had eaten it up. Was it really possible that Marcus hadn't seen it? Mack didn't want to know.

"They showed me some photos, said they were of Amanda, but I didn't take a good enough look to be sure. Just a big bloody mess. They said she hadn't gotten rid of the baby, and that it was mine, which made me suspect numero uno."

"What specifically did they ask you?"

"The usual questions. It's not like I'd never been in an interview room before, kiddo."

"Getting arrested at a labor protest isn't exactly the same as getting interviewed in a murder investigation. But if you want to be the expert, that's fine. I'll take my many years of prosecution experience back to bed. You can see yourself out."

Marcus eyed her, his smile fully falling away for the first time. "They asked where I was from the twenty-fifth to the twenty-eighth."

"What did you tell them?"

"I don't remember."

Mack remembered these semantic games from her childhood. Even credited them, in her kinder moments, with helping her become skilled at cross-examination. "You don't remember what you told them, or you don't remember where you were?"

"Both, actually. I'm a little shaken by the whole thing, I'll tell you. I haven't had any trouble in a long time, and they didn't go easy on me. That Barton guy is a tough character."

Mack had watched Dave do dozens of interviews over the years, and "tough" wasn't in the top fifty words she'd use to describe him.

"Did they tell you how they knew the baby was yours?" she asked.

Marcus shook his head. "I didn't ask."

"Did you know about the baby? I'm sure they asked that, right?"

He shrugged. "I guess they probably did. It's hard to remember."

"But then they let you go." It wasn't a question. If they had any evidence connecting her father to the baby, they would have kept him. Dave had overplayed his hand, hoping to get a confession. When that didn't work, though, they'd had to set him free.

"They let me go, but they made it pretty clear they'd be back. I don't think I'm out of the woods. Which is why I decided I should check in with you. I've seen your name in the news the last couple years. All your potential for better things aside, Kni—Mackenzie, you're not shabby at this lawyering thing."

"That almost sounded like a compliment, which, you know, thanks and all, but let's not get ahead of ourselves. I've never done any defense work, and I certainly don't intend to start now. I'm a prosecutor, remember?"

"But you must know people, right? I don't have all the money in the world, but I'm not destitute. It's not like the old days. I can afford to get ahead of this."

Mack scanned her mental list of defense attorneys she liked and respected. None she'd want to pawn this off on. "I think you should wait," she said. "In most cases, the public defenders are way better than anyone you could hire. They're in it for the cause and the courtroom practice, not the money. But you can't reach out to the PD's office until you're charged. If that happens—"

"Chas v'shalom," Marcus interjected.

Mack nodded mechanically. "Sure," she said. "If that happens, God forbid, then you can see whether or not the PD who gets appointed seems decent. If not, then you reach out and hire someone. But it's premature to start paying someone now, before we're even sure you're a suspect."

"We?" Marcus asked.

Mack drank the rest of her coffee and stood. Her mind was racing. "I don't know yet," she said. "I'm not sure there's anything I can actually, well, *do* for you in this situation. But I'm—I'm not ruling it out, how about that?"

Her father drained his mug and left it on the table. "I guess that'll have to do for now."

CHAPTER SIXTEEN

Mack tried to get her panicked thoughts in order. Whether or not her father had actually murdered Amanda Wagner wouldn't change her next steps. She wondered if she should have asked him. Would his inevitable denial have reassured her? Probably not.

She called Dave almost without realizing it, only noticing the time once it was ringing. He answered anyway.

"You interviewed my father without even giving me a courtesy call, Dave? Really?"

"I did *what*?" Dave said, sounding wide awake and already angry. "I didn't even know you had a dad."

Mack laughed despite herself. "Everyone has a dad, Dave."

"Well, sure. But I always assumed yours was dead, or had never been around, or something. You never talk about having two parents. Are you saying Marcus Wilson is your dad?"

"Nailed it," Mack said, the hot rush of anger leaving her body as quickly as it had appeared. "I know you didn't know. I'd already had this whole conversation with myself about how you couldn't know, but he came here after you let him go and I'm all...well, I'm out of sorts, I guess. I've never been close with him, so I don't really talk about him much. No wonder you didn't put it together. I mean, it's not like Wilson is such a rare last name. Sorry for Hulking out for a second."

A long pause.

"I'm not asking you about the interview," she said when the silence became uncomfortable. "And I'm not trying to interfere in your investigation. You do what you're going to do."

"Then why did you call?"

Mack sighed. "I'm not sure. I guess I needed to hear that he hadn't made up the interview. He believes he's the main suspect in the Amanda Wagner case. Without jeopardizing your investigation, is that accurate?"

Dave coughed into the phone. "I can neither confirm nor deny. But, Mack, I think you probably need to hand this one off to someone."

"I didn't think of that. You're right, of course. I'll talk to Sheila first thing Monday morning. If you need something before then...I don't even know. If you need something before then, call Jess, I guess. I'll give her a heads-up."

"Without getting too deeply into the weeds, I don't expect to need anything this weekend. Just have the new ADA call me on Monday. Anything else?"

"I just...would you be able to—I didn't get his phone number, when he was here. I don't have it. I could get it from my mom, I guess, but I'd rather not have to ask her. She'd think it was suspicious, ask a lot of questions. Did you get his number?"

"I can't give you that, Mack. You'll have to get it somewhere else—either from your mom, or, I don't know, maybe you have it laying around somewhere. Good night. I'm going back to bed."

He disconnected the call.

Maybe she had it laying around somewhere? What was that supposed to mean—she'd just told Dave that she had no contact with him. Where could she possibly have it?

And then it hit her.

"Shit," she said. "Shit, shit, *shit*." She walked into the third bedroom, which she'd turned into a small but functional office. The Wagner file was on her desk.

She flipped to the computer forensics summary report.

Cesar Chavez...Tinder.

No way.

She dialed the number.

"Knife?" her father answered.

CHAPTER SEVENTEEN

Beth was up and out first thing in the morning, none the wiser about Mack's late-night visitor.

"Did you sleep on the couch?" she asked, stepping out of the shower. "I woke up at one point, and you weren't there."

Mack was brushing her teeth. She spat into the sink before responding. "I wasn't tired, so I had the TV on for a while. I came in pretty early this morning, but you were snoring."

"No!" Beth said, laughing and dropping her towel. Mack watched her in the mirror. "I never snore."

Mack recognized the invitation but couldn't bring herself to accept. She hadn't been able to sleep after confirming that her father was Amanda's Cesar Chavez, and she was already paying the price. She was exhausted, and her head was throbbing. She knew she couldn't afford a day of rest, though. There was too much to figure out—too much to do.

"Are you coming hiking?" Beth asked.

"Wish I could, but I have some stuff I have to take care of," Mack said, pulling her hair into a ponytail. "Maybe we could see each other tonight? For dinner or whatever?"

Beth finished pulling up her black leggings. "Mmm," she said, adjusting her baseball cap. "I have plans tonight. But I think I have a free evening late this week, if that works for you? I'll have to check my calendar to see whether it's Thursday or Friday."

"Sure," Mack said. "Just let me know, and if it works, that's great. I'm going to get going. Feel free to stay as long as you want. Just put the garage door down when you leave."

She'd offered Beth a key weeks earlier, to make things easier, but Beth had demurred and had only been willing to accept the garage door code. "Can't lose a code," she'd joked. Mack had forced a smile in return. The offer hadn't *meant* anything, she told herself.

"I'm ready," Beth said. "We can leave together." She pulled Mack in for a chaste kiss, and Mack deflated a little more. She was sure Beth was busy with some other girlfriend—or some other boyfriend, for that matter—and she was getting tired of it. She wished she felt comfortable telling her what was going on with her father, but it seemed like too much too soon. Beth had made herself clear from the start. She was interested in someone to have fun with, not a relationship. And wasn't that what Mack wanted, too?

Once she was in her car and heading out of the neighborhood, Mack called Jess.

"Little early there for a Sunday," Jess croaked. "Don't you think, Wilson?"

"It is fully ten o'clock," she said. "So if I'm waking you up, that's on you. Besides, you're supposed to be meeting Beth in like half an hour. I need you to cancel on her, by the way."

Jess groaned.

"Get up and get dressed," Mack said. "I'm on my way over, and we're going hiking. Bring Shirley. I'll stop for bagel sammies on the way."

Jess groaned again.

Mack dropped the cheerful note from her voice. "Please, Jess? I have something I need to talk to you about, and I—I just…please?"

"Bring coffee," Jess said.

They ate the sandwiches and drank their coffee on their way east to the Broadway Trailhead, Jess' Chihuahua, Shirley, happily ensconced in the back seat with a squeak toy.

As they started into the desert, each carrying a large water bottle, Mack described the events of the previous night.

"Holy shit!" Jess exclaimed.

"Indeed."

Jess agreed that Mack needed to pass the investigation to another attorney. Even if the police never charged Marcus, even if they charged someone else, the mere appearance of impropriety would taint the case. A defense attorney would quickly determine that the prosecutor's father had been the main suspect. That would be the only thing the trial was about—whether Mack had somehow suppressed the investigation into him. Dan Petrou would never let her live it down.

Where they disagreed, however, was on how exactly Mack should do the passing of the file.

"Here's what I'm thinking," Mack said. They were stopped in the shade of an overgrown saguaro. Even though it wasn't summer yet, it still got warm by late morning. "And I know you're not going to like it. Just, like, hear me out. Okay?"

Jess didn't answer, and Mack couldn't see her eyes behind her sunglasses.

"Okay. So. I think I see Sheila tomorrow and tell her I've developed a personal conflict with the case and need to be walled off. She won't ask what the conflict is. She'll assume I'm shtupping one of the cops, and Lord knows she's not in a position to throw stones on that. We…well, we had a long conversation recently, and I don't relish telling her I have a conflict on an investigation, but at least it's precharging. It'll be okay."

Jess took a long drink of water. "That's lying," she said finally. "You're suggesting lying to Sheila."

Mack winced. "It's not lying. I wouldn't lie to Sheila. It's just…letting her draw a conclusion and not correcting her."

"So lying by omission," Jess said. "Which, as we all know, is just fine. No. What you're going to do is call Sheila today—as soon as we get back to the car—and tell her everything. You're going to throw yourself at her feet, claim the trauma is what kept you from calling until noon, and beg to be walled off rather than put on admin leave again."

"Admin leave? Wouldn't that be a bit harsh? I haven't actually done anything wrong."

"You didn't do anything wrong last time, either, friendo, and you almost got fired like, what, four different times?"

Mack thought through the previous year. "Three times, I think. But that one at least had something to do with me—it was my business card, I was the one who'd met the girl. This time, I didn't even know he was in Tucson until last night. And I certainly didn't know he had anything to do with Amanda Wagner."

"This is unbelievable, Mack. You don't even like him. You don't like him so much that people who meet you think you don't even have a dad. And now you're going to lie to protect him?"

"You don't understand," Mack said. "It's not about protecting him. It's about protecting myself from him. I've fought for everything I've ever had, and I won't let him take it away from me by going down in a spectacular disaster of his own making. I have spent my whole life trying to be more than just Marcus Wilson's kid, and now the best way to do that is to keep him out of Sheila's way."

"You want to protect yourself from him? Tell Sheila the truth. I've worked with her longer than you have. It's going to be okay. Really."

They compromised: Mack would tell Sheila the truth about the conflict of interest, but she'd wait until Monday morning to do it. That gave her almost twenty hours to work herself into a full-blown panic.

Mack took a deep breath and checked her outfit. She wore her favorite opening-statement power suit—navy blue with a red and white shirt. Her shoes were freshly shined. She was as ready as she'd ever be.

"Hi, there," she said in Sheila's doorway. "Do you have a second?"

Her boss looked up from a police report. "Come on in, Mackenzie. Did you have a nice weekend?"

Mack shut the door behind her and noticed that Sheila's face showed no surprise. Did she already know? How could she?

"I've had better weekends. That's actually what I wanted to talk to you about. You know the Amanda Wagner investigation? The young woman who was killed a few weeks ago?"

Sheila nodded.

"Well," Mack said, swallowing against the lump in her throat. "Well." Why was this so hard? She had practiced it a hundred times but couldn't get the words out of her mouth.

"Well?"

"Well," Mack said again.

Sheila smiled patiently.

"It turns out my father—who I haven't seen or spoken to in years and didn't even know was in Tucson, which is a whole different story, frankly—is the main suspect in her murder and so I have to hand the investigation off to someone else and also probably—no, definitely—need to be walled off the case because I don't want even the appearance of impropriety even though—as I said—I don't really have anything to do with him and would never compromise the investigation in order to—"

Sheila held up a hand. "I get the idea. Why don't you go ahead and type up a memorandum for me? Include your involvement in the case and all of"—she vaguely waved a hand—"this, and we can stash it in the file. I'll reassign the investigation to Nathan Moore, which I tell you only so that you can avoid accidentally becoming exposed to any information about the case as it proceeds—if, in fact, it does proceed. Sound reasonable?"

Mack nodded.

"Good. And let me just say this." Sheila paused and tented her fingers in front of her face. Mack almost smiled at the practiced gesture. "Family is complicated, and it sounds like yours might be particularly so. When things get...difficult...especially in this criminal law context, sometimes it draws people together. That's okay. Even here, that's okay. If you find yourself wanting to support your dad, it's normal and natural." She dropped her hands. "However. If we reach a point where you find yourself trying to help your father in any kind of legal way—regardless of whether or not you're using the resources of this office to do it—we'll have a problem. Emotional support, fine. Let this be the thing that repairs your relationship. But *any* kind of legal or tactical help, Mackenzie, regardless of whether he eventually gets charged with a crime or just remains a suspect, will constitute insubordination. Are you clear on this point?"

"Crystal clear."

"Excellent. I'll expect your written memo—which, again, should be thorough—no later than noon. Does that work for you."

It wasn't a question.

CHAPTER EIGHTEEN

Mack eyed the blank document before her, a cursor blinking on the screen. She didn't have the slightest idea how to explain everything in a way that wouldn't get her in trouble or make her look like an idiot, or, worst of all, reveal more about her childhood and relationship with her father than she wanted people at work to know. She thought about Christina Keller, the straw that broke the camel's back. Well, almost.

Christina and Mack had met during orientation week at Dartmouth, both freshmen, both out of place among kids who seemed born to the Ivy League. Despite their differences—Mack was openly gay and from a city, while Christina was straighter than an arrow and from farm country—they formed a fast friendship. It wasn't until late in their senior year, when Mack had her financial-aid package to ASU Law in hand and Christina had a job waiting for her at a nonprofit in Columbus, Ohio, when things took a turn.

It started with a bet. Mack lost her dollar when Christina kissed her late one night in their shared bedroom after way too much rum, but she didn't regret it. They went from late-night make-out sessions to a tentative relationship, and then to a commitment that came too fast and felt like too much, given the eighteen hundred miles about to separate them.

They made it work for almost two years, though, never going more than eight weeks without spending time together in person. The summer after her first year, she'd even arranged an internship in Columbus, and they'd lived together for eleven blissful weeks. Mack still remembered the night everything changed. It was mid-October, and she was studying, like she did every night, wrestling with a criminal-law textbook that was densely packed with things she didn't care about. Mack wanted to practice family law, and she chafed under the set curriculum, which included both criminal procedure and law. She chafed under everything about law school, so rigid compared to the liberal-arts education she had recently completed.

The phone call came from a number she didn't recognize. It had a Columbus area code, and she answered only because she assumed it was someone from her internship.

"Is this Mackenzie Wilson?" a gruff voice asked.

"This is she. Who's calling, please?"

"I'm Detective Earl Baker. Mackenzie, I'm so sorry to be the one to tell you this, but Christina Keller has been murdered."

Mack didn't remember the rest of the conversation, or much of the week that followed it. Christina had been killed at work—some guy had been dissatisfied with her nonprofit's services and shot up the place. Three people were hit, but only Christina had succumbed to her injuries. "Succumbed to her injuries"—Mack had found herself repeating that phrase on a loop, marveling at how clinical it made it all seem. Anything to avoid the mental image of Christina bleeding out on a dirty linoleum floor, the ring Mack had given her on a chain around her neck.

There were flashes of memory—a call to her mom, her trip to Columbus to pack up Christina's apartment, crying with Christina's mother at the funeral in Kenosha. Christina's mom had never liked Mack. She would have done anything, if only Christina had found a nice boy to settle down with, yet she had still sent Mack Christmas and birthday cards every year since Christina had died.

The only part of that time that was still crystal clear for Mack were the conversations she had with her parents at her mother's kitchen table in Shaker Heights. The leave of absence she'd taken from ASU was coming to an end. She had to go back, and her mom was trying to convince her to take the rest of the semester off and graduate late.

The knock at the door had startled both of them. Mack couldn't hear what her mom said to whoever was there, but she looked up from her steaming mug of tea to find her dad ambling into the room.

"I'll let you two talk," her mom said.

Mack didn't respond. She hadn't spoken to him in months and hadn't even known he was in Cleveland, but she was grateful to stop going around and around with her mother about whether or not she would be returning to school.

"Your mom filled me in," her dad said. "She said you're heading back tomorrow?"

Mack nodded.

"Maybe you should reconsider, Knife. It's not too late to do something else."

"I'm not dropping out of law school," Mack said. "Not now. I've worked too hard already and I'm almost halfway through. It'd be stupid to drop out now."

Marcus laughed. "It was stupid to go at all."

Mack didn't even flinch. Nothing he said could hurt more than what she was already going through.

"Come on," he said. "It's not like you were going to marry the girl."

"That's exactly what it was like, Dad." Mack fingered Christina's ring. The chain still had blood on it when Christina's mother gave it back to Mack, and she'd scrubbed it until her hands were raw and cracked. "We were going to get married after I graduated, and then she was going to grad school."

Marcus ran his hand through his blond hair—the same shade as Mack's. "My God, you really are dedicated to making the worst possible decisions, huh? Why not live a little, kiddo? Why are you so focused on growing up so fast? Have some fun, enjoy your youth. She was just one girl. There will be plenty of others."

Mack stood so fast the chair she was sitting in fell over. As she climbed the stairs to her childhood bedroom, she could hear her parents arguing.

Her mom didn't bring up her choice to go back to school again.

"What did that computer screen ever do to you?" Jess asked.

Mack looked up and blinked away tears.

"You look like you're ready to rip its circuits out with your bare hands," Jess clarified, dropping into the guest chair. "Or whatever. Do monitors have circuits?"

Mack smiled. "Just struggling over how much to put in this memo for Sheila. The investigation part is easy, but the stuff about my dad…I don't know."

"That's easy, too. Just put, 'We are not in relationship.' Done. Boom."

Mack typed the words and stared at them. "What kind of weird self-actualization seminar did you get that from?"

"Ha. No seminar. Just this therapist I was seeing. I went because of everything with Adam, and she was actually really helpful. And not just about Adam. I feel like I'm a lot clearer on what I want out of life than I was before."

"Is what you want out of life to help me on the Ferguson corpus hearing? Because if not, I will have to remain curious for now. I've got exactly fifteen minutes to get down to Judge Leyva's division."

"I'll walk with you," Jess said, taking Mack's rolling cart without asking. "So, how are things going with my new BFF, Beth?"

"Not so great, actually. Well, maybe not so great. I'm not sure."

"What's going on?"

"I just—I like her a lot. I find myself thinking, like, man, this could be it. This could be The Girl. But I'm approaching seventy percent confidence that I'm not the only person she's dating, and I don't know what to do about that."

"Have you put your cards on the table?"

"That sounds terrible. Can you imagine willingly making yourself that vulnerable to rejection? Gross."

Jess didn't respond but looked at her with such empathy that Mack wanted to throw herself off a bridge.

They arrived at the courtroom door, and Mack reached for the handle of her cart. Jess gripped it more tightly.

"Oh, I'm going in with you. I've been waiting for this with bated breath."

CHAPTER NINETEEN

Judge Leyva took the bench with his robes billowing around his slender form. He called the case and Mack announced her appearance along with that of Detective Debbie Wood. Hearsay is admissible in pretrial hearings, so she intended to admit what little evidence she had through Wood, then lean heavily on argument.

"Tom Colbey," the defense attorney said, rising and half-heartedly attempting to tuck in his white dress shirt. Mack found herself hoping the case ended in a jury trial, as there was no doubt she had more jury appeal than Tom did. "I'm here with my client Liam Ferguson who is in custody and who wishes to be heard before we commence with this hearing."

Judge Leyva faced Ferguson directly. "Sir," he said, in lightly accented English, "I am happy to listen to whatever it is you want to tell me this afternoon, but I advise you against telling me anything you don't want Ms. Wilson—the government's very capable lawyer—hearing. She will do her best to use it against you, as that is her job."

Mack recoiled. It was one thing to have a bias—everyone had biases, implicit or otherwise—but another to let it show so blatantly. If he was like this in a casual hearing, what would he be like in front of a jury?

Ferguson's handcuffs clanked against the table as he stood. "Yes, sir. I mean, Your Honor. I want to represent myself."

Mack leaned forward so she could see his face and remembered the old chestnut that a man who represents himself has a fool for a client. She might not respect Tom Colbey, but at least he—in theory—knew what he was doing. She would eat Ferguson alive.

"Why would you want to do a thing like that?" Judge Leyva asked.

"This guy"—Ferguson gestured at his attorney with his linked hands—"he doesn't have my best interests at heart. He's telling me this motion isn't going to work and I need to accept a plea agreement. Keeps telling me to come up with a number of years I'm willing to spend in prison."

Mack smiled. That was the best endorsement of Colbey she'd ever heard. Maybe he wasn't quite as stupid as he looked.

"I'm not taking no plea, though," Ferguson continued. "Because this is all just a big misunderstanding. There's no way a jury won't see through it. I'm taking this case to trial, and I'm going to win."

Judge Leyva leaned back in his chair and folded his hands over his stomach—his sermon posture, famous around the court complex. "We're not here to decide whether or not you're guilty, Mr. Ferguson, but I do want to give you a little guidance. Defense attorneys have two jobs. The first is to protect the rights of their clients. That's a very important job, because we know that any one of us could wind up in your unfortunate position, right? So we need a person whose job is to keep us safe when we're in the hot seat. But the second job is sometimes even more important. That job is to use their training and experience—and I've seen Mr. Colbey many times in my courtroom, and he is a very good lawyer—to assess when their client would benefit from taking a plea agreement. Defense attorneys call it 'mitigating the risk.'

We did a similar analysis when I was in family law, asking would my client benefit from reaching an agreement with the mother. If Mr. Colbey thinks that—regardless of whether this *should* be the outcome—if he thinks that a jury will convict you at trial, then he will advise you to take a plea agreement that would result in less prison time than you'd be looking at after trial."

He flipped open the folder in front of him. "Let's see. You're charged with—oh, my—you're charged with counts here where, if you're convicted by a jury, you will never see the outside of a prison yard again. In fact, if the government made all the decisions, when you died, they'd bring you back to life to let you die—let's see—one, two, three…six more times in prison."

"Judge," Mack said. "If I may, I think that's a misstatement—"

Judge Leyva held up a hand. "You'll have your chance later, Ms. Wilson, and I know you'll comport yourself well at such time. For now, though, your role is just to be an observer. Mr. Ferguson, do you understand what I'm telling you?"

"I do," Ferguson said. "But I want to represent myself, starting today."

Judge Leyva shrugged. "Okay," he said. "Unlike you, Mr. Colbey and I both get to go home at five o'clock, no matter what happens at your trial. Mr. Colbey will remain as advisory counsel. Do you want to proceed with this motion that your former attorney filed on your behalf?"

"I do. I read through it, and her response, and I'm ready."

"Ms. Wilson," Judge Leyva said blithely. "Call your first witness."

Mack approached the podium. "The State calls Detective Debbie Wood."

Mack and Debbie had prepared for the hearing and agreed on the scope of the detective's testimony. Mack wanted to keep it tight, especially now that Ferguson would be crossing her himself. Anything a witness said at a pretrial hearing could be used to discredit them if they testified to something different at trial, even if it was something that could be easily explained or something that didn't matter. Ferguson was unlikely to know that Arizona had full and open cross—he could ask Wood about anything, not just what she said on direct. If Mack was right, though, and that was more than Ferguson knew, limiting Debbie's testimony on direct might well help to contain the cross.

Avoiding impermissible leading questions, Mack guided Debbie through establishing the bare minimum they needed. There was a dead baby. Daisy had offered the forensic interviewer an explanation for how the baby wound up dead. The autopsy results weren't inconsistent with that explanation. There you have it, Judge—corpus. Ferguson's statements, such as they were, didn't form the basis for the charges.

Mack checked her watch. It hadn't even taken twenty minutes to get through her direct.

Judge Leyva turned to Ferguson. "Okay, sir, now it is time for your cross-examination of the detective. Go ahead."

Ferguson didn't stand. "I don't have anything for her."

Debbie shot a quick questioning glance at Mack, who shrugged. There was no telling what a *pro per* defendant was up to.

Judge Leyva looked similarly puzzled. "Are you unfamiliar with the process of cross-examination, sir? This is your opportunity to question the detective, get her to admit to things that help you—for example, if she made any mistakes in the investigation, or if there are details you want the Court to know that the State did not elicit because they don't help the State's case. Cross-examination is the greatest weapon in a defense attorney's arsenal, so I recommend that you, as it were, take your shot."

"Nope," Ferguson said. "Nothing for her."

Mack stood. "Can Detective Wood step down, then, Judge?"

"Of course. Thank you for your time, Detective. Ms. Wilson, do you have any additional witnesses?"

"No, Judge."

Judge Leyva turned to the defense table. "Do you have any witnesses to call today?"

"I call my daughter, Daisy Ferguson."

Mack turned around and eyed the empty gallery. As far as she knew, Daisy hadn't had any intention of coming to court that day.

Judge Leyva waited a long moment as nothing happened before turning back to Mack. "Ms. Wilson, did you subpoena Ms. Ferguson—who is, I believe, the listed victim in this case and therefore not subject to pretrial interview by the defense—for today's hearing?"

"No, Judge. You are correct that she's the victim in the case, and since her statements came in through Detective Wood, there was no reason for me to require her to be here."

"Mr. Colbey?" Judge Leyva asked. "Any chance you subpoenaed the witness?"

Tom stood and shook his head. "Wouldn't know where to find her if I wanted to, Your Honor."

"Well, Mr. Ferguson, we seem to be at an impasse. You have the absolute right to represent yourself, and I have already made that determination. The problem for you, then, becomes that defendants who represent themselves must behave the same way as lawyers. They must follow the same rules. They are held to the same standards. If you wanted a witness here, there is a legal process you needed to follow. I am not going to delay this hearing so that you can get up to speed."

Mack could hear Ferguson muttering under his breath, but she couldn't make out his words. She caught the eye of the detention officer and tilted her head, signaling him to move closer. If a defendant snapped, their attorney usually got the brunt of it, but Mack wasn't taking any chances.

"Now then," Judge Leyva said. "We turn to argument. Mr. Ferguson, this is your motion, so I will hear from you first and last. Go ahead."

Ferguson rose, and Mack noticed how big he really was—tall and broad-shouldered under his orange jumpsuit. She wondered how big Daisy was, comparatively, and hoped that the jury would hold his size against him. No surprise that Daisy had been terrified of him.

"This whole thing is unfair," Ferguson said. "They charged me with these terrible crimes—these crimes I never would have committed—crimes against my daughter, for Christ's sake, and they don't even make her show up and face me? That shouldn't be allowed. This whole thing is just revenge for me not paying for that girl to go to college. I didn't kill the baby, and they can't prove I did, because I didn't."

Was he done? Mack wasn't sure. After a long silence, she stood. "Judge, the defendant indicated before we started that he read the motion practice that resulted in this hearing, but he has declined to address the issue of corpus during his argument. The corpus rule exists to protect vulnerable defendants from themselves. What we have here, though, is not a vulnerable defendant. He is so competent, in fact, that Your Honor has granted his motion to represent himself. The State did not rely on any statements made by Mr. Ferguson in charging him with the murder of his child...his grandchild...the baby resulting from his sexual abuse of his daughter, Daisy. You have seen the evidence supporting the charge before you today, and I ask you to find that corpus does exist for this crime."

"Ms. Wilson," Judge Leyva said. "The defendant alleges— and advisory counsel alleged in his written motion—that the victim has a motive for saying the things she said. I myself am the father of four daughters, and we all know that relationships between parents and their children are often fraught. My question for you is simple. Are Ms. Ferguson's statements trustworthy? And I suppose my second question is just as simple. If her statements are trustworthy, how do you know that?"

Mack sensed danger ahead but couldn't see exactly where it lay. "Well, Judge, those are both good questions. But I guess I would come back to the issue of what the standard for corpus really is. It doesn't matter if Daisy's statements are reliable, although I absolutely think they are. What matters is that there's something out there in the world that points the finger at the defendant. It's not just his own words that will sink him—*if* the jury convicts him, which is of course up to them."

"I understand your point, Ms. Wilson," Judge Leyva said, a smile playing across his lips. "But I'm not sure you understand mine. I'm less interested in the word we apply to the motion— corpus or probable cause or motive. What I am interested in is whether there is enough evidence to present this count of murder to a jury, when your medical examiner has not conclusively ruled that there was a homicide at all."

And there it was. The judge didn't think there might be a corpus issue. He was using this hearing as a fishing expedition. A fathers'-rights advocate, he was looking for something—anything—to hang a ruling on so he could dismiss at least the homicide and maybe the whole case.

"Judge," Mack said. She paused, trying desperately to think. "Judge. The grand jury in this case, when given the statements by Daisy and the medical examiner's report, found that there was probable cause. Whether or not Daisy is a reliable witness is for the jury's consideration—it is not a pretrial determination for this Court. Credibility of witnesses is a standard jury instruction, and the things you're talking about—motive, bias, and prejudice—all go to the weight a jury should give the testimony, not its admissibility. The only motion we're here for today is corpus, and even with that only Count One is being challenged at this time. I know that Your Honor will rule accordingly."

The judge squinted at her, any hint of pleasantry absent now. "Mr. Ferguson, you get the last word today."

"I just think it's bull"—Tom elbowed him—"I think it's unfair that the girl doesn't have to get up and testify. I think that should be reason enough for you to dismiss the case right there."

"Thank you all," Judge Leyva said. "I will take this under advisement and rule by minute entry in due course."

CHAPTER TWENTY

"So, anyway, I'm just not sure what to do at this point." Mack and Beth were sprawled on Mack's couch, Beth's feet in Mack's lap, and Mack had spent the last half hour telling Beth about the Amanda Wagner case. Beth had noticed Mack's distraction as she had picked listlessly at her vegetable green curry over dinner. Mack hadn't wanted to burden Beth with the circular arguments she'd been having with herself all day, but Beth's gentle prodding—and the bottle of chardonnay they'd shared—had been enough to loosen her up.

"What do you mean, 'what to do'? What can you possibly do other than support him? He's your father."

"Yeah, well, fathers can kill people, just like mothers and grandfathers and the childless can."

"Sure, I guess, but not, like, *your* father."

Mack focused on her thumbs rubbing firm circles on the arch of Beth's left foot. "You can't really say that, though, because you don't know him. I mean, I don't even know him all that well."

"I don't care how well you know him. You can't seriously believe he murdered that girl."

Beth's eyes were closed, and she had a White Claw balanced precariously on her stomach. Mack stopped rubbing her feet and stood.

"It's not that easy. I mean, I don't know if I believe he killed her or not, but even if he didn't, I'm just not sure I want to throw my weight behind him. It's not like it won't get out that he's my dad, and this is a small town, especially in the legal community. People will know if I'm on his side, and there are folks who will be fine with it, sure, but there are more who won't be."

"Don't be ridiculous. Family comes first. People understand that. And besides, at this point, at least, there's no reason for anyone to know anything. He was interviewed, nothing more than that, right?"

"Right," Mack said. "Except he wasn't just interviewed. I mean, I told you about the texts. We'd already decided that whoever Cesar Chavez was pretty much had to be the killer. And the bottle. I mean, he drank Heineken my whole childhood."

"Heineken isn't exactly a niche beer, though, right? Or the only green bottle out there."

"Maybe not. But God forbid there's a fingerprint, or DNA, or something on the bottle. Even something innocuous—I mean, he had every reason to be in the house while they were dating. But isn't that suspicious, too? That he was a block and a half away from me, and clearly knew where I lived, and never thought it was worth coming by to say hello?"

"You're talking in circles, Mack. I can hardly keep up." Beth looked at her Apple Watch and finished her drink. "I have to run."

"Are you sure?" Mack asked. "I mean, I could really use some support right now. If you can stay, I'd appreciate it."

Beth was putting her shoes on. "I have plans tonight. But I'll call you."

Mack took a deep breath. It was now or never.

Now, she decided. "Are you seeing someone else?"

Beth hesitated. "Do you really want the answer to that question?"

Mack laughed. "I think I already know the answer, but I need to be sure."

"Then, yes, I am seeing someone else. Actually, more than one other person."

Mack sank back onto the couch. "Wow," she said. "I mean, I was pretty sure, but hearing it out loud…wow."

"Mack, we never said we were exclusive. In fact, I'm sure I told you when we started seeing each other that I don't believe in monogamy. It's just never worked for me. I thought you were cool with this. We have a lot of fun together, and I really like you, but I'm not interested in being tied into a relationship."

"So what now?"

Beth stood, her shoes tied, and swept her hair into a ponytail. "I guess that's up to you. I don't see that anything has to change. But if you're looking for something more concrete, then you need to make a choice that works for you."

"Will you"—Mack cleared her throat—"will you call me? Can we do dinner tomorrow, maybe?"

"I can't tomorrow, but I'll text you when I'm free, and we can figure something out. Good night, Mack. And seriously—call your dad."

Mack sat on the couch for an hour, studying the patterns on her IKEA rug. There was so much she liked about Beth—she was pretty, smart, funny, and had a full and exciting life, even without Mack in it. Most of all, though, Mack liked how easy things were between them. There was no drama. Well, there hadn't been any drama until Mack decided to open her big dumb mouth and ask the one question she knew she shouldn't have asked.

She picked up her phone and looked at the time. It was late, too late to call Jess, and Jess wasn't her first choice for sympathy, anyway. Not on this. Jess had been encouraging her to be honest with Beth about her feelings for weeks.

Was it so wrong to want a relationship? To want the security of knowing she wasn't competing for someone's attention? Mack didn't think so, but maybe she was just old-fashioned.

She knew who she wanted to talk to.

Anna.

The psychologist had always been the only one who could cut through to the heart of Mack's issue and help her see a way forward.

As she contemplated texting Anna—what that might mean, whether Anna would even be willing to talk to her at all, let alone about Beth—her phone lit up in her hand.

Her father.

Mack answered before she had time to think.

"How about breakfast tomorrow?" he asked without preamble. "I've been trying to lay low and avoid your friends in blue, but I've been craving pancakes. We didn't have a chance to catch up the other night, not really."

Mack tried to think of a reason to refuse, but she didn't have anything else going on the next morning, and pancake breakfasts were one of her only happy memories of her dad. She sighed. He had always known how to reel her in.

"Okay," she said. "How about Millie's? I'll meet you there at eight."

CHAPTER TWENTY-ONE

Millie's was already crowded when Mack got there five minutes early. Tucson was a small enough town that she often ran into people she knew while out and about. On a good day, she saw a cop or another attorney, but she'd never forget the time she looked up from a sandwich and found herself staring straight at the chef—whom she was in the process of prosecuting for grabbing the breasts of an underage family friend.

Her father arrived right on time, grinning, in a ratty old T-shirt, khaki shorts, and boat shoes—the uniform she remembered him wearing every weekend when she was a kid. Mack was surprised by how young he looked. The sun did agree with him, his tan setting off his bright blue eyes.

"Thanks for meeting your old man," he said when they were seated.

A waitress approached with a pot of coffee and returned their matching smiles. "So nice to see a father and daughter out together, just enjoying each other's company. We don't get nearly enough of that anymore. You make sure you appreciate these moments, okay?"

"Yes, ma'am," Marcus said. "We are surely blessed." He winked at Mack as the waitress moved on, dropping the good-old-boy act.

"Where'd you pick that up?" Mack asked.

"I did a little work in Marietta, Georgia, a while back. Not a great place to be Jewish, so I learned to fit in."

Mack noticed a trio of middle-aged men talking with their heads close together. She could have sworn she recognized the one in the middle, but she couldn't place him.

They each ordered pancakes, eggs, and bacon—blueberry and scrambled for Mack, chocolate chip and over medium for Marcus—and settled into an uncomfortable silence.

"So," Marcus said after some time had passed. "I guess you're still at the District Attorney's Office, huh?"

"Yep. It's been almost twelve years, now."

"You must like it, then?"

"Yep. It's what I've always wanted to do."

"Not always," Marcus said, flashing her a bright smile. "I remember when you were going to be a ballerina astronaut. And then there was your welder phase."

"You showed me *Flashdance* when I was way too young."

Marcus laughed.

"That was all your mom. I never liked that movie. If she'd been in a union, she wouldn't have needed the second job."

"Yeah, I remember. It was around the same time you made me do the report about why the Three Little Pigs should organize. Weirdly, Ms. Shields didn't love that one."

Marcus laughed again, and the three men looked over. She was pretty sure that the one she recognized had been a juror on a case she'd recently second-chaired, so she smiled at him. He ducked his head and looked away.

The waitress brought their food and Mack immediately went for a strip of bacon—Millie's was the best in town. "Have you been here before?"

"You bet. You know I'm all about breakfast food. I was happy you suggested it. Much as you try to fight it, you're just like your dad, huh?"

Mack didn't respond.

"So," Marcus said, trying again. "You seeing anyone?"

Mack groaned. "Let's not...do that, okay? We can have a pleasant breakfast, and talk about old times and cute childhood stories or whatever, but let's not pretend you're going to be a part of my daily life. Why start now, you know?"

A long moment passed.

"Look, Mackenzie...See, I can remember...Your mom and I did the best we could with you. Neither of us knew what the hell we were doing, especially as you got older and it was clear you were in a different league than we were. So we did the best we could. Your mom thought that meant staying close, making sure you had a hot dinner on the table every day. I thought it meant making a better world for you to live in. Maybe I—well, maybe I was wrong about what was best for you. Maybe you'd have turned out better if I was home every night, asking you about your day. But we made our choices, and here we are, kiddo. Do you wish things had turned out different?"

Mack chewed her pancake. "No. I guess I don't. There are a lot of specific things I wish had gone down in other ways, but I guess I wouldn't change where I ended up. Mom, though. You caused mom a lot of pain."

"Don't you worry about your mother. She's a tough lady, and she and I came to an understanding that's none of your concern many years ago."

Mack was surprised to find that she'd cleared her plate. The waitress poured her another cup of coffee.

"So what do you say?" Marcus asked. "Can we start over?"

They could never start over, and Mack suspected her father knew that as well as anyone. His choices would always be part of their history, part of what had made Mack who she was. She cleared her throat.

"I guess all we can do is try, right?"

CHAPTER TWENTY-TWO

"Most folks go for business casual," Jess said, peeking around Mack's office door and holding up a large coffee. "Some people even get crazy and wear shorts. But not Mackenzie Wilson. In a suit, even for jury duty!"

Mack groaned but accepted the coffee and a bagel sandwich. "I have a meeting on the Wagner case this afternoon—one last hurrah before I'm officially walled off—so I can't dress down. Frankly, I'm really annoyed about it."

"Of course you are. If it wasn't that, you'd be annoyed about something else. Jury service is the dream, and I'm not sure why you're in such a bad mood about it."

Mack chewed and swallowed. Egg and cheese on an everything bagel, was there anything better in the whole world? "Because no one is going to let me stay on a jury. I would love to serve, and we know no one is more critical of a prosecutor's case than another prosecutor. But no defense attorney in their right mind is going to let me sit. So it's a waste of a morning when I could be doing other things."

"That's fair."

"Glad you think so."

Jess sat and crossed her legs. "Want to hear about the date I went on last night?"

"I do, I do, I do."

"As you know, my profile says I'm a lawyer but doesn't say who I work for. So we meet at a bar near his house, we order drinks, we're chatting, and I tell him where I work. He says that is *so* great because he's actually currently being prosecuted by us for DUI, so if we get together the office will drop the charges."

Mack choked on her sandwich. "Do you"—she coughed—"do you think he targeted you?"

"No, he seemed so genuinely shocked and thrilled, I don't think it was a setup. I think he's just a drinker who thought for one glorious moment he had beaten the system. He was very upset when I shot that theory down."

They finished their sandwiches and stood, Mack stopping to glance at her hair in the mirror and pat a few stray strands into place.

"I'll walk you over there," Jess said. "The court complex can be confusing for newbies."

Mack grabbed her purse, reluctantly following her laughing friend.

As she checked into the dingy juror waiting room, presenting the postcard she had received and her driver's license, Mack scanned the other waiting faces. No one she recognized. That was something, at least—she wouldn't have to spend the morning making uncomfortable shop talk. She settled into a creaking chair with one broken arm and pulled out her laptop to prepare for her meeting, where she would tell Sheila and Nathan Moore—and perhaps some higher up members of the administration—about the status of the case. Aside from her father being the current suspect, Nathan would be taking over a blank slate.

Mack felt a prickling on the back of her neck and glanced around. Another prospective juror quickly looked away. He had been reading Mack's screen over her shoulder, no doubt titillated by the crime-scene photos she was scrolling through.

Mack closed her laptop with a sigh. What was she supposed to do all morning if she couldn't work?

She had just pulled up *BuzzFeed*, determined to lose herself in mindless celebrity gossip, when she heard a staff member call her name, along with a list of others. She was being summoned to a courtroom as a possible juror.

Mack lined up where directed, between a tall man wearing cargo shorts—she'd have to remember to tell Jess that her prophecy had come true—and a short woman wearing an American flag T-shirt. Perfect. Two people she'd never put on a jury, since the conventional wisdom was that anyone who wore shorts didn't take the process seriously and anyone wearing a patriotic shirt was trying too hard.

At the front of the line, a court employee was trying to get everyone's attention, and Mack smiled when she saw that it was Diana Muñoz, Judge Spears's former judicial assistant.

Mack waved and Diana came over, smiling broadly. She leaned in for a hug, and Mack returned it.

"What are you doing here, hon?" Diana asked.

Mack held up her placard. "Just my civic duty, like everyone else."

Diana laughed. "Girl, you can't be on this jury!"

"I know. Who are you working with now? Judge Spears retired, right?"

"Mm-hmm, his grumpy ass had enough after that Andersen trial. He finished out his time and went home. Moved back East where his grandkids are. I'm with Judge Moran now."

Moran was new to the bench, and Mack had only appeared in his division a couple of times. He came from a civil background, and word on the street was that he was finding Criminal to be a difficult adjustment.

"Wish me luck," Mack said. "I'm hoping for a quick release this morning."

Diana laughed again, squeezed Mack's arm, and led the line of seventy potential jurors through winding corridors, up the elevators, and to Judge Moran's courtroom.

Mack took the opportunity to scan the courtroom. She didn't recognize the prosecutor or the cop sitting next to him.

She made eye contact with the court reporter, Bertie Flack, and grinned. Bertie smiled back but raised her eyebrows. Mack shrugged and turned. She knew the clerk, Sarah, and the deputy, whose name she could never remember. The defense attorney was Holly Hart. They didn't know each other well but exchanged smiles nonetheless. She would be out of there by nine.

After introducing himself and the court staff, Judge Moran dove into the preliminary voir dire questions.

"Does anyone think they know me or any member of my staff?" he read from his binder full of scripts.

Mack was the only one to raise her hand. Diana brought her the portable microphone, and Mack rose when the judge asked her to. "Yes, Judge. I know everyone on your staff, probably Diana best, and I appeared in front of you on the Brecht case last week."

"You appeared in front of me?" The judge rustled through the stack of paper in front of him, and Mack assumed he was looking for the confidential jury information sheet that listed their names. "Are you a defendant in a case currently pending before the Court?"

"No, Judge. I work for the District Attorney's Office as a prosecutor."

The trial prosecutor turned to look at her. She still didn't recognize him, and he started shuffling through his own stack of papers.

"Oh, okay." Judge Moran flipped forward and back through his binder. Mack wondered if there was a script for what to do when a prosecutor was on a jury panel. Probably not, she decided. "Well, Ms...Waller, was it?"

"Wilson, Judge."

"Ms. Wilson, is there anything about your knowledge of me or my staff that would prevent you from being a fair and impartial juror in this matter?"

"No, Judge."

He gestured for her to sit, and she did so, expecting him to summon the lawyers to the bench, discuss the matter, and dismiss her.

Instead, Judge Moran had the young prosecutor stand to introduce himself and his case agent.

"Jeremiah Brigger, Judge. I work at the Tucson District Attorney's Office in the Felony Prosecution Unit, and this is Detective Quintano."

"Thank you. Does anyone know Mr. Brigger, Detective Quintano, or anyone at either of their offices?"

Mack again was the only one to raise her hand. The man in the cargo shorts smiled. Diana brought her the microphone.

"Yes, Ms. Wilson?" Judge Moran asked. "Who do you think you know?"

"Well, Judge, I don't actually know this prosecutor, but we do work in the same office. So I'm sure we know many people in common. And although I don't know this detective, I work with Tucson Police Department detectives every day."

"And is there anything about knowing those people that would make you not fair and impartial in this case?"

"No, Judge."

Again she sat, and, to her surprise, again Judge Moran moved on.

Holly introduced herself and her client.

"Does anyone know the defense attorney or the defendant?"

Mack's hand was, yet again, the only one raised. Several members of the jury stifled their laughter.

"I don't think I've ever had a case with Ms. Hart," she said, "but we've certainly run into each other in court and know each other enough to say hi to. Nothing that would make me anything other than fair and impartial."

Mack glanced at the courtroom clock. It was almost ten, and they would probably take a lunch break at noon, but Judge Moran still showed no signs of releasing her.

They proceeded through the rest of the morning, Mack raising her hand and answering questions along with the rest of the group about whether they knew any lawyers, had any knowledge of DNA, or had any biases or prejudice that the parties should know about. Other jurors chuckled openly each time Mack raised her hand.

Finally, the noon break came. Mack couldn't decide what to do. Should she come back after lunch, knowing she wouldn't wind up on the jury, or should she speak up now? She agonized over how it would look if she tried to pull rank but finally gestured to Diana.

"Can you ask Judge if I can talk to them before everyone leaves for lunch?"

Diana nodded and walked away. Mack stood awkwardly by the courtroom doors, watching.

When everyone else had left the room, Judge Moran waved her to the podium. "My judicial assistant indicated that you want to talk in private?"

"Yes, Judge." Mack took a deep breath. "If there is a realistic chance I will be seated on this jury, I will come back after the lunch break and complete jury selection. I'm happy to serve. But it seems hard to believe that any defense attorney would want me on their jury, and I have a meeting on a homicide investigation right after the break. Perhaps I'm wrong, and Ms. Hart thinks I would be a great juror?"

"She's not wrong, Judge," Holly said. "I'll be moving to strike her for cause."

Judge Moran looked confused. "What cause? She hasn't said anything to suggest that she couldn't be fair and impartial. Her employment alone is not grounds to strike."

"I would object to striking for cause," the young prosecutor said. Mack couldn't remember his name.

"What's the cause, Ms. Hart?"

"Aside from the presumptive conflict, since she works in the same office as the assigned ADA, there is no way, despite Ms. Wilson's assurances, that she can be fair and impartial. She knows too much about the system and knows that there are facts we don't tell jurors. I don't mean to impugn her integrity—I've worked with Ms. Wilson in passing, as she said, and have nothing negative to say about her—but the idea that she won't be speculating about material not provided for jury consideration is ludicrous."

Judge Moran turned back to Mack. "Your response?"

"I will do my very best to keep my knowledge of the system compartmentalized, Judge, but she's right. It's hard to imagine I won't draw some conclusions, even if they're unintentional."

The young prosecutor and his detective were whispering heatedly. After a long moment, the prosecutor broke away from their conversation. "I withdraw my objection, Judge. The State agrees that she should be stricken for cause."

"I still don't see anything other than speculative cause," Judge Moran said. "But since the parties agree, I won't interfere. You are released for cause. Do you need a note for your employer to prove that you had jury service this morning?"

Mack laughed. "No, Judge. I'm good. But thank you."

On her way out of the courtroom, she powered on her phone and found an email from Sheila canceling their meeting on the Wagner case, with no indication of when they would reschedule. That was odd, but Mack was grateful for a free afternoon and didn't waste any time thinking about it.

CHAPTER TWENTY-THREE

Mack's week was off to a dismal start. She was buried in police reports on three new cases that she'd picked up and needed to make charging decisions on. She skipped lunch, which always left her with a headache by midafternoon, but she needed the time to work. She hadn't heard from Beth and was reluctantly taking Jess' advice to leave the ball in her court. She'd reach out when she wanted to, and then it would be Mack's choice how to respond.

"But if you freak out and pester her," Jess said, "you'll chase her away. I know you're feeling spooked by this nonmonogamy thing, but it's not like monogamy has worked well for you in the past. Maybe it's time for a change."

But then Tuesday, Wednesday, and Thursday passed without word, and late Thursday night found Mack pacing her living room buried deep in her notes on Daisy Ferguson's forensic interview. Assuming Judge Leyva didn't gut her indictment, Mack felt confident about two things: the case would proceed to trial quickly because Ferguson would not want to delay, and Mack had the evidence she needed to convict.

She was contemplating her order of witnesses when there was a knock at the door. Peering through the peephole, she saw Dave Barton on her doorstep, looking pale and exhausted.

"Come on in," Mack said. "Can I get you a beer or some coffee?"

Dave shook his head and remained outside. "I can't stay. I just came by to give you an update."

"An update on what? We don't have any cases together."

He sighed. "I just arrested your dad for the murder of Amanda Wagner. I know you're walled off from the case, but after all we've been through, I wanted you to hear it from me."

Mack sat on the bench outside her door. "What sealed it?"

"DNA," Dave said. "We already had the baby and the DNA from the bottle. Some guys followed him to breakfast on Sunday and—"

"To breakfast with me, you mean?"

Dave cleared his throat and had the good grace to look embarrassed. "I didn't know you were who he was meeting."

Something clicked into place. "I thought I recognized a guy at the restaurant. Was that—"

"Yeah. Tim Schultz. He thought you made him."

"So you...what, exactly?"

"Once you guys left, we seized his coffee cup and silverware. Just in case there was extraneous transfer material, you know?"

Mack was impressed. "So he's the father? We were right all along?"

"He's the father."

"What about the other guy? Billy, or whatever?"

Dave shook his head. "We haven't figured that one out yet. The phone number subscriber info was probably fake. At least, that's what the forensics guys think."

"Well, that's pretty damning, right? I mean, why would Billy do that if he has nothing to hide? Shouldn't you be digging deeper?"

"Mack, it's not that I wanted to arrest your dad. I just went where the evidence took me. Yeah, Billy having a fake name on his cell phone is suspicious, but it's not illegal. Your dad's DNA is on the murder weapon. And…look, I don't know what he told you, but he lied about his alibi."

She nodded mechanically and hugged her legs to her chest. "No, yeah, no. Of course. I mean, thank you for telling me and all, but of course. I would never…You would never…"

She could feel Dave watching her.

"Does Nathan Moore know?" she finally asked.

"He knows we made the arrest. I called him when we got the warrant. We were worried—Well, that's not important."

"Worried about what?"

Dave took a moment to gather his thoughts. "How much do you really know about your dad's past, Mack?"

"Not a whole lot. He wasn't around much, you know? And there was no one to ask. He wouldn't have told my mom anything, and both of his parents died when I was *little* little."

"This isn't my story to tell."

Mack looked up at him. "Just say it. It can't be any more shocking than what you've already told me."

"He's got a bit of a record. Nothing—I mean, he's never done prison time or anything. But there's enough in there that we were worried he was armed and there might be a standoff. So I warned Moore when we were ready to make the arrest. Just in case—"

"Just in case things went to shit?"

"Yeah. But I don't know if Moore knows Marcus Wilson is your dad. You'd have to ask him about that."

"You just said he lied about his alibi. I thought he didn't have an alibi."

"Is that what he told you?"

Mack stared at her toes. Her pink toenails caught and reflected what little light there was. She'd picked the color the previous weekend, when Jess had taken her for brunch and pedicures in an attempt to distract her from what was going on with Beth.

"Yeah, that's what he told me."

"This so isn't a conversation we should be having, Mack. Can't you ask Moore?"

She couldn't ask Nathan anything, regardless of how much she wanted to know. She was walled off, and walled off meant a total blackout. No reports, no looking at the case status online, not even a casual conversation with Nathan in the hall. Radio silence was the order of the day.

"If I'm going to get anything, it has to come from you."

"If anyone knows I told you this, I'd be in deep trouble."

Mack laughed. "After last year? All the office gets from me is name, rank, and serial number."

"He told us he was at Bob Dobbs. You know that bar?"

"Sure, it's been around forever. I don't think I've ever been, but I've definitely heard of it."

"Well, he told us that's where he was, and his credit card records would prove it, and he named some witnesses."

"Should be easy enough," Mack said. "What fell apart?"

"He got the night wrong. I think he thought we didn't know when she died. He was at Bob Dobbs the twenty-eighth, not the twenty-seventh."

"Come on, Dave. That could be a lie, or it could be a mistake made by an old man. You didn't interview him until almost a month later. That's it?"

Dave didn't answer.

Mack was pushing too hard, and she didn't even really know why. Was it so hard to believe that he'd lied about his alibi? Regardless of whether he'd killed Amanda Wagner, her father had always had a tenuous relationship with the truth. He might have lied just for the fun of it or to protest what he viewed as an unfair interrogation.

"Ah," Mack said, realization dawning. "This is why my meeting got canceled Monday afternoon. You guys knew this was coming?"

"Yeah. Well, we believed it was, anyway." Dave sat next to her on the bench and put a hand on her shoulder. "Is there anything I can do for you? I could call Jess or, I don't know, drive you over to Dr. Lapin's or something."

Mack shook her head. "Here's the thing of it," she said. "If he was anyone else, I'd say, 'Fuck that guy. He's a killer and a villain.' And if he was someone else's dad, and she told me the things about him that I know about my own dad, I'd think, 'Of course her dad did it. Why doesn't she see that?' But he's my dad and I'm me, and I just don't know what I think. He's not some great guy, but I—I just…Do I really think he's a killer? I don't know."

"And that's okay," Dave said. "I know you're not someone who does well with uncertainty, and this situation is as uncertain as all get-out. It's okay not to be sure."

Mack forced a smile. Maybe some people were okay with not being sure, but she wasn't one of them. She needed to know, one way or another, the truth about Amanda Wagner's death. There was no one else who could help her figure it out. She would have to deal with it alone.

CHAPTER TWENTY-FOUR

The Ferguson minute entry came out bright and early Friday morning, and Mack's hand hesitated over the keyboard.

"Whatcha looking at, there, sport?" Jess asked. "Computers can't hurt people. Not yet, at least."

Mack explained, "If I don't open it, I can't know if that asshole judge destroyed my case."

Jess walked around the desk and stood behind her. "Deep breaths. Leyva might be dumb, but he's friends with some smart judges. Let's just hope he reached out to them before ruling. I'm going to open it. Okay?"

Mack closed her eyes.

She heard Jess scrolling and muttering, then felt a nudge.

"Listen to this," Jess said. "This is beautiful. It's the conclusion of the ruling. 'The Court has a serious concern about the reliability of the charged victim's testimony. As the State correctly pointed out, though, that concern goes to the weight that the fact-finder must give to the evidence, not to the admissibility of the evidence. The State also correctly noted that the motion before the Court is limited to the issue of corpus delicti on Count One. Had the defendant challenged the sufficiency of the indictment on other grounds, the Court's analysis might well have been different. Under these very limited circumstances, however, the Court finds that the State has met its burden. The defendant's motion is therefore denied.'"

Mack exhaled shakily and opened her eyes. "Holy guacamole. He definitely talked to someone. This is incredible."

"It really is shockingly good for you."

"Is there anything else in there I need to know about right now?"

"He set a trial date. Thirty days. Says it won't get continued unless Ferguson specifically asks."

Mack sank back in her desk chair. "Which he won't. Well, okay. Looks like I'm trying a murder case next month."

"Yep. In the meantime, let's hope your defendant isn't smart enough to read this ruling for what it is. I mean, it couldn't be clearer that he wants Ferguson to file another motion to dismiss."

"Agreed," Mack said. "But it'll be, what, a week until Ferguson gets this in the jail? And then he'd have to write and file something. By then, I've got a good shot at precluding it as untimely, if—"

"If you get assigned to someone other than Leyva for trial."

Mack looked at her wall calendar. "Thirty days. That's not much time. You busy?"

Jess cleared a small patch on Mack's desk and sat. "TBD, I think. I've got a couple of things that really want to get started, depending on judges and defense attorneys and the alignment of the stars."

Mack laughed.

"Pivot," Jess said. "Back to why I actually came in here this morning."

Mack pushed back her chair so she could make eye contact without craning her neck.

"How are you doing?" Jess asked.

"With which part, my dad or Beth?"

"Start with your dad."

"I'm okay, I guess. So far, at least. I rode the elevator with Nathan Moore this morning, which was weird. But I couldn't tell if it was weird because he knows, or if it just felt weird because I was making it weird."

"Sure, that could go either way."

"If I did the math right, grand jury won't be until Monday. I haven't talked to him."

"To your dad?"

"Yeah. I feel like I'm hypersensitive to my phone right now. Like, it could ring at any second and be him, and then what do I do? Pick up? Listen to the message telling me I'm receiving a call from the Pima County Jail, and that call is being recorded and monitored? I'd rather sit naked on a hot grill."

Jess laughed. "Now that's a vivid image."

"Seriously. Can you imagine anything more mortifying than Nathan Moore listening in on your dad's jail calls and—oop!— there you are? Because I can't."

"I don't know," Jess said. "I like Nathan okay."

"That's not the point. I like Nathan okay, too. But it wouldn't just be Nathan. It'd be his paralegal and his intern and whoever second-chairs the trial and then defense counsel—probably more than one—and *their* paralegal and intern and then it'll somehow get leaked and soon Dan Petrou is publishing a new special feature on the Tucson District Attorney's Office's favorite loveable scamp. What *has* that Ms. Wilson gotten herself into this time?"

"Alrighty then, what about Beth? What's going on there?"

"A whole lot of nothing. It's dead in the water, but I don't want to be the one who pulls the plug."

"Way to mix your metaphors, there, my literary friend. What do you mean?"

Mack started clicking a pen repeatedly until Jess grabbed it and set it down out of reach. Mack reluctantly recounted her last conversation with Beth. "So there you go. I have spent the last week studiously not thinking about it."

"Oh," Jess said. "So it's *dead* dead. I don't even think there's a plug to pull at this point."

"Listen. I have a bunch of work I need to do to get ready for Ferguson. Can we finish this later?"

Jess nodded and left.

Mack ducked out of her office around noon to grab a salad from her favorite deli, right across the street from her building. As she walked in, though, she immediately regretted it. There was Nick Diaz, sitting facing the door and sipping from a steaming paper cup. She couldn't turn back now.

"Come sit," Nick called.

Mack nodded and went through the short line, trying to come up with an excuse to avoid him. She didn't want to be seen with him, especially after what Sheila had told her, and she also didn't want to deal with the inevitable awkwardness of the conversation. Mack hadn't had time to even think about Melissa O'Connor's invitation to join her team—and it was likely that the offer would magically disappear come Monday, anyway.

"Happy Friday," Nick said when she was settled. "I haven't heard from you lately."

"You know me. Busy, busy. Not a whole lot of time for politicking."

Nick watched her pick at her salad. "Are there any questions I can answer for you? Help you make your mind up?"

"Now that you mention it, actually, yes. Do you know Dan Petrou?"

Nick took a long drink from his cup and Mack recognized the gesture. He was stalling. "A little, I guess. Just from around town."

She waited.

"He came to me last year," Nick said. "Asked me what I knew about a few things going on at your office."

"Me?"

"He asked about you. But I never gave him anything directly about you, Mack. I swear it."

"So you did give him other things? How do you even know anything?"

Nick shrugged and attempted a smile. Mack's glare shot him down.

"I hear things. I still have friends in your office, and, besides, people get chatty at happy hours. By early last year I was already working with Melissa, and we knew she was planning a run. So I slipped him little things—nothing that could hurt you—just little bits about Campbell, what he was doing, inconsistencies, stuff like that. You weren't the one we were after. We were after Campbell."

"Did Melissa know?"

"Know what?"

"Know what you were doing? Does she know now? Does she know you're trying to recruit someone whose life you blew up last year, whether you meant to or not?"

"No." Nick's head dropped, and Mack had to struggle to hear him. "I never told her. She wouldn't have liked it—me going to the press, doing anything underhanded. She thinks she can win this just by the virtue of her ideas."

Mack closed the lid of her salad. She wasn't hungry anymore. "It wouldn't be fair to hold your boneheaded moves against your boss, so I won't. But I do have one more question, and I want you to tell me the truth. If I think you're lying, I will dedicate myself to bringing down Melissa and you until your careers are as screwed as mine was after those articles, okay?"

Nick looked up.

"Were you working with Michael Brown?"

"Michael…you mean that guy in the exec office? Campbell's lackey, or whatever?"

"Yes."

"Never. Honestly, Mack, I've never worked with him. Never even spoken to him. I couldn't even pick him out of a lineup."

Mack studied his face. How could she ever have thought he was handsome? She stood. "Tell Melissa I might be in touch with her directly. I don't want to go through her unreliable middleman again."

CHAPTER TWENTY-FIVE

"Something about seeing your face makes my stomach hurt," Mack said to Dave, ushering him into her living room that Monday evening. "What's that about, do you think?"

Dave grimaced and pulled the collar of his light-blue dress shirt away from his neck.

"I assume this is another conversation that never happened?" Mack asked.

He sat at her kitchen table and accepted the beer she handed him. "Yeah," he said when it was half-gone. "In fact, have you and I ever even met?"

She chuckled. "You had grand jury today."

"Yeah. No hesitation. They indicted."

"So I'm no longer the daughter of the main suspect in Amanda Wagner's murder. Now, I'm the daughter of the defendant."

Dave finished the beer and shook his head when Mack offered another. "That was the last time, Mack. No more status updates. Anything else you want to know, you'll have to get someplace else."

"That's okay. You've gone out on a limb already. Several limbs, I guess. I wouldn't ask you to keep doing it."

They sat in silence, Mack picking at the label on her own beer. She had been working her way through a six-pack when Dave knocked at her door.

It had been ten days since she'd heard from Beth, not that she was counting.

The Ferguson case was a disaster. The victim advocate told her that Daisy had stopped answering her phone after hearing that her dad was representing himself. Now they were frantically trying to get a subpoena issued and track her down, but she didn't have a stable residence.

"Can I ask you one more thing, though?"

"Seriously, Mack?"

"Why did you tell me anything at all? I mean, you didn't have to, and I wouldn't have blamed you."

Dave stood and walked to the fridge. He looked at the remaining beers for a long time before taking a bottle of water and sitting back down. "Fair question. I guess to answer it, I have to say some things about my relationship with my son. I just think about what it's going to be like when Ricky grows up and I don't see him every day anymore. Who knows what'll happen between now and then, you know? I mean, he's still just a kid and thinks his dad being a cop is pretty cool. But what if he grows up into a leftist radical or something? I'll still love him—that comes with the territory—but he'll have to make his own choices."

"I don't think you're making the same kind of mistakes that my dad made."

"Yeah, maybe not. But I'm making a whole other set. That's what parenting is. Trying not to make the same mistakes your parents made but making different ones, instead. So, I just...I mean, I think about what I'd want you to do for him if the situation was reversed. Even if he grows up and doesn't tell people about me. Denies he has a dad. Hell, tells people I died. I'd want him to know the truth. Then he can make his own decisions...and you can make yours. So, that's it, I guess. I just think you needed to have the information."

"Thanks," Mack said softly. She cleared her throat. "Thank you."

Dave looked at his watch and grimaced. "I have to go. But, well, I suppose you need to know that Moore and Sheila and I met after grand jury this afternoon. Amanda's mom supports this case going capital. Moore is going to file the death notice at the arraignment."

A rush of dizziness hit Mack, and her vision went gray at the edges. "They've already decided? They're not giving him an opportunity to present mitigation?"

"They want to avoid the appearance of impropriety. There's some indication—I don't know what it is, you'd have to ask Sheila—that Petrou's got ahold of this already. If it looks like they're giving your dad special treatment, they think O'Connor will run away with the election."

"They're going to try to fry my dad because Campbell needs extra votes?"

"No, they're going to pursue the death penalty because he killed a pregnant woman and her unborn child." Dave grimaced. "Allegedly. Or whatever."

Mack saw Dave to the door without another word. She finished the six-pack and lay awake for more than an hour before finally drifting off.

She was waiting outside Judge McPhee's division the next morning when she saw Eric Flagler waving at her from down the hall. Her head was pounding, and she wasn't in the mood for small talk. The fingerprint technician she was waiting for was almost forty minutes late, and she had three other courtrooms to get to before the morning calendars ended and trials started for the day.

She'd worked with Eric before—tried back-to-back molest trials with him in front of Judge McPhee before she moved to Homicide and Eric moved to the death-penalty unit at the public defender's office. She liked Eric but knew better than to underestimate him. His long dark hair, gathered into a neat manbun, gave him an aura of approachability, but his skill in front of a jury was undeniable.

"How's things in the big leagues?" she asked as he slumped onto the bench next to her, taking off his leather messenger bag and letting it drop to the floor. Mack frowned. The courthouse linoleum was notoriously disgusting, and she never let her own bags touch it.

Eric smiled. "I was actually hoping to run into you this morning. I manifested it as I ate my overnight oats."

Mack arched an eyebrow.

"I think we have a defendant in common."

Mack scanned her mental roster of cases. "I don't think so. I don't do death cases."

Eric nudged her shoulder.

"Oh," Mack said. "You got—"

"Yep. We met at his arraignment this morning. There was a bit of a mix-up. We had the duty PD set to stand in, but then Sheila herself showed up to file the notice. So they called over, and I was the lucky winner. We didn't have long to talk, but he told me about you."

She could feel sweat trickling down her back and hoped her face wasn't as red as it felt.

"Are you okay, Mack?"

So much for that. She forced a smile. "I'm glad he got someone good. He asked me about hiring someone, and I told him to wait and see."

"I tell people the same thing. He did ask me to give you a message, though. Said don't tell your mother what's going on."

Mack snorted. "She'll see it on the news soon enough, if she hasn't already. She has enough Google alerts set up that she knows if I blow my nose in the courthouse."

"He also told me he's been worried about calling you. Asked me if I'd set up a jail visit."

"The first time he's shown any sense...ever, as far as I know. Tell him I appreciate the lack of calls. Keep it up. I'm not so sure about a visit. If I go and my name shows on the visitor list, Nathan will be sure to see it."

"What if you come in with me on a legal visit?"

Mack struggled to keep her voice low. "Are you out of your mind? I work for the office—in the unit, no less—that is actively trying to kill him. I walk into that room and your attorney-client privilege is blown out of the water. Not to mention that I walk into that room and you are presumptively ineffective. I mean, for all that is holy, you can't possibly think that's a good idea."

"We're just spitballing right now. I assure you that I have his best interests in mind. At this point, I'm sounding out my client's potential character witness, who has, I've been told, a pretty good way with a jury."

"You don't want me as a character witness, Eric."

He shrugged. "Sometimes someone with nothing good to say is the exact right person to keep the client off death row. It just depends on how they say it."

Mack saw her fingerprint technician get off the elevator and look around confusedly before heading for the courtroom.

"Have you gotten discovery yet?" she asked Eric, standing and grabbing her tote bag off the bench.

"Fifteen thousand Bates-stamped pages, all neatly arranged on a disc. You want a copy?"

Mack shook her head. "Let me know when you've gone through it, though. And talked to him more. I don't...I mean, I want to help. I think. I don't know what that's going to look like yet, but I at least want to have another conversation about it."

"That's all I can ask for," Eric said. "At least for now."

CHAPTER TWENTY-SIX

It was unseasonably cold the next Tuesday, and Mack was bundled in a scarf and heavy jacket as she walked to court. She had agreed to cover a quick reset for her colleague Nan Chin but hadn't noticed that it was in Judge Moran's division. She hoped she could skate through without any attention being called to her behavior during jury selection.

The defense attorney—Holly Hart, she saw when she checked the calendar—wasn't there when she walked in, so she made herself comfortable at the prosecution desk and pulled out her phone. A soft touch on her arm made her look up.

"I can't tell you how hard I laughed last week," Diana said.

Mack smiled. "I'm glad someone did. Did they finish the trial?"

"Yep, guilty on all counts, shockingly, including the severed misconduct involving weapons."

"Oh, unknowable universe."

Holly walked in and made a beeline to Mack.

"I'm marginally offended you didn't want me on your jury," Mack said.

"I'm sure you would have been just fine. And actually, it wouldn't have changed the outcome any. Just would have impacted my street cred, you know?"

Judge Moran took the bench and called Nan's case. Mack stood at the prosecution table, ready to introduce herself.

"Before we get started," Judge Moran said. "I just want to take a minute to apologize to Ms. Wilson."

"Oh, that's not necessary, Judge."

"No, it is. I have felt bad all week for not recognizing you. I didn't have my glasses on and wouldn't have expected to see you out of context. I apologize for making you wait until the break to dismiss you."

When the hearing was over, Holly approached Mack for a second time. "He must have talked to another judge. Someone set him straight about never keeping a prosecutor on the jury."

"Someday, perhaps as my retirement goal, I will make it onto a jury. I will sit in judgment all day long, and it will be glorious."

That night, when Beth finally called, almost three weeks after their argument in Mack's living room, Mack was buried under a pile of blankets on her couch binging *Love Island*. Her heart sank when she saw the contact photo on the screen. Beth never called—only texted to set up the next time they would see each other.

"Hi," Mack said. "I was starting to think I wouldn't hear from you again. Everything okay?"

"Totally fine! I'm going to be in your neighborhood— more or less, at least—and thought you might be free for a late dinner?"

Mack sat up and shivered as the blankets fell away. "I haven't heard from you in over two weeks and the last time we talked it was kind of a big fight, and you...aren't going to mention it? Are we pretending it didn't happen?"

"It wasn't that big a deal, Mack. Honestly. Just water under the bridge."

Mack took a deep breath and slowly released it. It was time to put her cards on the table. "It may not be a big deal for you, but it is for me. Look, I haven't told you all that much about what happened last year, but a big part of my trauma was that my girlfriend up and abandoned me at the first sign of trouble."

Mack could hear a rush of air on the other end that meant Beth was driving somewhere.

"And you've made it abundantly clear that you're not my girlfriend, and for a while I thought I was okay with that. For a while, I really *was* okay with that. But…well, I think I want you to be."

"Are you asking me for a monogamous relationship?"

"Yeah, I guess I am. And it's okay if that's not something you're interested in, but…well, they indicted my dad. And I was sort of, kind of, part of the investigation against him. Which is a lot. And I just…I don't think I can do breezy, whatever, whenever, right now. I think I need someone who shows up every day. I mean, not like I need to see you every day, but, like, two weeks is a really long time."

"Mack, I like you—"

"Here it comes."

"—but I'm not cut out to be anybody's girlfriend. I'll inevitably let you down, and you won't get what you need. And I know what I need, and it isn't any kind of serious relationship, even with you."

Mack's eyes filled with tears, and she willed her voice to remain steady. "Okay, well, thank you for being honest with me, I guess."

"If you change your mind and want to keep doing what we've been doing…"

But Mack knew she wouldn't. She had enough to deal with.

* * *

Mack cried for four minutes. Then she sat up, wiped her nose on her tank top, and thought what to do next. She didn't need a girlfriend, not really. Not enough to go trolling online, at any rate. She knew what Jess would say—that she deserved someone who would value her and who was worthy of the love she had to give. Easy for her to say. She would miss Beth, but soon enough she would forget. It would be as if Beth had never happened, and she could go back to her well-ordered life.

What she needed, Mack decided, was to get her act together. She sent Jess a quick text, announcing the end of her situationship, and marched into the bedroom. She washed her face, scrubbing until her skin was as pink as her swollen eyes. She'd spent enough time dithering. She had to get Ferguson in shape for trial, and she had to make up her mind about her father. She looked at her watch. It was too late to call the victim advocate to set up a meeting with Daisy, but perhaps she could make some progress somewhere else.

Eric answered right away.

"I'll do the legal visit," Mack said. "You can keep my name off the paperwork, right?"

"Shouldn't be a problem. They don't ever ask the paralegals or mitigation specialists for their names or IDs. Can you just do your best not to look like a lawyer?"

Mack laughed. "I'll try. I'm not—well, I'm not committing to anything, okay?"

"Sure."

"Really, Eric. Don't assume this means more than a single visit."

"I don't assume anything. That's a fatal mistake for a defense attorney, as you know. He'll be glad to see you. By the way, did you ever tell your mom?"

"No," Mack said. "And she hasn't mentioned it. I think—well, I know this sounds paranoid, but—"

"After the year you've had? I think you're entitled to some paranoia."

"I think my office buried it. I think they didn't want to risk Petrou putting it together—you know, about me—so they haven't done any press, and maybe even, like, made deals with reporters not to say anything about it."

"You're right, that totally sounds paranoid. It's not unheard of, though."

"What's that old joke? Just because you're paranoid doesn't mean they're not out to get you?"

Eric laughed. "Mack, while I've got you, I've gone through the discovery and I'd like to talk a bit."

Mack was immediately on edge. She didn't want to know what additional evidence they might have gathered against her father.

"Your name is all over the reports."

"My name? Why? You mean, like, normal ADA stuff?"

"Mostly. You were present at the autopsy. You talked to the victim's mom. But some of it is witness stuff. You were there when they did the surreptitious DNA collection, stuff like that."

Mack rubbed the back of her neck. "Yeah, well, that's kind of unfixable, right?"

"Right. But..."

There was a long silence.

"Eric?"

"I'm here. I'm just...well, I'm trying to figure out how to say this without alienating you. I've always respected you, Mack, and I don't want to tank our working relationship."

"Say what you need to say."

"I think your multiple layers of involvement on the case can cut both ways. I think Nathan could use it to paint your dad in a bad light—either he knew how to cover it up because of you, or, I don't know, maybe you were even helping him."

"That's bull, Eric. I've never even talked to my dad about my work."

"I know," Eric said, his voice soothing. "But there's the other side, too. A less...scrupulous, let's say, defense attorney could paint it as...well..." He cleared his throat. "You've got this well-known grudge against your dad, and then he winds up getting arrested on a case where you had your hand in the pot at every stage. You were on scene that night. You were at the autopsy. The DNA collection. Everything."

Mack paced her living room. "Are you seriously going to tell the jury that I framed my father for murder?"

"I don't want to, because I don't think that's what happened. But their case is strong, Mack. Really strong. And I have to do what makes sense for the client, you know? Nathan told me he won't entertain a plea. Trial will be quick—Judge Leyva has already said no delay tactics. And Marcus won't let me try for mental-health mitigation."

"How quick are we talking, here? Three years instead of six?"

"We're set for ninety days. I think I can push it a little, but not much."

"That doesn't make any sense," Mack said. She thought back across every capital case she'd ever followed. "Death cases take years. Without exception. I can't understand why this one would be so different."

Eric sighed. "Marcus and Nathan are the exact wrong people to be on opposite sides. I think they're both playing chicken, confident that the other one will blink and delay, but neither one of them is going to."

"Now I'm not sure how to say something without alienating you."

"Out with it. We might as well just career screaming into the void on this call."

"We all know you guys delay death cases. I mean, the State's case doesn't get better with time. Witnesses forget, they die, alibis are harder to challenge. Why are you letting this happen?"

"Trust me, I wish I had control of the situation. I warned Marcus, but he insists the only way to get past this is to get through it. He wants his day in court as soon as possible."

"Has he said—I mean, I guess you don't have to tell me, but has he told you whether or not he did it?"

"He hasn't said," Eric said. "And I certainly haven't asked. PD 101—you don't ever ask that question."

"Maybe I'm being stupid. I just...I want to know, one way or the other."

"You're not being stupid. If I were in your shoes, I'd want to know, too. My dad died when I was a kid, and I never knew him that well. I like to think he was a good guy, but he died drunk-driving. Single-car accident."

"I had no idea, Eric. I'm so sorry."

"That's okay. It was a long time ago. I don't bring it up for pity. I bring it up because I think I know what you're going through, in a way. I mean, it's different, right? He just killed himself. But I think about him. I remember riding on his shoulders. I felt so tall, like he was the strongest guy in the world. But then I think about my stepdad, and how we fought when I announced my intention to join the Marines after high school. Would my dad and I have fought about that? If he hadn't wrapped his car around a tree that night, would he have done it some other time? Killed someone else, maybe? I'll never know. So I just choose to remember the good things about him. And you can choose, Mack. You can choose to support your dad, who is going through a really hard and scary thing. And even if he, ultimately, did what your office says he did, you can still support him just because you're his daughter. You don't need to endorse him, or, like, nominate him for father of the year. You can just make the choice to support him."

Mack opened her refrigerator and closed it again, frustrated. She'd meant to pick up groceries and a new bottle of vodka, but she'd forgotten.

"Did you join the Marines?" she asked.

"No. I had a buddy in high school who got popped for drug sales—and when I say he was a dealer, I mean the smallest-scale, dime-bag garbage. And even that was probably oregano. But we thought he was a BFD, and he wound up doing a little jail time, and then his parents shipped him off to some military school in Utah. I decided he'd gotten a bum rap, so I figured I'd be a defense attorney and protect the rights of dumb little weasels like him."

"How'd you wind up doing death cases?"

"Promise I still won't alienate you?"

"Blanket anti-alienation clause applies to this conversation. Proceed."

"I think the death penalty is state-sanctioned murder, and it doesn't even apply to the right crimes."

"What would the right crimes be?"

"I don't know. But I feel like if you can get death for killing two drug dealers, but scumbags who rape toddlers get to live in relative comfort in prison for the rest of their lives, we've gone awry. Like, as a society."

Mack considered it. She didn't disagree with him, really, but she wasn't sure she should admit it.

"The thing that gets me is the economic side," she finally said. "It's so expensive to get the death penalty on someone, and then it takes twenty years to pull the plug. Compare that to the cost of keeping a perp in prison for the rest of his life, especially if we keep him in solitary confinement and don't give him any enrichment activities—"

"Enrichment?" Eric snorted. "Isn't that what they call it for zoo animals?"

"Yeah, well. Some crimes are so heinous that people give up their right to be considered people. I don't have a problem with that. Not my circus. Sorry, am I being rude about your clients?"

"They'll survive. This insult, at least. Hey, my wife is summoning me. Apparently it's way too late to be on a work call."

Mack looked at her watch and was shocked to see how long they'd been chatting. "Duh, of course. Just, um, I guess just let me know about the jail visit, okay?"

They hung up and Mack looked around her living room. Her father had been right—there were no pictures of him. Not that she had many pictures up, anyway, and none of her childhood. A few of Mack and her mom or Mack and Jess in recent years. The one of Christina she'd had reprinted after Benjamin Allen stole the original from her old condo. Her decor was mostly limited to art prints of world landmarks she hoped to visit someday. She turned on her laptop and navigated to a folder of old photos. Maybe it was time to make some changes.

CHAPTER TWENTY-SEVEN

It took almost a week for Eric to set up the jail visit, which gave Mack almost a week to consider canceling. No matter how often she told herself that she had permission to be unsure whether or not her father was a murderer and permission to support him despite her mixed feelings, it wasn't sinking in. She kept wondering if the murderer of Amanda Wagner and her unborn baby deserved the death penalty, and she kept concluding that he did. Amanda would have suffered terribly in the moments before her death—Mack knew that from the autopsy report. She would have known that she and her child were dying. Whether she might ultimately have decided to terminate her pregnancy or not, she hadn't chosen to terminate it that night at the hands of a murderer.

If Mack's father had killed Amanda, he deserved the death penalty. But did she really think he was a killer? Late at night, unable to sleep, she prowled her home and considered the question. There was DNA and cell phone evidence. He had lied to the police. That was enough for Sheila and Nathan to charge him and probably meant he'd done exactly what they said he did. Neither of those prosecutors played fast and loose with the law.

On the other hand, Mack had known him her entire life. He was the one who had tucked her in at night, the one who sang her lullabies. On the other hand, the lullaby he sang was "Mack the Knife," and a guy who thought *that* was an appropriate lullaby for a toddler was probably capable of murder.

If her father hadn't done it, though, who had? Billy, the other boyfriend in Amanda's contacts, still hadn't been identified, as far as Mack knew. Perhaps he was worthy of further investigation, though she knew she would be in a world of trouble if she even suggested that to Dave. She had been told in no uncertain terms to stay out of it.

She slumped on the couch and rummaged through the cushions for the remote. Another middle-of-the-night reality-TV binge lacked any appeal, but she knew she would just toss and turn if she tried to go to bed. She'd already run six miles on the treadmill and that had done little to tire her.

She thought about Eric Flagler. She had put out some feelers—subtly, not mentioning his connection to her father's case, just asking other prosecutors what they thought about him. The consensus was that he was a good attorney, about the best the PD's office had to offer, but he was, like the rest of them, hampered by a lack of resources and a significant caseload. Mack trusted him to protect her father's interests, but he couldn't coordinate the kind of investigation into Billy's identity that a private attorney could. A private attorney like Robert Miller, for example. Mack had known Professor Miller since taking his trial-advocacy class back in law school, and she had come up against him most recently during the Steve Andersen trial. She'd been impressed with his courtroom skills, and she knew that his investigator was a top-notch retired cop.

Mack scrolled her contacts, then realized it was much too late to call. The last time they talked he'd invited her to call if she ever wanted to change sides, and she'd laughed him off. She wondered what he'd say tomorrow if she called him about this instead.

The face staring back at Mack from the mirror was thinner than it should have been, and the bags under her eyes were so dark they looked almost like bruises. The scar on her cheek—left by Benjamin Allen and now faded into a dull white line—ached, though she knew that was psychosomatic. She wasn't sleeping, and the combined stresses of her father's situation and the upcoming Ferguson trial had driven grocery shopping out of her mind. She tightened her hands around the edge of the counter. Given her lack of expertise with makeup, there was nothing she could do about the way she looked.

"Sack up, Wilson," she said out loud. "There is too much to do today. We don't have time for navel-gazing. You are Mack fucking Wilson, and Mack fucking Wilson can handle whatever today holds." She gave the hand in the mirror a fist bump and nodded. She was as ready as she'd ever be.

She leaned into Jess' office and found her friend staring intently at her phone. "You okay?"

Jess shook her head and looked up. "Just peachy. I'm trying to set up a date for tonight, and this guy is just impossible. He lives on the north side of town, okay?"

"Okay," Mack said. "Lots of good options over there."

"Correct. So I suggested meeting at Vivace, but he doesn't drink. I suggested ZinBurger, and he's a pescatarian. I suggested Ra, but he doesn't eat sushi. I asked him where he wanted to go, and he says he's a homebody and I should just come over."

"You need to cancel. You're not going to some stranger's house on a first date."

"No, I'm not." She gestured at the black silk shell she was wearing and her perfectly curled hair. "But it feels like such a waste to just take all this home at the end of the day. Plus, he's a plastic surgeon, so I'd really like it to work, you know?"

"You've got a thing for plastic surgeons?"

"I've got a thing for anyone who will do my Botox for free."

Mack laughed.

"Seriously, though, do you know how much I've spent on poisons these last few years?" Jess touched the skin next to her eyes. "At this point, I don't know how I'll ever financially recover, and it's just getting worse."

"You have the skin of a child," Mack said.

Jess scowled but immediately caught herself. "Ugh, I'm trying to stop frowning. It's terrible for my wrinkles. Anyway, speaking of people who need to up their skincare regimen, how are you this morning?"

"I have a meeting with the victim on Ferguson. If you're free to do the trial, you should come with me and get to know her."

Jess looked at her computer. "I'm still not sure about the trial, but I'm free this morning. Let's go."

Jason McCormick, the victim advocate, greeted them at the door to the conference room. "She's inside," he said, wringing his hands. "But I'm not sure she's going to stay. She is…well, she's understandably upset. Detective Wood tried to calm her down, but I think it actually had the opposite effect."

Jess raised her eyebrows. "What did Debbie say?"

"Well, she was talking about what it will be like to be on the stand, and how after you ask questions, then *he* gets a chance. I guess—I had explained to her after the evidentiary hearing that he was representing himself—but I guess she didn't really understand what that meant."

"That's not great," Mack said.

Jason nodded.

Mack and Jess exchanged a look. They both had plenty of experience getting a reluctant victim back on their side, but it was never fun. They took matching deep breaths and walked into the conference room, Jason trailing behind them.

"Daisy?"

The young woman who stood to shake Mack's hand was shorter and heavier than she'd expected, with a snub nose and short black hair. She looked nothing like her father, and Mack wondered if that had played into the abuse. He was punishing her for not resembling him.

Once introductions had been made, Daisy sank back into her chair at the head of the table.

"Jason says you have some concerns about your testimony," Mack said. "And since we're gearing up for trial, I want to make sure those are addressed."

"I know I told Debbie that I could do this—that I could testify, I mean—but I didn't know he'd get to talk to me directly. I thought he'd have a lawyer, like on TV."

"Totally. When we think about a criminal trial, that's how we think about it. Two lawyers asking questions, and the judge arbitrating—keeping the lawyers in line, I mean."

"I know what arbitrating means. I'm not stupid."

Mack flushed, and Jess jumped in. "What Ms. Wilson is saying is that you had the right idea, and in normal cases that would be exactly what would happen. But your father—"

"He's not my father."

Jason cleared his throat. "Daisy has taken her mother's maiden name, Larson, and asks that we refer to the defendant as Mr. Ferguson."

Mack smiled. "Of course. So Mr. Ferguson made the choice that he didn't want a lawyer to represent him. He wanted to represent himself. And unfortunately, as long as a defendant is competent to make that choice, we have to respect it."

"He can question everyone else," Daisy said. "I don't care about that. But he shouldn't be allowed to talk to me. Not after what he did."

"I agree with you," Mack said. "But it's not up to us. The law says that if you were still a kid, I could ask the judge for special permission to have someone else ask you the questions. But because you're a grown up, there's nothing the judge can do. So why don't I explain the process, so you know how it'll work on the day you testify?"

Daisy looked like she was ready to bolt, and Mack hoped that a simple logistical conversation would help keep her in place.

"Okay, so after opening statements, the judge will tell me to call my first witness, and I'll say, 'The State calls Daisy Larson,' and then—"

"You can't call me that in court! The whole reason I changed it is so he can't find me."

Mack glanced at Jess, who made eye contact and raised an eyebrow. This girl was definitely on edge.

"No problem. I'll say we're calling Daisy Ferguson, then, and you'll walk up to this woman called the court clerk—Jess, you be the clerk."

Jess stood and raised her right hand and signaled to Daisy to do the same. Mack surreptitiously looked at her watch. She was used to doing this kind of role-play with children, but Daisy was an adult, and this felt like a waste of everyone's time. Mack's appointment to meet her father at the jail was inching closer.

"Once you're sworn in, you'll sit in the witness chair and answer questions. For now, let's pretend that Jason and Debbie are the jury, okay? So you can look at them while you're answering my questions."

Mack was surprised when Daisy played along, turning to face the "jury." She'd never tried this approach with an adult, had always thought it would seem condescending. Maybe she needed to adjust her idea of where Daisy was developmentally.

Mack ran through some of the standard "getting to know you" questions she used with teenagers—what was Daisy's favorite subject in school, what did she like to do when she wasn't working, what had she done the previous Saturday—making notes all the time. There were ways in which Daisy sounded exactly like the young adult she was, but other ways in which she seemed much younger. They would need to accommodate that at trial.

"Then I'll start asking specific questions about the abuse," Mack said. "I'll start with something like 'Tell the jury why you're here today,' and you don't have to worry about getting every detail in right away. I can and will ask follow-up questions on anything we need that you might leave out. Okay?"

"Where do I look when you're asking all these questions?" Daisy asked.

"You have options," Jess said. "You can look at the jury. There will be fourteen or fifteen different people, so you can look at some or all of them. You can look at Ms. Wilson or Debbie or

Jason, because they'll all be there. If I'm there, you can look at me."

"Do I have to look at, you know…him?"

"One time," Mack said. "At one point I'll ask you whether your father—"

"He's *not* my father," Daisy said, her hands balling into fists.

Mack looked up from her notes and took a deep breath. "I get it. I'd feel the same way in your shoes. But from the jury's perspective, I want to hammer it home for them that this isn't just some guy who did bad things to you." She swallowed, aware of a sudden tightness in her throat. "Most of the jurors are going to be parents, and I want them to understand that the person who had the highest burden in the whole world to take care of you betrayed you."

Daisy looked at her steadily, and Mack held eye contact. Whatever her recalcitrant victim was looking for, she must have found it.

"Okay," Daisy said.

"Okay," Mack said. "So at one point I'll ask if your father is in the courtroom and, if so, where he's sitting and what he's wearing. You'll look at him then, just for a second."

"What if I don't want to?" Daisy was slouched so low in her chair that Mack could barely maintain eye contact.

"Unfortunately," Jess said, "you're going to have to be even braver and stronger than you already are. You're already brave for coming forward and telling Debbie what happened. And testifying is hard work. And then that will be the hardest moment—looking at him and saying, 'That's him. He's the guy.' But you're a strong person, so we know you can do it."

Daisy looked at each of them in turn. "Thank you all for everything you've done, but I think I'm out. We haven't even talked about what happens when it's his turn to ask the questions, and I think this is more than I can handle. I'm out of the house, so it's not like he can get me again. I just want to be done with it."

"Here's the thing, Daisy," Mack said, trying to decide how to say what needed to be said. She snuck another glance at her watch and was shocked at how much time had passed. "You're under subpoena to come to trial. Normally, that doesn't really mean anything. I tell someone to come to trial and they do, and we all move on. But, well—"

Jess took over. "What Ms. Wilson is trying to say is that, if you don't come on your own, you can actually get arrested, and then you'd have to sit in jail until it was time for you to testify."

Daisy was upright in a flash. "You can't be serious. No way that's a real thing."

Four nodding faces looked back at her.

"It's true," Jason said.

"I've had to arrest victims," Debbie said. "It sucks for everyone, but it's allowed."

"I—I'll…" Daisy was standing now, gathering her purse and straightening her clothing. "I'll leave. I'll leave town, and you'll never be able to find me."

Mack shook her head. "That's not how it works. You've got a job and an apartment, you can't just up and leave. And even if you did, we'd find you. It'll be much easier if you just cooperate, okay? Look, how about if I set up a tour of the courtroom, and then, after you've seen it, we can practice again."

Daisy nodded grudgingly, and Debbie saluted Mack as she followed the girl, who practically ran out of the room.

Mack slumped in her chair and rested her forehead on the table. "Think she'll show up?"

"I do!" Jason said.

But Jess shook her head. "Get the warrant ready now. It'll save you time later."

Mack had to hurry to get to the jail on time. Stepping into the lobby, she was hit by the stench of unwashed bodies, industrial cafeteria food, and fear. She'd shed her suit jacket, hoping that her slacks and blouse would make her look more like a paralegal, but Eric frowned at the sight of her.

"No paralegal has ever looked that good," he said. "Can you at least, I don't know, have worse posture or something?"

Mack curled her shoulders forward and put her head down.

"That works."

Eric signed them in, and the guard clearly recognized him.

"Hey there, Mr. Flagler," she said. "Long time, no see. You got someone new with you today?"

"Yes, ma'am, Laverne. This is Kenzie. She's helping me out on this one."

Mack waved but kept her head down.

"Welcome, Kenzie. You stick with Mr. Flagler, okay? He'll show you the ropes."

"I will, thanks."

Laverne buzzed them into the first security checkpoint, where Eric removed his belt and they both sent their bags through an X-ray scanner. After being wanded by another deputy, they were buzzed into a second checkpoint, where they were patted down and told to wait.

"I don't know how you keep your hair long," Mack said. "I always feel like it takes a week of shampooing before I get rid of the smell."

Eric shrugged. "Honestly, I don't even notice it anymore."

"Well, let me tell you, it's foul. And it stays in my nose for days."

"My wife agrees with you. On jail days, she makes me strip down in the garage and throw my clothes straight in the washer. Then I shower in the guest bathroom."

"You'll have to tell me what shampoo you use. I don't come here often, but when I do I feel like my water bill instantly doubles."

They were buzzed through a third door into another, smaller lobby, which had six meeting rooms branching off it. A guard met them and showed them into one of the rooms.

"He'll be just a minute," the guard said and closed the door.

Mack looked around at the same industrial-gray paint that was all over the courthouse and her own office building.

"I've never been in these rooms," she said. "When I meet with a victim or a witness, they put us in an interview room."

"These cubicles are okay," Eric said. "They're just for legal visits, so no audio or video recording. Chairs and table are bolted to the floor, so there's not much risk. Just a heads-up, he'll be in chains. Once they show him in, though, they'll leave us alone unless they hear a commotion. You can even hug him if you want."

Mack shuddered. Deciding to come had been hard enough, and she could already feel her heart racing. She'd pass on the hug.

Eric sat quietly, reviewing his file, as they waited. Mack couldn't bring herself to sit.

"Not much room in here, huh?" she said, making conversation.

Eric shrugged. "I usually have another attorney, a paralegal, an investigator, and my client, and we all fit okay. Are you claustrophobic?"

Mack pressed her lips together and took shallow breaths through her nose.

Five minutes later, there was a knock at the door. It opened to reveal her father, paler than he'd been the last time she'd seen him. Thinner, too. Jail was definitely taking its toll. Still, his face broke into a broad smile when he saw Mack. He leaned toward her and raised his chained arms, but she backed away.

"I wasn't sure you'd come," he said. He didn't seem offended by the lack of a hug, just settled himself onto one of the bolted-down chairs and kept smiling.

"I wasn't, either," Mack said, taking a seat across from him. "But here we are."

They made small talk about the food and the conditions. His cellmate was "a real nice guy" who was charged with killing his girlfriend's two-year-old son. Both men were in protective custody because of the nature of their crimes.

As the conversation died down, Eric cleared his throat. "I want to get a little business taken care of," he said. "Marcus, Mack's surprised you're pushing this to trial so fast, and—as you and I have talked about before—I agree with her. Are you willing to revisit the idea of delaying the trial?"

"Nope," Marcus said. "Not even for a day. Not for a minute! This has been such a nightmare. I want my trial, and then I want to walk out of here, and I want it to happen as soon as possible."

His demeanor, Mack thought, was good. Credible. He didn't sound like a man who knew he'd be convicted of capital murder—he sounded like an innocent man determined to fight. If she were a juror, she would believe him. Of course, she'd believed him as a kid every time he promised to take her to the zoo or the movies or give her a ride to school. The fact that he never followed through, that Mack's mom was left to comfort her, never seemed to matter the next time he promised something he wouldn't deliver.

"There's something I'd like to talk about," Mack said. "But, Eric, I'm worried it will offend you."

"I'm a defense attorney. If you're not planning to literally spit on me, I'll be okay."

Mack took a deep breath. "I think you should hire Robert Miller. He's probably the best defense attorney in the state, and his resources are unbelievable. If you want to prove that someone else did this—"

"Hold on there, Mackenzie," Marcus said. "I've been very happy with Eric, and I'm not sure I want to go switching horses midstream."

Eric cleared his throat. "You should hear her out, Mr. Wilson. I've seen Rob in trial and he's incredible. It's just—well, there are a few things about him to consider."

Marcus snorted. "You just don't want to lose your money if I go with someone else."

"No, I'm paid by the state. If you change attorneys—hell, if you have a heart attack and die right here in front of us—I'll have a new client tomorrow, and my life will go on just fine."

Mack covered a smile with her hand. "I've been thinking about Miller's fee. I don't think you have enough money for anyone private, let alone him. Right?"

Her father nodded.

"Well, I don't either, but I have my house, and I could take out a mortgage against it. You wouldn't be the one hiring him. I would. He'd be what's called *Knapp* counsel. So Eric would still be your primary attorney, but Robert would help with two specific things—the trial, and the investigation into a third-party defense."

"What does that mean?" Marcus asked.

"It means that our defense at trial would be to name the person we think committed the murder," Eric said.

"And how much is this going to cost?" Marcus asked.

"I haven't talked to Professor Miller yet, but I would think right around forty thousand."

Eric whistled. "I knew Miller was steep, but I didn't know he was that steep. For what it's worth, I'm not offended at all, and I encourage you to think about it, Mr. Wilson. Technically, Mack can hire him with or without your consent. But, frankly, I hope she won't." He turned to Mack. "If you're counting on a third-party defense, I can't tell you strongly enough how fruitless I think that's going to be."

"But if he didn't kill Amanda, then someone else did."

Eric nodded. "Absolutely. You know that, and I know that, and any juror with an ounce of common sense will know that, too. But the evidence against him is strong, and it will take a heck of a lot to overcome it."

"So what's your plan?"

"The same as in most murder cases. Hold the State to its burden. No one saw Marcus kill her, and the State can't prove he did. There are innocent explanations for every fact in the case. The beer bottle was old and he did drink out of it, so that's how his DNA got there. He misunderstood the date the cops were asking about, due to his anxiety based on previous interactions with police. They can't prove he actually followed through with his text and showed up at her house."

"Are you going to testify?" Mack asked her father.

"We haven't decided yet," Eric said. "Remember, all we need is one juror on our side to hang it, and it'll be harder for the State to try him a second time."

Mack was sweating, and the stench of the jail was overwhelming. This was all too much, too real. She hadn't expected their conversation to be so granular, to find herself considering strategies from the defense perspective. She had to get out of there.

"I—I have another meeting," she said, feeling like she was speaking underwater. "I am going to have to step out. Eric, are you able to stay?"

The defense attorney shook his head. "We've done everything we need to do today. I'll walk you out. Marcus, I'll be in touch in a couple of days, and we can talk through a road map of what's coming next."

Eric knocked on the steel door, and soon a deputy swung it open and ushered them back into the lobby.

There was a roaring in Mack's ears.

"Are you okay?" Eric asked. "You look kind of pale and clammy."

Mack stepped outside and focused on not passing out. She closed her eyes. "Just got to be too much, I guess."

Eric squeezed her shoulder. "Easy does it. Let's talk next week. Whatever you're going to do about Robert, you should do it soon. If he's going to get anywhere without continuing the trial, that will be tough."

"I'll think about it, I just…I need time to think about it."

CHAPTER TWENTY-EIGHT

The final trial-management conference in the Ferguson case was fast approaching, and neither Jason nor Debbie had heard from Daisy since their ill-fated meeting. They had subpoenaed her for the hearing, not because they needed her to appear, but because it would make a good test for the trial, when her presence would be necessary. If she showed up for the hearing, there would be no need to ask the judge to issue a warrant. In case she failed to appear, however, Mack reluctantly drew up the warrant paperwork.

That only took ten minutes, and then Mack found herself with an hour to kill. She was, for once, caught up on her cases. One thing she liked about homicide cases was that they generally took longer to resolve, and that meant more time for motion practice, interviews, and all the other procedural work that went into a case.

For the first time since before she had started in Sex Crimes, there were no emergencies demanding Mack's undivided attention, and she didn't know quite what to do with herself.

The office's internal file-management system was up on her screen from the warrant paperwork, and before she realized what she was doing, she found herself typing her father's name into the search box.

"What are you staring at so intently?" Jess asked.

Mack jumped, clicking frantically in an attempt to close the search window, but only succeeding in maximizing it.

"Are you watching porn? I haven't seen your face this red since…well, I don't even know when."

"Keep your voice down," Mack whispered. "Close the door."

Jess shut the door and sat. "Are you up to no good?"

Mack shook her head. "I just, well, I thought I'd see if there were any new motions or anything. In…in my dad's case."

Jess came around the desk in a shot and pulled the mouse from Mack's hand. "My dude. You're not even in the public docket, you're in our file management? How stupid can you be?" She closed the search window.

"I wasn't generating anything, I hadn't even opened any documents. I just wanted to see what was going on."

"No. Nope. No 'oopsies!' here. They log every view of every file, and you are walled off from that case for a reason. If they catch you looking at it, you are so totally screwed. You'll be fired before you have time to say 'I quit.' This is the most terminally boneheaded thing you've ever done, Mack, and I've known you to do some stupid things."

Jess' voice rose as she ranted, and Mack slumped lower and lower in her chair. "But—"

"No. Absolutely not. No buts. No nothing. All I've heard you say about the guy for the whole time I've known you is how worthless he was when you were a kid. He flaked out on every birthday party, he showed up late and reeking of booze at your bat mitzvah. And now you're going to risk your entire career to—to what, to check on the status of his case? And worse than that, if you don't immediately tell Sheila—if *I* don't immediately tell Sheila, I'm an accessory! You're putting *me* at risk for this guy I've never met and never will."

"I'm sorry," Mack said. "I never meant to put you at risk, obvi. I didn't even know you were in the office this morning."

She sighed and ran her hands through her hair. "Haven't you ever just needed to know something?"

"Sure. I needed to know whether Ben Affleck went to rehab after his divorce from Jen Garner. I needed to know whether the green curry last night had shrimp paste in it. I needed to know whether the mole on my back was something I should worry about. But I have never needed to know whether my office had sufficient evidence to kill my dad."

Mack started to cry, covering her face with her hands.

Jess' face froze. "I'm sorry, Mack. I shouldn't have said that. This thing with your dad has nothing to do with you. It's not your fault, and of course you're curious what's going on. You've just...you've got to find a better way."

Mack grabbed a tissue. "It has everything to do with me, Jess. It's who I am. It's who I come from. What if—what if I—okay, look. Last year, when I was a murder suspect, you said, 'Of course you didn't, you could never!' which was so kind and so sweet, and Dave did the same thing. Again, such kind, much sweet. But what if I could? What if my dad is a killer, and so I could be a killer and it just happens I wasn't the killer last time? But I could be next time? What if I need to be alert every minute of every day so I don't just...just snap?"

"Okay, now *that's* the stupidest thing you've ever said. Look, I know you think you've got everything under control. But this...this is not what 'under control' looks like, and I think you know that."

Mack sat absolutely still for a very long time, staring at the diplomas on the wall. At last, she pinched the skin between her thumb and index finger until the pain brought her back into her body.

"You need to see somebody," Jess was saying.

Mack wondered what she'd missed.

"A therapist. A trauma specialist, probably. I know you're not talking to Anna, or whatever, but I can talk to her. I can get a referral. You are careening toward disaster, my friend."

Mack nodded woodenly. "Trauma doctor. You'll get me a name. Got it."

Jess put a hand over Mack's and rubbed at the fingernail-shaped indentation she'd left in her skin. "I came in here to tell you I got placed for trial this morning. Super messy child-abuse death. We're screening for three months, so I won't be able to help with Ferguson. I'm not—well, I don't want to add insult to injury, but do you think maybe you should have someone else do the trial with you? Just, under the circumstances, you know?"

Mack could feel the beginning of a panic attack. There were cruel words on the tip of her tongue, itching to be free. Jess had been engaged to a serial killer—who was she to tell Mack what to do? Who was she to recommend a therapist? Mack knew for a fact she hadn't gone to the doctor Anna recommended more than half a dozen times before deciding she was smarter than the psychologist and had nothing to learn from them. What kind of person couldn't even tell when their own fiancé was a sexual sadist? She could almost hear herself saying the words, feel them leaking out of her in a low hiss.

"I have to go," she said instead, rising so abruptly she bumped her knee on her desk. She was grateful for the pain—it gave her something to focus on instead of rage. "Court."

"Mack—" Jess said but stopped herself. She was still sitting there when Mack left the room.

Adrenaline pushed Mack into the court complex, but she started to shake as she stepped into the courtroom. She looked in vain for Daisy, but—she glanced at her watch—she was almost fifteen minutes early. She forced herself to take long slow breaths, in through her nose, out through pursed lips. The anger ebbed from her body, left her numb and tired and wishing she could fast-forward through the rest of the day.

Judge Leyva hadn't yet taken the bench, and the occupants of the courtroom were chatting easily. Mack couldn't make out individual conversations, but that was okay. There wasn't anyone she wanted to talk to.

The third *psst* got her attention, and she looked around the room for the source of the noise. No one she recognized in the gallery, and the other attorneys were all talking in small huddles. That left the chain—the in-custody defendants who waited, chained together in the jury box, for their matters to be called.

Oy vey, not Liam Ferguson. He was the last person she wanted to interact with, though, because he was representing himself, he could talk directly to her without an intermediary. When she located him on the chain, however, he was intently focused on a stack of papers in his lap.

She looked more closely at the inmates, and her stomach dropped at the fourth face from the end. Her father.

"Mackenzie!" he stage-whispered. Some of the other defendants were looking now, trying to figure out who he was talking to.

The deputy noticed. "No talking on the chain," he called.

Unbelievable. She literally could not believe that the inmate trying to get her attention was her father. It was just too weird. She signaled to the deputy, who approached, looking bored.

"Can you tell him I can't talk to him without his attorney present?"

The deputy swung around and looked at the nine men on the chain. "Which one?" he asked loudly. "I didn't see who was making noise, just heard the commotion."

Mack cleared her throat and beckoned the deputy closer. "The fourth one from the right. Wilson?"

The deputy straightened. "Wilson! No talking on the chain or you will be taken back to holding. Don't bother the nice district attorney, okay? She doesn't want to talk to you."

If she tried hard enough, maybe the ground would open up and swallow her whole. Her prayers were interrupted by someone squeezing her shoulder, and she opened her eyes to find Eric Flagler smiling reassuringly.

"I caught the tail end of that," he said. "Do you want to say hi, or should I tell him it's against the rules?"

"Let's see how the calendar goes," Mack said. "If some people clear out, I can. But I don't want...well, I don't want to draw any attention, you know?"

Eric nodded and walked over to his client, leaning in close. Mack hadn't even known he had a hearing this morning. She flipped open the daily calendar that court staff left on the prosecution and defense tables. Marcus Wilson, hearing on motion to modify. A motion to modify release conditions? On what planet would a capital defendant get out of custody?

"Seriously?" she said to Eric, who had returned to the defense table.

He shrugged. "My client wanted me to file it. I told him it was pointless, but not unethical."

"What possible basis could you have?"

Eric looked at her, straight-faced. "Ties to the community."

"Jesus." She was his only tie to the community, as far as she knew. At least, now that his girlfriend was dead.

Mack weighed whether or not it was fair game to watch the hearing, should her father's case get called before Ferguson's. Technically, courtrooms were open to the public. The office couldn't forbid her from attending and hadn't tried. But it certainly wouldn't look good for her to be there, especially given her adventure in the file-management system earlier that morning.

Judge Leyva interrupted Mack's internal debate by rushing onto the bench, waving at everyone to take their seats before his bailiff had even finished announcing "All rise." Mack looked at the lawyers, now silently jockeying to be called first. Nathan Moore wasn't among them, but Tom Colbey was. She made eye contact and nodded.

"Judge, I think we're ready on Ferguson," Tom said, approaching the podium. He motioned for Ferguson himself to stand.

"Good morning, everyone," the judge said, once Mack, Tom, and Ferguson had stated their appearances for the record. "Happy Monday to all and thank you for spending some of your day here with me. We are set for trial next week, are we ready to proceed?"

"The State is ready, Judge," Mack said. "I do have one administrative matter for the Court to handle, but that can wait until the end of the hearing."

"I am ready," Ferguson said. He handed Tom a thick pile of papers. "But I have some motions that need to be dealt with. I've just given advisory counsel copies for Ms. Wilson and for Your Honor."

Judge Leyva accepted the pile he was handed and leafed through the pages. "Okay, what do we have here?"

"There are three motions. Number one is a motion to dismiss for malicious prosecution and preindictment delay."

Mack swallowed a laugh. Malicious prosecution? Liam Ferguson was about to see how malicious she could be. And preindictment delay? He'd caused his own delay by bullying Daisy into silence for so many years. That wasn't in the State's control.

"The second is a motion to suppress the alleged victim's testimony because she lacks the capacity to testify."

More nonsense. Just because Ferguson had access to a legal library and a slew of jailhouse lawyers didn't mean he had the intelligence to use their input appropriately.

"And finally, a writ of habeas corpus because I'm being unlawfully detained."

At that one, even Judge Leyva let the hint of a smile cross his face. "We'll take these in order. Ms. Wilson, have you seen these before this morning?"

"No, Judge, and I would request the full statutory response time so that I can file my written responses. Well, actually, before that, I would request that all three motions be stricken as untimely. We're one week out from trial, as you stated, and these motions were all due no later than thirty days before trial. One remedy, of course, would be to push the trial date out. However, since Mr. Ferguson has been so insistent on exercising his speedy trial rights, I think the Court should make him elect a path—pursue the motions and continue trial, or retract them and proceed with trial as set."

"Let's see if we can find some middle ground, shall we?" Judge Leyva asked. "For example, this third motion I've reviewed as you were speaking, Ms. Wilson—I apologize for not giving you my full attention—and it appears that this is, in fact, a habeas writ. Habeas writs, Mr. Ferguson, are a federal law matter. This is not the correct court in which to file this. I am going to declare your third motion moot based on my lack of jurisdiction. Ms. Wilson, anything to add on that one?"

"No, Judge," Mack said, thinking through the issue. "But if I come up with something, I'll put it in writing."

The judge smiled. "Moving on to the second motion, regarding the victim's capacity to testify. Ms. Wilson, you'll correct me if I'm wrong, but don't we have a presumption canonized in our Arizona law in favor of anyone being capable of testifying?"

"Honestly, Judge, I'm not sure. I'm unfamiliar with this issue."

"I see that you have a statute book right in front of you, yes?"

Mack grabbed the book. Her office made sure there was one in every courtroom for just such a circumstance.

"I think if you turn to the evidence rules, perhaps 601, you'll find something informative."

Mack flipped through the pages, looking for the rule. She read it twice to herself before risking looking up at the judge. "You are correct about the presumption, Judge."

"Even a stopped clock is right twice a day, isn't that what they say?" Judge Leyva asked.

The attorneys waiting to have their own cases heard all chuckled. Mack hadn't realized that anyone was paying attention and looked around, hoping Nathan Moore hadn't made it to court yet. Her heart sank as she saw him in the front row of the gallery, apparently listening intently. She smiled at him, but he ignored her. He must have been taking "walled off" as far as it could go.

"Okay, then. So, Ms. Wilson, you're going to respond in writing to this motion to dismiss and to this motion regarding the victim's capacity to testify, citing to the applicable rule."

"But, Judge, the timeliness issue—"

"Ms. Wilson, you've been practicing in my court for years, and I have no doubt that you will respond thoroughly, professionally, and within forty-eight hours."

Forty-eight hours? That was insane. Under normal conditions, she would have ten days to write these responses.

"Unfortunately," Judge Leyva continued. "It will not be I who reaps the rewards of your no doubt scintillating discussion of these issues. I see that you have been assigned to Judge McPhee for trial, and my loss is her gain."

Mack's fury dissolved. Judge McPhee was about as ideal a judge as she could imagine. She'd keep Ferguson under control during trial, which was all anyone could ask for with a pro per defendant. Judge Leyva had done what he could to undermine Mack's ability to effectively respond to the last-minute barrage of motions, but it was just a parting shot. He knew it would be smooth sailing once she got to Judge McPhee.

"Reurge the timeliness issue before McPhee," Nathan Moore whispered to her as he approached the prosecution table. "That might get somewhere with her."

So she wasn't totally cut off, after all.

Judge Leyva looked ready to call the next case, and Mack reviewed her notes from the hearing.

"Wait, Judge. I have another thing to take care of on the Ferguson case."

Leyva looked at her, his smile still in place. Mack scanned the gallery one more time for Daisy. She never liked issuing warrants on witnesses, and certainly not on victims. It just made her complicit in their revictimization. But her ability to hold Ferguson accountable depended on Daisy showing up to testify.

"The listed victim in this case was subpoenaed to this hearing. She is not present, however, and has not made contact with me or my office. As a result, I am asking that a warrant be issued for her arrest. All the necessary paperwork is prepared, I just need your signature."

Ferguson stood and banged a hand on the edge of the jury box. "I would strenuously object to that, sir. If she chooses not to be present, that's just more evidence of her lack of seriousness—another reason for this bullshit case against me to be dismissed."

"Mr. Ferguson, please consider your words and actions carefully while in my courtroom or in any courtroom," Judge

Leyva said. "That kind of language will not serve you here. Now, as it happens, I am inclined to agree with you that Ms. Ferguson's absence today tells us something important about her allegations. But that issue is no longer in my hands, it is for Judge McPhee to address. The issue for me is whether the State has its paperwork in order. And judging from Ms. Wilson's history and reputation, I am sure it does."

Mack approached the bench and handed the judge the packet of papers—a copy of the subpoena, the warrant application, and the warrant tabbed for his signature.

"Thank you, Judge," she said. "That's all I have this morning."

Leyva signed his name with a flourish and returned the papers to Mack. "Always lovely seeing you in my division. I am sorry we will not have the opportunity to share this trial. Mr. Ferguson, other than your brief linguistic struggles this morning, you have been a pleasure to have in court. I wish you all the best in your trial. Be careful of Ms. Wilson. She's a dangerous opponent."

Mack slid into the pew next to Jason, who had arrived during the hearing.

"He must really like you," the advocate whispered.

"I'd rather he just make the right rulings and forgo the flirting, but I'll take what I can get. He's more or less harmless."

"Does he do that to other people, too?"

"Only women, and not all women. I think he knows there's no risk with me. He's been happily married for something like forty years, so this is just his 'harmless' little fun." She handed Jason the warrant paperwork. "Can you give this to my paralegal when you get back to the office? I'll text Debbie and let her know she can pick it up. I have another hearing this morning."

She didn't think it was necessary to mention that her other hearing was her father's hearing.

CHAPTER TWENTY-NINE

His case was the next one called, and Mack slid lower on the bench. She wasn't breaking any rules by being there, but she didn't want to call attention to herself.

"Marcus Wilson," Judge Leyva said, reading the calendar. "I just saw a Mack Wilson, and now a Marcus. Who knew that would be such a common name this morning?"

Mack flushed. Did that mean that the judge knew about the connection, or was he just being his normal, overly familiar self? It was impossible to be sure.

"There sure are a lot of us running around," her father said.

Mack sighed, grateful for his discretion, but, figuring discretion was the better part of valor, she slipped out of the courtroom before the hearing continued.

Almost twelve hours later, she was still at her desk, ostensibly working on the newly filed motions in the Ferguson case but really thinking about her father.

She had her music on shuffle, which turned out to be a mistake. Normally, she only listened to classical while working—

no lyrics to distract her—but for some reason she'd hit shuffle this time. She wasn't sure when she'd downloaded a Paul Simon greatest-hits album, but he was one of the few musicians her parents agreed on when she was a kid.

As the opening vocals and percussion of "Slip Slidin' Away" came through her earbuds, Mack was hit by a visceral image of riding in her dad's car. She must have been about six, because she had her T-ball uniform shirt on, and she'd quit playing in second grade. The car was an old Pontiac with a cracked leather bench seat. He let her sit next to him on the way to McDonald's, though her mom made her sit in the back on a booster seat until she was ten.

She could almost smell his Old Spice and the little air freshener and the hot, earthy scent of Ohio in August through the open windows. The backs of her legs stuck to the seat with sweat. The Pontiac's air-conditioning had died even before Mack's dad bought the car. She remembered asking why he'd bought a car where they had to physically roll down the windows when her mom just had to press a button.

He'd turned up the volume, humming along. He had a great voice. Mack's mom always used to say that he could have been a singer, if things had gone differently.

"Dad," Mack said. "What does that mean?"

He kept singing.

She hated when he did that. He would never just answer her questions. He always made her work for a response.

"What does that *mean*? It doesn't make any sense—if you get closer to something, you're not sliding away!"

He rolled to a stop, and even thirty years later Mack could feel his eyes on her. "It's hard to explain, Knife. It means…well, you know how sometimes I have to work far away from home?"

"Yeah."

"And you know how that makes you sad and makes Mom sad?"

"Yeah. Mom cries. I don't, though."

He smiled and tousled her hair. "That's my shadow. Wilsons don't cry. But that's what the song is about. It's about how sometimes grownups have to do things they don't want to do. And you can try and try, but you just can't quite get yourself to where you want to be."

Mack thought about that. She still didn't get it. "Can I get the boy toy with my Happy Meal?"

Her father's laugh drowned out the song. "You bet."

"Burning the midnight oil?" Sheila asked, dropping into a chair. Mack blinked. She hadn't noticed Sheila come in, so intent was she on that memory. She hadn't thought of it in years—it was possible she'd never thought of it before—so why had it come up now?

"More like the ten-p.m. oil," Mack said. She leaned back in her chair and squinted at the overhead lights. They were on a motion sensor and Sheila had awakened them. "God willing, I won't still be here at midnight. Sometimes I think the stupider the motion is, the harder it is to respond to. I'm really struggling to make this more than just 'nuh-uh,' you know?"

Sheila smiled. She was wearing leggings and had a light sheen of sweat across her forehead. She plucked at a speck of lint on her tank top. "Nathan told me about your trip to see Judge Leyva this morning."

Mack felt like she'd been punched in the throat. She hadn't even seen anything happen in her dad's case, and anyway, a courtroom visit was totally allowed. There was no need to panic, yet she couldn't force herself to stay cool. She picked up a pen and began clicking it.

"Your victim is in the wind?"

"Oh," Mack said, exhaling deeply. "That. She's been hit or miss since defendant went pro per. We met last week, and I explained the warrant process, so we'll see what happens. I don't think it'll come to an arrest, but I wanted to be ready. The last time I had to arrest a victim, it was actually kind of a blessing for a while. She was a sex worker and had been pretty brutally raped by a john. By the time trial came around, she was about seven months pregnant and strung out, bad. We got her in custody and kept her there for two or three weeks. When she testified, she was past the worst of withdrawal and talking about getting out of the life."

"What happened to her?"

"We kept in touch for a while. And I kept in touch with her sister. The baby was okay—not drug-dependent at birth."

"And your victim?"

Mack cleared her throat. "Went back to the life. She didn't... um, she didn't make it. Took too much her first time back after the baby."

Sheila looked at her appraisingly. "You cared about her."

"I did. I helped her—well, the advocate and I helped her—get into a program. The baby was adopted at birth, and the program was supposed to help Nikki get job skills. She seemed to be on the right track. The rape messed her up—mentally, of course, but physically too. She almost died from her injuries. We were hopeful that the conviction would be the closure she needed to move forward."

"You can't save people who don't want to be saved," Sheila said. "And we're not lifeguards. That's one thing I've learned in this job."

"Sure. Can't save them all. But you never know which ones you can save. So, you know, I keep trying."

"That's how prosecutors burn out."

"Can be. It's also how we maintain the fire to keep on fighting. To keep writing late-night motion responses."

Sheila nodded noncommittally. "He told me you also stayed for the hearing after yours. For Nathan's hearing."

Mack fought the urge to argue. "I actually left right after they called the case. I didn't see anything substantive. Although if I had—"

Sheila raised a forestalling hand. "Courtrooms are public. You had every right to stay. I just..." She weighed her words. "I hope that you're spending time taking care of yourself. I'm not asking you to confide in me—that would put unfair pressure on you given the supervisory nature of our relationship. I just hope you have a satisfying life outside of this building."

Mack forced a smile. "I was actually getting ready to leave when you came in. My running group meets tonight."

"Perfect," Sheila said. The sound of her hands hitting her thighs surprised Mack. "Let me just get my purse, and we can walk out together."

Cursing herself for choosing that specific lie, Mack stood and gathered her own bags. She looked at her watch. If there was no traffic, she could be in her sweats, on the couch, cold beer in hand, within thirty minutes. She'd always found running to be a solitary activity.

CHAPTER THIRTY

Her second time in the jail's visitation-room lobby, as she and Eric waited to be ushered into their meeting with her father, Mack felt no calmer than she had the first time.

"Is it me?" she asked. "Or did this room shrink?"

Eric looked at the industrial-gray cinderblock walls. "If shrinking it would save the city money, I wouldn't be surprised."

"Hey, I've been meaning to ask you. I checked the public docket on the case the other day, and I see you're not challenging the seizure of the DNA. Don't restaurant patrons have a privacy interest in their discarded place settings?"

He laughed. "That's an argument I haven't heard before. I can't get too deep into it because of the confidentiality piece, but suffice it to say that your dad and I talked about it and decided not to go forward."

"Why not? Was it a lost cause?"

"Definitely not a lost cause. I think there were points to be scored, especially about the reliability. They may have had probable cause for his DNA, but there was no way to control whose DNA was going to be on the mug and silverware, right? It's not just the customer who touches stuff in a restaurant. Anyway, he made the decision because you'd need to testify at the evidentiary hearing if we challenged it, and he knew you wouldn't want to. He wanted to keep you out of it."

Mack's hands shook. "Really?"

A guard ushered them into a legal-visit room and Eric sat, opening his file on its small table. "Really. He said he knew you didn't want to be involved, and he didn't want to make you make a choice."

Five minutes later, Mack was still thinking about that when her father was led into the room. He and Eric began to chat.

"Can I ask you something?" she interrupted them, gripping the back of an empty chair and watching her father's face settle into studied neutrality.

"I figured this was coming," Marcus said. "Ask me whatever you want, and I promise I'll answer you."

Mack realized that he expected her to ask him whether or not he was guilty of the murder. "No, no, not that. I just want to know if you remembered taking me to McDonald's in the Pontiac after T-ball."

His expression cleared. "Sure, I remember taking you to McDonald's. You always wanted the boy toy. You were...well, we just called you a tomboy then. Your mom thought I shouldn't indulge you—you should learn to like the girl toys. But I didn't see the harm. But, kiddo, I didn't buy the Pontiac until you were thirteen. I always drove Fords when you were little."

Mack searched her memory. "Are you sure?"

Marcus laughed. "Very. Because your mom finally put her foot down when I missed your bat mitzvah because I was stuck in Pittsburgh when the Galaxie wouldn't start. It took a while to find something I liked, but I had a buddy who was looking to get rid of the Pontiac and gave me a good deal. God, I hated that car. It didn't even have a tape deck, so there was no way to play music in it. I just had to listen to whatever was on the radio. Why are you asking about that old gas hog?"

Mack knew exactly why she was asking. If her memory was accurate, then maybe she had finally understood her dad. He was just a guy who was trying to provide for his family—trying to create a better world for his daughter—but life took him away from where he should have been. It was the closest she had come to being sure he hadn't killed Amanda Wagner. But if the memory wasn't real, then what did that mean? She had to try one more time. "You don't remember listening to Paul Simon with me in the car?"

He frowned. "Never. I never liked his stuff. Always thought Art's voice was better. Your mom liked him. Always kept his cassettes in her car."

"Okay, well, thanks for indulging me." She produced a smile, though the realization that she couldn't trust her own memory had her on the verge of panic. "Eric, I really need to get moving, but let's touch base next week?"

She forced herself not to run out of the building, and the measured sound of her heels clacking against the linoleum helped regulate her breathing.

"It smells like the jail in here," Jess said, coming into Mack's office and closing the door behind her.

"Yeah, that's where I spent my lunch break."

"With your…"

Mack nodded.

Jess cleared her throat and gathered the ends of her hair into her hand, examining them closely. "I…Well, I want to apologize. For how I handled things the other day."

"Thanks," Mack said. "You don't need to, though. It turns out you weren't wrong. I just got defensive in the moment. When I got a little distance from it, I knew that. I mean, I knew looking up his case wasn't allowed. I just wasn't thinking and wound up typing his name. Like automatic writing or something."

"Even so. Even if it was intentional, I mean—I shouldn't have yelled. I understand why you did what you did. I don't agree with it, but I get it. I just…I don't want any part of it. Okay? I don't want to put myself or my job at risk for him."

"*I'm* sorry for putting you at risk. For what it's worth, I would never have let you get in trouble. I would have quit, if it came down to it."

They sat for a while in an uneasy silence.

"I guess," Jess said, her voice tight and high. "I guess I've been pushing really hard since the Adam thing, and I just snapped."

"You've seemed pretty fine to me. Are you not fine?"

Jess let her hair fall and rubbed the balls of her thumbs against her eyes. "I'm really very not fine."

When she took her hands away, Mack could see tears on her cheeks. "Oh, friend, it's okay to not be fine. You had a terrible thing happen to you."

"Nothing actually *happened* to me. I was in a relationship, he turned out to be a liar, we broke up."

Mack blinked, trying to process. She couldn't understand Jess any more than she'd understood her dad earlier that day.

"You—you got engaged, and then found out that your fiancé was a serial killer and my ex-girlfriend was his next victim, and then watched our cop pal shoot him to death. That's…that's not the same as what you just said."

Jess waved her hand. "Tomato, to-mah-to. My point is just that *Anna* should have trauma—*she* got drugged and kidnapped. *You* can have trauma—Adam threatened to kill you. Dave had to shoot a man for me—*that's* trauma. But what happened to me? I don't feel like I have the right to trauma."

"Dude, it's not…it's not pie. There's enough trauma here for all of us. I don't pretend to know how Dave and Anna are dealing with what happened. I see Dave, but we don't talk about it. And Anna, well. You know. Anna."

"Thanks. I think—I think maybe I stopped going to therapy too soon. I did the six sessions that were free through the office, and then I 'graduated.' Maybe I need to go back."

"I think that's a great idea."

They fist-bumped across the desk. The air felt clearer than it had earlier.

"Did you see Petrou's teaser this morning?" Jess asked.

"No, I try to never know what that jerkface is up to. I won't even watch KGUN anymore."

"You might want to rethink. He's launching a new podcast, *The Desert Murder*."

Mack groaned. "Of course he is. Because he needs more exposure. Barf. What's it about?"

"Seriously? It's about a death-penalty case that's starting soon? And got a whole bunch of media attention back when the murder happened?"

"You're just messing with me. That's funny. Ha ha ha."

"It's not a joke. It's why I came to apologize to you. I've been feeling bad and kept meaning to do it, but when I saw that this morning...well, I figured you're about to need the support."

"Does he know about me?"

"I'm not sure if he knows you're involved on a personal level. But even if he doesn't—which is best case, of course—there's going to be some scrutiny. You were the original prosecutor, and then Moore wound up with it. Even if he doesn't know why, he'll probably try to make something out of that."

Mack glanced at her watch, frustrated to see that the afternoon had flown by before she'd had the chance to get any real work done. "I'd better call my mom. She has news alerts set up for his stuff, and I need to warn her."

CHAPTER THIRTY-ONE

"Hi!" her mom said enthusiastically. "I was just thinking about you. Were your ears burning?"

"Hi, Mom, how are you?"

They chatted easily about her mother's latest adventures in retirement. Mack enjoyed hearing about her friends at the community center. Mack's mom and aunt often traveled together and had just returned from Niagara Falls, so she heard about that, too.

"What's up with you, sweetie?"

Mack took a deep breath. She had been dreading this conversation for weeks, but there was no putting it off any longer. "I'm actually calling to tell you about a new true-crime podcast that's coming out."

"Ooh, one of your cases?"

"Well, I worked on it for a little bit, but no, not really. It's Petrou—"

"I hate that guy."

"I know, Mom. Me, too. But the defendant in this murder case, it's...well, it's Dad."

For a moment, there was no response, and Mack bit her cheek to stop herself from taking the sentence back, trying to write it off as a bad joke.

"Your father? You—you must be mistaken. There must be some kind of mistake."

"No, Mom, no mistake." She related the facts, explained the strength of the State's case.

"Mackenzie, you don't honestly believe your father killed some girl. I know you have your issues with him, but you know him better than that."

"Honestly, Mom, I'm not sure what I believe. It's…it's pretty bad. I got called to the scene the night she was killed and, well, I think they're doing the right thing. Going for death, I mean. She suffered pretty terribly."

"That doesn't mean your father did it."

"No, no, of course it doesn't. But, well, if I had that much evidence against anyone else, you wouldn't even question it. You know?"

Her mother's breathing was ragged. Mack wondered if she should call her aunt, get someone to go sit with her.

"Anyway," Mack said, itching to get off the phone. "I know you have a news alert set up for Petrou and I didn't want you to hear about this on a podcast. I know Dad hasn't called you, and I—well, he asked me not to tell you, but…" She let the sentence trail away.

She waited for her mother's reaction, but the silence stretched out interminably.

"Mom?"

"I'm here."

"Are you—are you okay?"

"I'm fine, dear. Please ask your father to call me, if you can. I have to go now."

The call ended before Mack had time to say goodbye. She set her phone on her desk and rubbed her eyes, trying to stave off the headache she could feel brewing.

"Is this a bad time?" Sheila asked from the doorway.

Mack looked up. "Come on in. I just…well, just got off the phone with my mom."

"I assume you heard about Petrou's podcast on the Wagner case?"

Mack admired the way Sheila leaned so perfectly against the doorframe. She looked breezy and natural, but Mack got the feeling the pose was practiced. Studied. She wished she was anywhere other than pinned by Sheila's stare.

"I did."

"Mr. Brown asked me to chat with you about it, make sure you weren't planning any kind of unsanctioned public response. I told him none of my employees would ever do such a thing, but he insisted."

Mack sat up straight in her chair, winced at the cracking of her vertebrae. "Wouldn't that be an unconstitutional content-based prior restraint on my speech?"

Sheila smiled. "I have no idea. Con Law was never my thing. Can I reassure the folks upstairs that you have no plans to make an ill-advised statement, regardless of the constitutionality of their request?"

Mack glanced at her watch. She was late for the motions hearing in front of Judge McPhee. "Yeah, that's fine. I wasn't planning on saying anything, anyway. Petrou would just find some way to use it against me."

By the time Mack made it through court security and slid into her seat at the prosecution table, Ferguson and Colbey were both staring at her and Judge McPhee was already on the bench.

"Sorry, Judge," Mack said.

"Let's jump into it, folks. I've got Judge Leyva's ruling on the habeas motion, which I'm not going to revisit. I've got the motion to dismiss and the…well, I'll call it the competency motion, for lack of a better name. Mr. Ferguson, they're your motions, so you get first and last word."

Clearly, Colbey hadn't prepared him for oral argument. Mack tried to take notes while unpacking her tote bag. She wanted the paper copies of the motions and her responses in front of her when she addressed the judge.

"...and so that's why this case should be dismissed, because that girl shouldn't be allowed to testify, and without her testimony they don't have a case against me."

"Ms. Wilson?" Judge McPhee asked.

Mack stood and buttoned her jacket. She took a sip from her water bottle to give herself one last moment to prepare. She was still rattled by her encounter with Sheila and found herself struggling to stay present.

"Judge, the defendant is desperate for this case to go away, and he's bringing up whatever he hopes will make it go away. Unfortunately for him, as I address in detail in my written responses, there is no legal basis for his requests. The simple fact is that Daisy is competent as a witness. He's arguing about her credibility, which is a matter for the jury's consideration, not Your Honor's. There is sufficient evidence for this to be resolved with a jury trial. Again, his quarrel is really with the weight of the evidence, not its admissibility. So unless you have any questions, Judge, I'll rest on the pleadings."

"I do have a question, Counsel." Judge McPhee took off her glasses and put one earpiece to her mouth. Mack had never seen anyone do that in real life before. "Let's imagine a world in which you receive an investigation that involves an alleged victim who you believe is not competent to testify. What would that victim look like?"

Mack considered it. "A child who was preverbal but had penetrative sexual trauma, maybe? Or an adult, for that matter, who was nonverbal and didn't have an alternate means of communication? But, Judge, I've had victims *draw* their abuse on the stand if they can't say the words out loud. In our state law, the bar for who can testify is truly on the floor. Anyone who can speak can testify. The rest, even when it comes to mental-health conditions resulting in delusions, all goes to credibility."

"Surely, Ms. Wilson, you must have had investigations where you didn't believe the alleged victim. Are you telling me that an unbelievable victim, whether because they're subject to delusional beliefs or because the investigation has proven them to be a liar, is still capable of testifying?"

"Judge, respectfully, you've changed the question. Prosecutors have discretion in charging. Have I declined to charge cases where the charging standard was not met, where I didn't think I had a reasonable likelihood of conviction? Sure. And often that's because there are issues with the victim's statements. But that's different from capacity to testify. Once a case is charged, we've got a presumption of capacity. And then—one more point on that, Judge—the defendant in this case maintains that his daughter should be found incapable of testifying based on his assertion that she's a liar, but he has presented no proof to support that claim. It is his burden to overcome the presumption of capacity, and he has failed to meet that burden. Thank you."

Judge McPhee looked like she had another question, and Mack waited tensely. She'd given the best arguments she had in her written responses and hadn't expected questions during oral argument. Now her charging discretion was at issue, on top of everything else, and she was the one who'd put it there. As Mack's panic increased, Judge McPhee shook her head.

"Okay," she said. "Mr. Ferguson, you get the last word."

"Ma'am, I didn't have the opportunity to go to law school, so I'm not sure I followed everything the government's lawyer just said. But I do know that Daisy is a liar, and I will prove it during trial, if you don't grant my motion to dismiss. Once you review everything, I think you'll see that there's nothing to the government's case other than my daughter's testimony. That's not justice. That's not how the American legal system is supposed to work. So I'm sure you'll agree with me that dismissing the charges is the only appropriate solution."

"Thank you both for providing me with these thoughtful pleadings and arguments this morning. I'm going to go into chambers briefly and then will come back and rule. A written ruling will follow later today. Please stick around."

Mack smiled at that. She could leave, sure, but Ferguson was in custody. Even now, a deputy was taking him back to the holding tank to wait for the judge's return. When he was gone, Colbey stood, stretched, and walked to the prosecution table, sitting on the edge. He offered Mack a cookie from a plastic bakery clamshell. She accepted it with a nod of thanks.

"I hate pro pers," Colbey said. "They take so much of my time, and I don't even get to do the fun part. Plus, their arguments are exhausting. I always feel like the State and I are in the same boat on these."

He hated pro pers? All he had to do was sit there! Mack, on the other hand, had to treat them like lawyers while dealing with their thoroughly unlawyerlike demeanors, pleadings, and arguments. Her victims had to tolerate cross-examination by their own abusers. Mack had never yet seen a pro per acquitted, and their juries not only had to tell them that they were guilty, but also that their lawyering was unbelievable. Everyone in the courtroom was victimized by pro pers *except* for advisory counsel, and Colbey and Mack certainly weren't in the same boat.

She stood, brushing cookie crumbs from her fingers. "I'll be in the hall, okay? Just come grab me when McPhee gets back on the bench."

She didn't have to wait long. Less than five minutes later, Colbey found her pacing outside the courtroom and gestured her back in. "I didn't mean anything," he said. "Earlier, that is. I hope you weren't offended."

"Of course not. I'm just anxious for these rulings, you know?"

Judge McPhee gestured for them to sit. "The short version is that I'm denying both motions. I don't agree with the defendant that he's proven the victim should not be permitted to testify. I don't agree that the State's case rests entirely on her statements. There's DNA evidence, there's the body of a small child, there are secondary sources—including documentation—that support the State's case. What weight the jury will give to any of that evidence is, as the State says, up to them. Questions?"

Ferguson leaned close to Colbey and whispered furiously. Mack could only make out the occasional word, but she got the gist of it. He'd been counting on winning both motions and was in a tailspin. Good.

"Judge," Mack said, standing. "I wonder if it might be fruitful to discuss settlement at this point."

Judge McPhee waited for Ferguson to respond, but the man apparently hadn't heard Mack. She tried again, but still there was no response. Finally, the judge cleared her throat.

"Sir," she said, when Ferguson looked up, red-faced and out of breath. "The State has suggested that there might be a possibility of resolving this case without going to trial."

"What does that mean?"

"Are you interested in a plea agreement? I don't know if one was ever on the table. Ms. Wilson?"

Mack started to respond, but Ferguson was already talking, his voice more strident than ever. "I will never be interested in a plea agreement. I have done nothing but deny these spurious charges since their inception, and the only way this case will end, based on your unjust ruling, is in a trial."

Judge McPhee looked unhappy. "Okay, then. We will pick a jury tomorrow. Any last issues anyone needs to bring up?"

CHAPTER THIRTY-TWO

Jury selection was, as usual, largely uneventful. Mack and case agent Debbie Wood watched the parade of bored faces as a hundred members of the community filed into the courtroom and took their seats. No one they recognized, which was good, and no one who immediately stood out as an undesirable juror—no unnatural hair colors or facial tattoos.

It was difficult to pick a jury with a pro per defendant, because Mack had to balance her subjective desire to make a good first impression with her objective need to control the courtroom. Judge McPhee's first responsibility was to protect the defendant's constitutional rights, so Mack couldn't rely on her to keep Ferguson under wraps. She would have to do that work herself.

By the afternoon break, they'd whittled the group down to forty, and Judge McPhee started the final round of questions when they were again settled in the gallery.

"This is your last opportunity, ladies and gentlemen. Is there anything anyone wants to tell us but hasn't had the chance to say? Either we didn't ask the right question, or you just remembered, or you weren't sure it was important—whatever the case, now is your time."

A petite, elderly juror in the front row raised her hand and waited for the judicial assistant to bring her a microphone. Mack had nicknamed this woman "Gramma Lela" in her notes, and she hadn't yet said anything to distinguish herself either way. She was seventy-four, a retired administrative assistant, never married, no kids, no history of jury service.

"Yes, thank you. I want to say that I—well, I wouldn't call myself a psychic, necessarily—but I am a person who is in touch with the spiritual realm, and I could tell as soon as I walked in here that this man is—"

Judge McPhee cut her off before she could poison the pool. "Thank you, ma'am. We'll come back to you later."

After a few other comments—a juror with a vacation he'd forgotten, one whose boss said she couldn't be spared for a month—Judge McPhee dismissed the panel into the hallway so that Mack and Ferguson could each make their final strikes.

"Can we address the psychic, Judge?" Mack asked before the judge could leave the bench. "The State moves to strike for cause."

"Oh, right. I should have let her finish, and then as long as you two agreed to abide by her ruling, we could dispense with the need for a trial."

Mack laughed, thankful for a bit of levity. Ferguson remained stone-faced. Colbey whispered in his ear.

"I'd like to scratch the panel," Ferguson said. "They were tainted by her comment, and there's no way they'll be fair now."

Judge McPhee looked to see if Mack had a response, but she shrugged. If the panel was all stricken, they'd just start fresh the next day. Mack had no place else to be.

"I disagree," the judge said. "Since I didn't let her finish, there's nothing to taint them. She is stricken for cause, and the parties will make their peremptories at this time."

Mack and Detective Wood went into the jury room with the list.

"You get any bad vibes off any of these mutants?" Mack asked.

"Nothing in particular. These are the ones who weren't smart enough to find a way to get kicked off, right? Isn't that what you guys say?"

It was exactly what Mack and countless prosecutors across the years said. She flipped through her notes, making three quick lists: people she wanted to strike, people she expected Ferguson to strike, and a second tier in case there were strikes left over.

Colbey leaned into the jury room doorway. "Lord help us, everyone. I wonder what Miss Cleo was going to say."

Mack handed him the list and smiled dryly. "I guess we'll never know, Tom."

When Judge McPhee finished reading the jury instructions, she gestured for Mack's opening statement. Mack looked at the Shinola watch she always wore for jury selection and openings—a bit too expensive, but not ostentatious. She wanted jurors who knew about watches to approve of her choice to buy American but not focus on it. She took a deep breath and gripped the podium for a moment. No matter how many times she stood in front of a jury, the first thirty seconds filled her with anxiety.

"Ladies and gentlemen," she said, making eye contact with each juror in turn. "This is a case about power and control."

And just like that, she breathed more easily. This might even be fun.

"So when you've heard all the evidence, after Daisy has testified and you've heard from the doctors and police and scientists, I'll come back up here, and at that time I will ask you to find the defendant guilty on all counts. Thank you."

"Thank you, Ms. Wilson," Judge McPhee said. "Mr. Ferguson, you can stand and give your opening statement from your table."

Ferguson stood clumsily, his balance impacted by the locking leg brace he wore under his pants, and Mack saw that his suit was too tight on his bulky frame. Colbey had brought it to him—that was one of his few duties as advisory counsel—but Ferguson had gained weight on the jail's processed food and he was surely wearing a shock belt, and the jacket constricted his waist, chest, and shoulders. It reminded her of an old Chris Farley bit, and she had to force herself to focus on his words.

"The government wants you to believe that I committed the worst crime anyone could ever commit."

Mack thought about objecting but decided it wasn't worth it. She would let him dig the hole she'd bury him in.

"But the only proof they'll give you is no proof at all. The government scientist will testify that it's ninety-nine percent likely that I am the father of the alleged baby. I tell you, folks, that my innocence can be found in that one percent."

Mack didn't even know what he was talking about.

"The girl that they're going to parade in front of you is a liar—"

"Objection, Judge," Mack said. That was a bridge too far, even with the wide latitude she was giving him.

"Sustained. Sir, please refrain from giving your own judgment on the State's witnesses."

Ferguson glared in Mack's direction before continuing, "The girl you're going to hear from, well, let's just say you can draw your own conclusions once you hear her story, which won't make any sense. Instead, you'll find that the police and the government have worked together to frame me, based solely on the allegations made by a girl I raised from birth and did nothing but love and take care of."

Mack stopped listening. There was only so much word salad she could tolerate. Instead, she pulled her notes for her direct examination of Daisy closer and reviewed them. Daisy would be her first witness the next morning, and Mack wanted to be sure she presented the strongest picture possible.

A nudge from Wood brought Mack back to the present.

"So that's why, folks, at the end of this trial, you'll find me innocent."

They were off to the races.

CHAPTER THIRTY-THREE

"One moment, Your Honor," Mack said. She looked at Debbie Wood and asked, "Anything I missed?"

The detective shook her head. Daisy had hit on each of the charged sex offenses, as well as the murder of her baby. There were no major points on the checklist Mack had given Debbie that hadn't been discussed. Mack was still riding high on the relief she'd felt that morning when Daisy had walked into the courtroom ten minutes early, nervous but ready to go.

"No further questions for this witness at this time."

Judge McPhee nodded. "Thank you, Counselor. Okay, Mr. Ferguson, cross-examination?"

Mack tightened her fingers on the arms of her chair. She had been dreading this moment since Judge Leyva gave Ferguson the okay to represent himself.

Direct examination had gone smoothly enough. Daisy wasn't a rocket scientist, but she had told her story in a clear and credible way. She knew dates, and she could explain her inability to disclose for so long. Mack believed her and got the sense that the jury did, too.

Ferguson pulled a thick pile of papers toward him and began reading with his head down, still seated. "Daisy, where did we live when you were five years old?"

"Objection," Mack said, standing. "Relevance, Judge."

Judge McPhee's neutral expression didn't change. "That seems premature, Ms. Wilson. Overruled."

Daisy didn't speak. She had glanced at her father once, when Mack asked her to identify him for the record, but since then her eyes had been locked on the desk in front of her.

"That means you can answer," Judge McPhee clarified.

"What was the question?" Daisy asked.

"Where did we live when you were five years old?" Ferguson repeated. Mack hated the sound of his voice. It was nasal and too high for his stocky build.

"Aunt Nancy's house."

"Right. And what happened at Aunt Nancy's house?"

"What do you mean?"

"When we moved to Aunt Nancy's, who slept where?"

Mack nudged Wood with her elbow. "How could she possibly know that's what he meant?" she whispered. "Do you know anything about Aunt Nancy? Do we know where this is going?"

The detective shook her head. "No idea. Never came up in the forensic."

"You slept upstairs," Daisy said. "I think in your own room, and I slept on the couch, because there wasn't a bed for me."

Mack wondered how far she should let this go. She couldn't begin to imagine what the relevance of the sleeping arrangements at Aunt Nancy's house was, but she needed to give Ferguson as much leeway as she could. Save the fighting for when it counted.

"Did you like sleeping on the couch?"

"You know I didn't. Cousin Trevor—"

Mack sprang to her feet. "Objection, Judge." She couldn't think of the grounds for the objection, but she needed something other than *"I'm not sure what she's about to say, but it sure sounds like someone else abused her, too."* She tried to convey that to the judge without speaking.

Judge McPhee nodded. "Sustained. Move along, Mr. Ferguson."

"Can we talk about this, Judge?" Ferguson said. "Because this is crucial in order to—"

The judge raised her hand, and Ferguson stopped talking.

"I'm going to excuse the jury for a bit," Judge McPhee said. "Let's take a five-minute break. Nothing to worry about, just a thing that happens sometimes to give us a chance to work things out so that you are not unduly inconvenienced."

Mack motioned to Daisy to stand, along with everyone else in the courtroom, as the jury filed out.

"Okay," Judge McPhee said. "Let's back up. Since we can't do sidebars in the traditional way, what with Mr. Ferguson being in custody, this is how we'll need to deal with any issues that come up. I appreciate you refraining from a speaking objection, Ms. Wilson, but now's your chance. What's the objection?"

"This is a tricky situation, Judge," Mack said. "Because clearly the defendant and the witness have a whole lifetime of shared knowledge that no one else in the courtroom is privy to. So I'm at a disadvantage. I don't know what Daisy was about to say about Cousin Trevor, but it sounded like maybe there's going to be a rape-shield issue. And based on the way we got to Trevor's name, it seems like that's where the defendant is going. So I would like to—or you can, Judge, if you want—voir dire the witness on what's coming, and then we can go from there."

"I'm inclined to agree with you, Ms. Wilson. Mr. Ferguson?"

"What?" Tom nudged him with an elbow. "What, Judge?"

"What is it that you think this witness will say?"

"Well, I expect her to say that Trevor touched her. That's what she told me when she was young, to try to get a bedroom. She was really angry that no one believed her, and that's when all of this started."

Judge McPhee turned to Daisy. "Is that what you would say if you were asked?"

Daisy looked at Mack, who nodded and smiled encouragingly.

"I'm lost," Daisy said. "What question am I answering?"

"You heard what your fath—what the defendant said just now, right? How he expected you would answer a question about your cousin Trevor?"

Daisy nodded.

"Was he right? If you were asked that question, is that how you would answer?"

"I don't really see what Trevor has to do with this. He touched me *years* before the defendant did. I told him when it happened, but he didn't do anything. Neither did Aunt Nancy."

Judge McPhee nodded decisively. "Thank you, Daisy. Why don't you go ahead and step out of the courtroom, so I can talk to Ms. Wilson and the defendant."

Once Daisy was in the hallway with Jason, Judge McPhee dropped her pleasant attitude and glared at Ferguson.

"Sir," she said, clearly weighing her words. "You are not a lawyer, and so you don't know how things work in court, let alone in my division. So I'm going to take a moment to educate you and then ask you to make a decision, and then we'll figure out how to proceed. Information about a victim's sex life is generally not admissible in a trial, unless the information meets one of a few exceptions. When defense attorneys want to admit that kind of information, they have to file motions in advance. That's called a rape-shield motion. Now, if you were represented by Mr. Colbey and told him about Trevor, he could have filed a motion saying that that information met one of the exceptions to the rape-shield protections, and Ms. Wilson could have responded to the motion, and the lawyers would have duked it out before trial started. But you've made the choice to represent yourself. You probably remember that you had to complete some paperwork when you made that choice. A big part of what that paperwork said is that you would be treated the same as a lawyer—held to the same rules, in other words, even though you haven't had the benefits of going to law school or practicing law. Do you remember that?"

"Yes, Judge."

"Good. Now. I am a firm believer in the idea that victims have a right to privacy. In fact, that right is enshrined in our Arizona Constitution. So I don't respond well when someone tries to circumvent the procedure for legally violating that privacy. I have granted defense rape-shield motions before, and I am certain that I will again—probably much to the chagrin of Ms. Wilson and her colleagues. But I will *only* do so if the defense attorney or defendant has followed the correct procedure. Which you have failed to do. So, you will not be asking Daisy any more about Trevor or any other sexual activity she may or may not have engaged in with anyone other than yourself. The choice for you, sir, is whether you want to have Mr. Colbey take over and represent you. He cannot get you out of this particular hole. It's too late for him to file that motion, and I would deny it if he tried. But he could, perhaps, keep you from stumbling into any further mare's nests."

Ferguson shook his head. "I don't want him to represent me."

"That's fine. Ms. Wilson, do you have any motions for me at this time?"

Mack stood and buttoned her jacket. "Well, Judge, I'm not sure exactly what motion the Court is anticipating," she said, stalling for time. "As you know, the State can't request a mistrial."

Judge McPhee leveled a glare at Mack, and she blinked under the scrutiny and scrambled to think what the judge was driving at.

"Perhaps, Judge, the State could move to strike any mention of Cousin Trevor? And move to preclude any further mention thereof?"

Judge McPhee gave a minuscule nod. "Granted. I will read a curative instruction to the jury. Any other issues before we resume?"

Ferguson stood. "Now I would like to request a mistrial, because I'm being hamstrung from presenting my defense."

"Denied. Ms. Wilson?"

Mack shook her head and remained standing until the jury and Daisy, fetched by Wood, were all back in their seats.

"Ladies and gentlemen," Judge McPhee said. "Thank you for your patience. Before our break, you heard mention of someone referred to as Cousin Trevor. That reference has been stricken. That means that, legally, it never happened, and you are not to consider it for any reason. You are not to question or wonder why the reference was stricken or what the results might have been from that line of questioning. Any questions?"

No hands went up.

"Good, then. Mr. Ferguson, this is still your witness."

His failure to stand annoyed Mack each time, but she resisted the urge to object. She didn't want the jurors to see her as a bitchy woman trying to destroy a man representing himself. Young female prosecutors couldn't be too careful.

"Your mom died when you were seven, right?"

"She did." Daisy was slouched in the witness chair, staring at her joined hands on the desktop.

"And after she died, you started having some behavioral issues, right?"

Mack stood. "Objection, Judge."

"What is the basis for your objection?"

"Relevance."

"Overruled. The witness can answer."

"What was the question?" Daisy asked. Mack wondered if she wasn't really listening, or if she somehow couldn't hold on to a question when there was any discussion before she was permitted to answer.

"You started acting out after your mom died, right?"

"You started abusing me after my mom died. I don't know if that's what you mean by acting out."

Mack hid a smile behind her hand.

The second day of Daisy's cross-examination continued in much the same vein. Mack objected to over half of Ferguson's questions, and they kept having to take breaks to address the issues.

That evening, Mack and Jess sat on Mack's couch, a six-pack of Angry Orchard between them and *The Bachelor* on the television. "So the problem is that they have this whole universe of backstory between them that I can't know. So I couldn't file anything in advance, and Judge McPhee and I are feeling our way through the dark as they have a conversation in a language we don't speak."

"Sounds infuriating."

"Oh, it is. And the real sticking point is that I keep objecting, but I have no idea what the actual objection should be. Is it relevance? Maybe, but I have no way of knowing, because I don't know what the answer is going to be."

"Meanwhile, you look like a bitch, and so does your victim."

"That's correct."

"I watched a little bit today, though. She seems good. Firm."

"Yeah," Mack said, thinking about Daisy's demeanor on the stand. "I think this is the only time she's had any control in that relationship. She's so used to him being the one in charge, and I think in a weird way she's taking her power back on the stand. I just hope her power doesn't come at the expense of my conviction."

Jess shook her head and took a long pull of her cider. "Rock and a hard place. You just have to wait it out. How long could Ferguson possibly keep her on the stand?"

When Mack walked into court on the morning of the third day of Daisy's cross-examination, Judge McPhee was still on the bench dealing with her morning calendar.

"Good morning, Ms. Wilson."

Mack didn't look up from the bag she was unpacking. "Good morning, Your Honor."

"Can you approach? And Mr. Flagler, too, please."

Mack whipped her head around. She hadn't even noticed Eric when she entered the courtroom.

"Do we have any cases together?" she whispered, as they walked to the bench.

Eric shook his head. "I only have the one case right now. I'm just here covering for someone."

"So why does it feel like we're being called to the principal's office?"

"Mr. Flagler," Judge McPhee said, once the white-noise machine was on and they were huddled around her desk. "Let me alleviate your concern. You're here so that what I have to say to Ms. Wilson won't be an *ex parte* communication."

"Phew, Judge."

"Now." Judge McPhee turned to Mack. "Without getting into the specifics of the case you're trying, I wanted to advise you to look carefully at the rules of evidence. Specifically, I want to make sure you're familiar with six-eleven. Are you?"

"I will be by the time we get started this morning, Judge."

Judge McPhee waved them away.

"What was that about?" Eric asked when they returned to the prosecution table.

"Not sure yet," Mack said, pulling her statute book toward her. "But I'll know soon." She flipped through the book until she got to the rules of evidence. "'The Court should exercise reasonable control over the mode and order of examining witnesses and presenting evidence.' What does that mean?"

Eric leaned in closer to see for himself. "'To avoid wasting time and protect the witness.' You got a witness who needs protecting?"

"I sure do. She wants this to be my objection?"

"Looks like it. Must be nice to be the State."

Mack nudged him with her shoulder. "You'd be objecting, too. Pro per defendant has had his daughter on the stand for days, literally. This is day three. It's been torture."

"Okay, fine. Maybe it wasn't bias, this time. She just wants out of here."

They walked into the hall together.

"Actually, I'm glad to run into you," Mack said. "I had a question I wanted to ask you."

"Of course you do."

Mack paused, taken aback. "I'm sorry, have I been overstepping? Just tell me to back off."

Eric sighed and rubbed the back of his neck. "No, you're fine. I'm just stressed. This trial is coming up way too fast."

"Have you filed a motion for change of venue? Because I know Amanda's murder got a ton of press here in town, and with Petrou's new podcast coming out, it's hard to imagine the jury pool won't be tainted."

"Thought about it but decided not to. The only other place we could realistically do it would be Phoenix—nobody else has the resources to try a death case. Problem with Phoenix, though, is that their prosecutors love the death penalty. If we were trying to change counties, one of the big arguments would be that your office shouldn't be prosecuting him at all."

"Because of me?"

"Well, yeah, frankly. I mean, I get that there's no factual conflict, and I know he doesn't want to drag you into this, but that would be my strongest argument."

Mack nodded. "Maybe it's worth it, just to get death off the table?"

"That's not what will happen. If it goes to Phoenix, they'll work extra hard to kill him, just to prove they're not giving preferential treatment to someone from out of town. My goal, at this point, is to keep him alive. Keeping it here is the best way to do that."

"Thanks," Mack said. "It's nice that we all have the same goal." Her stomach churned. She had never expected to have a serious conversation about keeping her father off of death row.

Eric waved as he loped off down the hallway, and Mack slumped onto the bench outside Judge McPhee's courtroom.

The last thing she needed was to be focused on her dad's situation during Daisy's testimony, but she couldn't help it. If Eric was making strategic decisions based on her father's desire to keep her out of the spotlight, that made her responsible for the outcome whatever it might be. She was still unsure if he had murdered Amanda, but she was sure of one thing.

She didn't want to be the cause of him getting the death penalty.

"Everything okay?" Wood asked, her shadow falling over Mack's face.

Mack stood and shook the tension out of her arms and shoulders. "No, but nothing to be done about it right now. Let's get to it."

Even with the new objection in Mack's arsenal, it was day four of cross-examination before Ferguson got to the meat of the charged crimes.

"You didn't see me shake the baby to death, right, because it never actually happened?"

"Right. I mean, that *is* what happened, and I *did* see it." Daisy had been almost totally shut down all morning, and nothing Ferguson said seemed to faze her—until this question.

"You told the jury it happened after lunch. What did you have for lunch that day?"

"Objection, Judge, six-eleven," Mack said in a single breath. She had said the same thing one hundred times or more since her conversation with Judge McPhee the previous day, and the judge granted approximately seventy percent of them.

"I'll allow this one," Judge McPhee said.

Mack understood why. If the judge let Daisy answer the questions that were harmless, that would give Ferguson less ammunition for an appeal. McPhee must be convinced that the jury was going to convict. Mack hoped that was it, at least.

"I don't remember," Daisy said.

"What time did you have lunch?" Ferguson asked.

"I don't remember."

"Did we eat lunch together?"

"I don't remember."

Mack wondered how much of Daisy's memory loss was legitimate, and how much was frustration with her father and the trial. On the one hand, the trauma of seeing your baby murdered could wipe mundane details out of the mind of a person with an otherwise accurate memory. On the other hand, Daisy's memory seemed hazy at best. She was missing details Mack would expect her to know.

"Did you feed the baby?"

Daisy paused, and Mack wondered if she should object. This, though, seemed relevant.

"You fed it," Daisy said. "I never fed it."

"You never fed your baby?"

"Objection," Mack said. "Asked and answered."

"Sustained. She answered, sir. Next question."

"What did I feed Baby Henry that afternoon?"

Daisy shrugged and looked at Mack. "I don't know. I wasn't watching. Whatever you normally fed it, I guess. Formula?"

Ferguson made a big show of writing something down. "So you had some lunch—you don't know what—and I fed Henry—you don't know what—and then you went to take a nap, right?"

"No. Then I was trying to do my homework."

"I thought you said I didn't let you go to school?"

"You didn't always, but I was in school then. After—after it was born, because they asked at the hospital. You let me go the next year."

"They asked who the father was at the hospital, right? And you told them it was a boy from school?"

"You told them. You didn't let me answer."

Ferguson hit the desk with his hand, and Mack jumped out of her seat. "Objection, Judge. Six-eleven. The defendant is clearly badgering this witness, and I—"

"Sit down, Ms. Wilson," Judge McPhee interrupted. "And kindly remember that I do not allow speaking objections in my court."

Mack sat, chastised.

"Now. Your objection was to the defendant's gesture?"

"Yes," Mack said.

"Sustained. Sir, I will remind you that grandstanding is not allowed in my court, either. You will comport yourself calmly and respectfully."

"Judge, I really think this is unfair, because—"

Judge McPhee banged her gavel. Mack had never heard a judge actually use the ceremonial object before. "The jury will excuse us while we address a procedural matter. All rise."

"What procedural matter?" Wood whispered.

Mack shrugged. She was in the dark again.

When the door clicked shut behind the last juror, Judge McPhee exploded. "Mr. Ferguson, I have given you *wide* latitude in your examination of the victim in this case, but I will not tolerate you poisoning the jury with your expostulations."

That was as close to yelling as Mack had ever heard her. Judges often yelled at prosecutors soon after yelling at defense attorneys, just to avoid any perception of bias, and Mack shrank in her seat. She didn't want to be the next target.

"So Daisy gets to sit up there and lie and refuse to answer questions and I just have to take it? Is that what you're telling me?"

Judge McPhee took a deep breath and held it for a five count before releasing. Mack watched her settle back into her typical judicial temperament.

"The victim is not refusing to answer questions, and you will not accuse her of lying unless you can back it up with something more than your word. I am not going to argue with you, sir, and I'm certainly not going to let you argue with me. I will again remind you that your right to represent yourself is not without limitations. If you cause another uproar, you will be removed from this courtroom and Mr. Colbey will take over in your absence. Do I make myself clear?"

Ferguson opened his mouth to respond, but Colbey placed a restraining hand on his forearm.

"Yes, Judge," Ferguson said.

"Good. Bring the jury back in. Ms. Ferguson, do you need a break? Some water? Nothing? Okay."

Mack watched the jury file back in and take their seats. They looked annoyed, and she couldn't blame them. They kept getting kicked out right when things were getting interesting.

"Let's go back to what happened with Henry," Ferguson said. "You said I shook him. Why did I do that?"

"I don't know," Daisy said. She seemed tired, her head hanging low. "I think it was crying."

"I had raised another child, right?"

"You mean me?"

"Objection, Judge," Ferguson said. "I'm the one asking questions, so please direct the witness to answer them."

Mack bit her tongue. Colbey must have given him that idea. That meant he was going above and beyond what was required of advisory counsel.

"She's just looking for clarification," Judge McPhee said. "Is she the child you meant?"

"Yes, Judge. I raised you, right?"

"I guess."

"Never shook you?"

"Not that I remember."

"You remember crying a lot as a little kid?"

"I remember crying a lot when you abused me."

Mack covered her laughter with a cough and took the water Wood offered her.

"So despite me having raised you without shaking you, you want the jury to believe that I'm the one who shook Henry?"

"You are the one who shook it."

"Weren't you the one who shook him?"

Daisy sat up straight. "What? Me? I would never."

"Are you sure? Haven't you been talking for days now about how much you don't remember, but this you remember crystal clear?"

"I'd remember killing a baby."

"One would hope. How long did it take Henry to die?"

"I don't know."

"Where in the house were we?"

"In the kitchen—no, in the living room."

Mack wondered if she should object, just to disrupt his flow, but this was the first long stretch of questions he'd asked that weren't obviously problematic. Daisy would have to keep up.

"Didn't you say on direct that you were in my bedroom?"

"I don't think I did. If I did, I was confused. We were in the kitchen."

"And this happened before lunch?"

"Yes."

Mack looked up. Daisy had consistently said it happened after lunch. "Judge," she said, looking at the clock. "Perhaps this would be a good time for a break."

Judge McPhee frowned. "No, we have time. Keep going, Mr. Ferguson."

"Didn't you take naps before lunch?"

"Yes."

"So you wouldn't have been awake at the time you say you saw this terrible thing happen?"

"I guess not."

"Isn't it true that when you came to find me at lunchtime, Henry was already dead?"

"No, it's not."

"It's not?"

"I—I don't think it is. I don't remember."

"No further questions, Judge."

Mack did what she could to fix things on redirect, but the damage was done. Over four days, Ferguson had worn her down to the breaking point. It was easy for Mack to understand why Daisy had put up with her father's abuse for as long as she had. Now, after four days of aggressive questioning, she was fried beyond comprehension.

"Any questions from the jury?" Judge McPhee asked when Mack was finished.

Several hands went up. When the jurors had given their sheets of paper to the bailiff, they were dismissed to the jury room so that Mack and Ferguson could discuss their questions.

Mack flipped through the twenty or so pages and sighed.

Why can't you remember something so traumatic?

First you said it was after lunch and then before. Which was it?

Why could you remember things when the State asked them but not your father?

It was going to be a long afternoon.

CHAPTER THIRTY-FOUR

The next several trial days were filled with police officers and other witnesses who were crucial to proving Mack's case but not fascinating. Dr. Rosie Green, the medical examiner, testified, describing her autopsy of Baby Henry, whose body was located by police right where Daisy said it would be, buried in the backyard of Aunt Nancy's house. Although her findings were made more difficult by the years that had passed between his death and her examination, nothing she said contradicted Daisy's version of events. The questions the jurors were asking showed that—other than Daisy's own testimony—they seemed to be accepting the State's case. Mack was cautiously optimistic about the verdict. Once Daisy was off the stand, Ferguson himself had relaxed a little. He hadn't taken more than a couple of hours with anyone else.

Mack was eager to get her last witness—the DNA analyst who would discuss paternity of the baby—on the stand, and was busily making final notes for his testimony when Jess hurried into her office.

"Podcast dropped early," she said, closing the door behind her and dropping into a chair. "Should I put it on?"

"Okay, but I don't have a ton of time. I need something to eat before heading to court."

Jess fiddled with her phone and set it on Mack's desk. Dan Petrou's voice filled the office.

"The neighbors heard screaming—that's what started it all. When police arrived on scene—accompanied by Mackenzie Wilson, the assistant district attorney who has been the subject of much media scrutiny in recent years—they found the body of thirty-two-year-old Amanda Wagner. Amanda had been brutally murdered, and her body carried a secret. A pregnancy that she had not yet revealed, not even to her own mother."

"Pause," Mack said.

Jess tapped her screen.

"You know this is garbage, right?" Mack asked. "They knew she was pregnant that night. It wasn't a secret in the context of the investigation."

"Well, sure. But also, he describes you as the subject of media scrutiny, conveniently leaving out that the only media scrutinizing you is him."

"Like I said, garbage. Go on."

"Police quickly discovered that Amanda's cause of death wasn't gunshot wounds, as they had originally thought. Instead, she had been stabbed to death with a broken bottle—a bottle taken from her own fridge."

"More trash," Mack said. "They didn't think she was shot at the scene. There was no cordite smell, no bullets were recovered. This is dumb."

"Shh," Jess said. "I don't want to miss anything."

Mack went back to her questions for the DNA analyst while Jess continued listening to the podcast.

"So this is really just a *Dateline* rip-off?" Jess asked when the episode finally ended.

"Sounds like it," Mack said without looking up. "Which seems right. Petrou seems like the kind of guy who wants to be a national news reporter but doesn't have the chops. This is just sensationalism masked as journalism. The case isn't even that interesting."

"That sounds like sour grapes to me."

"No, really. I mean, from the outside—the only things Petrou sees—it looks airtight. DNA, fingerprints, cell phone evidence. Open and shut, really."

Jess looked at her across the desk. "Open and shut."

Mack nodded, her throat tight. Her fingers flexed repeatedly against the desktop.

"Do you want to go get a sandwich?" Jess asked. "I'll walk with you."

"Never mind. I've lost my appetite."

DNA evidence was tedious at the best of times. Paternity evidence was even worse. Paternity evidence on a product of consanguinity was the worst of all—there was no way for Mack to craft a compelling story. She just had to get the science on the record and lay the basis for the analyst's conclusions.

"So how can you tell that there isn't interference caused by the fact that the father of the baby is also the father of the mother?" Mack grimaced at her own question. It was inartful, and a real defense attorney would surely have objected. Luckily, Ferguson didn't seem to notice the issue.

"Right, that is a good question," Leonard Joost, the DNA analyst, said. Mack had worked with him before, and jurors loved his calm manner and Afrikaans accent. "But unfortunately, there is no easy answer. Basically, we have got the mother's full profile and the putative father's full profile, and we compare those to the baby's full profile, and that is how we can tell whether the putative father is, in fact, the biological father."

"So the fact that the mother's profile and the father's profile are the same at some alleles doesn't matter?"

"Not really. I can look at the data and tell immediately if someone is not the father—if there is one allele where there is a mismatch, that person can be ruled out. In this case, you can see that we have matches at all seventeen alleles. I can say with ninety-nine percent confidence, which is the highest level of confidence in my profession, that the source of Profile B is the father of Baby Boy Ferguson."

"And were you given a name for the source of Profile B?"

Leonard flipped through his report. "Yes. Liam Ferguson."

"No further questions," Mack said, gathering her charts and returning to the prosecution table.

Ferguson stood to begin his cross-examination. Mack was surprised, since he had stayed in his seat while questioning the previous witnesses.

"He must think he has something," she whispered to Wood.

The detective nodded.

"I can't imagine what. The DNA stuff is so impenetrable, he can't possibly understand it well enough to challenge it."

"You don't know what you don't know," Wood said. "Maybe he thinks he's got it locked down."

Ferguson addressed the witness. "You testified that you can say with ninety-nine percent confidence that I am the father, right?"

"I said that I can say with ninety-nine percent confidence that the father was the source of Profile B, who is identified as Liam Ferguson."

"But I'm Liam Ferguson."

"Oh," Leonard said, looking confused. "Then, yes, you are the father."

"Why can't you be one hundred percent confident?"

Leonard took a sip from the cup of water Mack had handed him when he took the stand. "Because that is not how the science works. I do not compare the entire genome. As I described on direct, based on these alleles we can absolutely rule out putative fathers, but we cannot one hundred percent rule them *in*. If, for example, you had an identical twin, well, he could also be the father."

"Do I have an identical twin?"

"I do not know, sir. That is beyond the scope of my analysis."

"So what would you call that one remaining percent?"

"I do not understand your question."

"Well, I'd call it reasonable doubt. What would—"

"Objection, Judge!" Mack said.

Judge McPhee turned away from Joost. "What is the basis for your objection?"

"It calls for the witness to comment on the burden of proof."

Judge McPhee looked at the ceiling for a moment. "Sustained. Move along, Mr. Ferguson."

"Wouldn't you agree that the real father could be in that one percent?"

Leonard frowned. "I do not understand the question. You are the father. There is no other possible real father."

Ferguson kept trying. He rephrased his question several times, but to no avail. Leonard, with his concrete approach to the world—perfect for a DNA scientist, Mack thought—was unshakable.

Ferguson finally gave in, and there wasn't much for Mack to do on redirect. She was not surprised when the jury had no questions. They probably didn't really understand the testimony, and it would be up to Mack to argue it appropriately during closings.

"Ms. Wilson?" Judge McPhee asked.

"Judge, the State rests."

CHAPTER THIRTY-FIVE

The text from Eric came in late that night. *Hearing at 9 tomorrow to affirm trial date. I know he'd like to see you, if you can.*

Mack didn't respond but checked her calendar. Ferguson planned to testify in his own defense, but that wasn't until later in the morning. She probably wouldn't go to her father's hearing, but it was nice of Eric to make the suggestion.

Still, the next morning she found herself walking toward Judge Leyva's division without really thinking about it.

When she entered the courtroom, Eric was already talking to her father. Judge Leyva was not on the bench, and Nathan Moore was nowhere to be seen, so she joined them.

Her dad smiled when he saw her, but she noticed that he'd lost his tan. His skin was sallow against the orange jumpsuit, which was looser than it had been when he'd been taken into custody.

"How are you feeling?" she asked. "You know, about everything?"

"You really want to know?"

Mack crossed her arms over her chest, feeling defensive. "I wouldn't have asked otherwise."

"It's just...you haven't asked me that. In this whole time, you've never...well, you've never really seemed like you cared how I was doing."

Eric turned away, suddenly very absorbed in his file. Mack thought about it. Was it possible that she'd never stopped to consider how he was doing? If he killed Amanda Wagner, he was probably dreading a verdict. If he was innocent, he was probably still dreading a verdict—for different reasons. She cleared her throat. "Well, I haven't wanted to, you know. I haven't wanted to make you focus on it."

Marcus laughed. "I focus on it every waking moment, Mackenzie."

She pulled back as if he'd slapped her face, uncertain how to respond. "You can call me Mack. I mean—if you want to. That's what people call me."

"Mack. I like that. Well, Mack, I'm struggling. It's...I've been in jail before, but never like this. It's hard in there."

"Is there anything—I could send you stuff, I think. Books, or whatever. Is there anything you want?"

Mack flushed under the strange look her father was giving her. Grief and joy and something else she couldn't identify.

"I'd love that," he said. "What's your favorite book? Why don't you send me that?"

Mack nodded and stood. "I'll have to think about it, but I'll talk to Eric and figure out how to get it to you. I'll...if there's anything else you need, just let him know, and I'll make sure you get it."

Eric touched her forearm, and they left the courtroom together. Mack could feel tears gathering in the corners of her eyes, and she rubbed her sternum to stop them from falling.

"That...he really appreciated that."

Mack cleared her throat. "Good. I feel bad for not doing more for him."

"You don't need to feel bad. That's the last thing he wants. It's interesting, I wind up becoming a lot closer to these clients than to the clients I used to have. Attorney, friend, father confessor, I do a little of everything. And, I just...you should know how much he loves you, Mack. He may have been a terrible father, but he loves you."

"It's funny—not, like, funny ha ha—but I feel like we're closer now than we ever have been. I still—well—I'm still not sure how I feel about the whole situation. But it hasn't been the worst thing in the world, getting to know him a little bit at this point in my life."

Eric went back into the courtroom, and Mack sat on the bench in the hallway for several minutes, steeling herself to face another day of Ferguson.

When she walked into Judge McPhee's division, she found Diana Muñoz behind the bailiff's desk.

"What are you doing here?" Mack asked.

Diana pointed to the electronic recording system, indicating that the courtroom was being monitored. Mack leaned in close, so Diana could whisper.

"Judge is in a foul mood today, so be careful. I'm subbing for her normal bailiff. She called out last minute."

"Perfect. Our pro per defendant is testifying, so I can use all the bad mood I can get."

When a defendant was representing himself, there were two ways he could testify. He could get up and just tell a narrative. No questions to answer, just tell the jury what he wanted them to hear. He could also give prepared questions to advisory counsel, who would have to read them exactly as written—even if he knew they were objectionable. Either way, Mack could then cross-examine Ferguson normally, as though he were any other defendant.

Colbey walked in and veered toward Mack and Wood, offering them his half-empty bag of Swedish Fish.

"It's a little early in the day for me," Wood said.

Mack took some candy.

"I can't get enough sugar right now," Colbey said. "Normally, I want salt in trial, but this one is killing me. I can't believe I have to ask his asinine questions today. You might want to be quick with your objections, Ms. Wilson."

Mack chewed and swallowed the gummy in silence. She couldn't trust herself to be polite.

"Mr. Ferguson, please introduce yourself to the jury," Colbey read mechanically from the sheet of legal pad when Ferguson had taken the stand and the jurors were seated.

Ferguson turned toward the jury in an exaggerated manner and smiled broadly. "I'm Liam Ferguson. I'm fifty years old, I'm an Air Force veteran, and I'm a dad."

"Objection, Judge." Mack had been waiting for this, but when he hadn't brought it out through Daisy, she'd thought maybe she was wrong. She'd contacted the Air Force after Ferguson had said the same thing to Wood in his interview. They'd told her that Ferguson never made it through basic training.

"Overruled," Judge McPhee said, without seeming to consider it. "You can deal with whatever the objection is on cross."

"How many children do you have?" Colbey read.

"Just the one daughter, Daisy, who the jury heard from earlier in this trial."

"Mr. Ferguson, did you commit the crimes you're on trial for?"

"I did not."

They continued that way through the morning. Colbey read the questions Ferguson had written, giving Ferguson the opportunity to perform "dutiful father" for the jury. By the lunch break, they still hadn't gotten to the substance of the charged offenses. Instead, they'd covered Ferguson's early childhood, his relationship with Daisy's mother, and his struggles raising a difficult daughter as a single dad. Mack objected periodically, but Judge McPhee had lost interest. Diana hadn't understated her bad mood, and Mack had misunderstood how it was going to impact her case.

"Do you know how Daisy got pregnant?" Colbey asked.

"I think so. I think I've put it together, after the fact. I didn't realize it at the time, but now I'm pretty sure."

"Please explain it to the jury."

"We were still living with my sister Nancy. Daisy slept in the living room, but it was too loud in there for her to do her homework, so she would go up to my room after school so she could have some privacy. Well, one day I was in my room before she got home, and I...well, I was a single man, remember." He smiled bashfully, and Mack's throat burned with bile.

"So that afternoon, I decided to...you know. I had a box of condoms that I'd gotten somewhere along the line, so I...you know, in the condom, so it wouldn't make a mess, and tossed it in a trash bag near my bed."

Wood leaned in close to Mack. "This is so disgusting. I feel sick."

Mack nodded but didn't respond. She didn't want to miss a word of this new defense.

"Later that afternoon, I went into my bedroom while Daisy was supposed to be doing her homework, and I caught her masturbating—which had happened before—but she was using the condom I had put in the trash."

Mack's jaw dropped. "Judge, I'm going to request a bench conference at this point."

Judge McPhee looked up and blinked. "We're almost at the afternoon break, so the jury will excuse us a little early. We will address this and get you back in here after our court reporter has had her requisite fifteen minutes."

Mack collected her thoughts as the jury filed out of the courtroom. Several older male jurors were shaking their heads, presumably, Mack thought, at what they'd just heard.

"Ms. Wilson?"

"Judge, I'm not even sure where to start. First, any allegations about the victim masturbating should have been subject to a rape-shield motion, just like any allegations about Cousin Trevor. That testimony fits squarely within those protective rules, so I'd ask to preclude it, strike it, and I'd ask the Court to give a curative instruction. Second, odd as it feels to say this, it appears that the defendant is attempting to introduce a third-party defense, and—"

"With the condom being the third party?" Judge McPhee asked.

"Yes? Or with Daisy as the third party? I mean, it appears that he's saying he's not the one who got Daisy pregnant, *she* is, using his…masturbatory emissions, which were left in the condom. However, since third-party defenses must be alleged before trial, it's too late in the game for the introduction of this…new…story."

Ferguson started to speak, but the judge stopped him. "Ms. Wilson, I understand your argument and am not insensitive to it. I think that, if I were in your shoes, I'd probably raise the same issues. I'm also not insensitive to the argument that pro per defendants are to be held to the same bar as lawyers. All that being said, however, I'm not going to keep any of this out. This is his defense as to a single count. You will be given the opportunity to thoroughly cross-examine him, and I have no doubt that you'll make your points to the jury. It's up to the jurors what they decide to do with them."

"Okay, Judge," Mack said. She reached for the lukewarm coffee that had been sitting on the prosecution table since she'd set it down midmorning. She needed something to jolt her out of the panic she was beginning to feel.

"We'll bring the jury back in," Judge McPhee said. "And, Ms. Wilson, I'd advise you to school your face before they are seated. I understand that you might not like my ruling, but pulling faces is unprofessional, and I expect better of you."

Mack's face reddened and she could feel herself beginning to sweat. What was going on? She had always respected and even liked Judge McPhee, so why was she being so hard on her?

Mack's phone buzzed with an email from Diana.

Girl, you weren't pulling faces. Get it together and win this thing. Don't let Miss Robe-Thang get you down.

Mack smiled, grateful for the pep talk.

When the jury was seated, Colbey returned to the podium with his handwritten questions. "What did you do when you found Daisy mas—doing what she was doing?"

Ferguson glared at him, and Mack knew he'd made a choice not to read the word aloud.

"I told her that it was natural for her to have those feelings, and even natural for her to act on them, but she needed to make sure she was in private when she did that and she needed to not use my trash for it."

"Why do you think Daisy eventually accused you of abusing her?"

Mack considered objecting but let it go. Judge McPhee obviously wasn't in the mood for it, regardless of whether or not this was an appropriate topic for Ferguson to address.

"She was angry. She was eighteen and thought I should pay for her to go to college and get an apartment. I told her I wished I could do those things for her but I just didn't have the money. She told me she was going to make me pay one way or another, and then she went to the police. So I think it's pretty clear."

"Let's move on to the death of Baby Henry. Please tell the jury what actually happened that day."

"Objection. Advisory counsel is testifying," Mack said. She knew it wouldn't work, but she had to do something to signal to the jury that Ferguson was twisting things. Lying to them.

"Overruled."

Mack kept her face very still. She felt her cheek with her hand. It was still warm.

"What was the question?" Ferguson asked. "Oh, right, what actually happened to the baby. Well, I came home from work that afternoon and Daisy was in bed. She was upset. She was upset a lot back then. In retrospect, it was postpartum depression, but I didn't realize it then. She was in bed, and I couldn't hear Henry, which I thought was odd. It wasn't even seven p.m., so he should have been awake and should have been really hungry. I was the one who fed him dinner. So I asked her where the baby was, and she just kind of shrugged."

"Did you find Henry?"

"I did. I went to his crib, and he was laying there, cold and stiff. I ran back to Daisy and—I admit this—I lost my temper. I started yelling at her to tell me what had happened to her son. My grandson."

"What did she say?"

"Objection, Judge. Calls for hearsay." No one would accuse Mack of going down without a fight.

"Overruled."

"She told me she didn't know what happened. But she seemed—I don't know—out of it, I guess. So I slapped her. One time, the only time I ever raised a hand to her. And she told me that Henry had been crying while she was trying to take a nap. So she shook him, and that just made him cry harder. She shook him and shook him, and finally he stopped crying, so she put him down. But he wasn't breathing. She asked me to take care of it."

"What did you do next?"

"I'm not sure what order things happened in. It was obviously a really stressful time, and all I was focused on was keeping Daisy safe. So I'm not sure what I did next, but I know that later that day I dug a hole in the backyard, and I buried Baby Henry."

Mack rolled her eyes, disgusted. She hoped the jury could see through his story—although making up emotional memory loss was a nice touch.

"Do you love your daughter, Mr. Ferguson?"

"I do. Even with all of this trouble that I'm in now, and all the lies she's told, she's still my little girl. My deeply troubled little girl."

CHAPTER THIRTY-SIX

Mack looked at the piles of paper on her desk. They were organized by topic, with highlighted police reports, notes from Daisy's testimony, and draft cross-examination questions for each major issue she wanted to highlight. She had been at it for hours and had made almost no progress. She hadn't prepared in advance—couldn't do so until she knew what insane story Ferguson would come up with on the stand—and now she was overwhelmed.

She knew what she had to do next, and she did it without letting herself think too much.

"Well, never let it be said that Mack Wilson isn't full of surprises," Anna Lapin said.

"Hi."

"Hi, yourself. Is everything okay?"

Mack hesitated, then took the plunge. "I need your help."

Anna inhaled unsteadily.

"It's a case," Mack said quickly. "It's not, like, a personal thing."

"Of course. How can I help?"

Mack marveled at how smoothly Anna's professional mask slipped into place. "I have a pro per defendant, and he's taking the stand tomorrow. I can't figure out how to cross him."

"Hmm. Tell me about your case."

Mack briefly described the facts.

"What's the goal?"

"Of my cross? I'd love it if he made a full confession. So far, he's denied anything helpful. But I'd settle for the jury seeing that he's a lying psycho."

"You've crossed dozens of defendants without help. Why does this guy have you freaked out?"

"He kept his daughter on the stand for four full days. I've never seen anything like it. He's clearly not stupid. There are brain cells there, even if I don't like what he's doing with them. I'm worried that he's really messed things up in terms of the jury's ability to understand the facts. They haven't seen him as a crazy control freak. They just saw a father and daughter arguing for four days, and most of them have kids. They probably haven't argued with theirs for four and a half hours a day for four days, but they know what it's like to argue with a kid. And then he testified, and it was just so full of lies, but he sounded pretty credible. And I just…I don't want to…it's really important that I get him."

"What makes this case so important?"

If Mack knew Anna, she was crossing her legs and leaning forward, sure she was on the verge of a breakthrough. "They're all important. I've asked you the same question on other defendants."

"Sure. But not for the last eighteen months. Before that, I figured it was just 'cause you liked me."

Mack frowned. "This case is important, because I won't be able to face Daisy if the jury doesn't convict. I'm not sure she'll survive a not guilty, and I don't want to be responsible for that."

"Narcissistic injury."

"Excuse me?"

Anna laughed. "Not you. That's how you cross him. He sounds like a classic narcissist. He made her sit on the stand for so long because it kept her focus, and the jury's, on him. So how do you break him down? You pierce his ego. Wind him up and let him go."

"Should I start with bad cop, or try to play nice?"

"You can go either way, I think. It depends on the specific manifestation of his narcissism. I mean, there are narcissists who work really hard to keep people from realizing that's what they are, because they've found they can be more successful with a different approach. They only turn on the real crazy behavior—the rage, violence, manipulative stuff—if sweetness doesn't work. But there are others who start from that power-and-control place and never bother to mask it. You know he has the capacity for that kind of rage from the daughter's testimony, so, if you can get the right injury, you can make hay with it."

"What's the right injury?"

"Could be anything, and it's hard to say conclusively without knowing him. But I'd start with his ability as a father or his intelligence. It sounds like those are areas where he really focuses on his strengths, has a lot of pride. So that's what you want to cut at."

"So someone crossing me would poke me in the 'trial dog'?"

There was a long pause, and Mack realized that she'd crossed a line from professional to personal. She winced at the misstep.

"Someone crossing you would be well-served to poke at your personal life, rather than your professional life. Your ability to show up as a friend, for example." Anna's tone had turned snippy. "Look, Mack, I was pretty excited when I saw your name on my screen just now. I thought maybe winter was thawing at long last."

Mack bit her cheek to stop from snapping back.

"If you have something like this come up again, I think you need to call another provider. I can give you some phone numbers if you need them, but anyone who's doing risk assessments should be able to weigh in. If you want to work on rebuilding our friendship, I'd be happy to engage in that process and see what comes of it. But this whole—I don't know—this whole 'Let's only engage professionally' thing isn't working for me."

"You're right," Mack said. She stretched her neck, feeling the vertebrae crack. "It wasn't fair of me to call. Not like this. I could have texted you or called someone else. Dr. Flores would have been ecstatic to hear from me."

Anna laughed. "Carlos has never been ecstatic about anything in his life."

"Okay, maybe not ecstatic. But he would have picked up the phone."

"So why call me?"

"I don't know how to answer that question without sounding like either a selfish asshole or a manipulative asshole."

Anna laughed again, and Mack felt her shoulders relax. She wasn't ready to throw herself back into a full-fledged friendship with the psychologist, but she couldn't deny that she missed Anna. Until she'd been so unceremoniously dumped the year before, she'd always felt, whether they were dating or just friends, like Anna understood her better than anyone. Even Jess. She could be vulnerable with Anna in a way that felt hard and raw and worth it. She didn't feel like that kind of vulnerability was possible anymore—not right now, at least—but she knew she owed Anna some measure of the truth.

"I don't want to get into the whole thing, but I'm kind of going through a weird time right now. And this trial on top of that has been…well, difficult. If I can't put our personal relationship aside for five minutes for the greater good, well, what kind of jerk does that make me? That's not the person I want to be. Certainly not the prosecutor I want to be."

"Is this about your dad? I've heard some things through the grapevine."

"Of course you have. God, this town is way too small."

"How are you doing with it?"

Mack could feel herself closing off. This was too much for their first real conversation in a year and a half. "I'm…struggling, to be honest. But that's as much as I want to go into it right now. I need to keep my focus on this trial."

"Sure, of course." Anna's tone was unchanged. "I'll let you get back to work on that."

"Thanks." Mack cleared her throat. "And thanks for, you know, taking my call. For your help. I really appreciate it."

"I'd say anytime, but, well…you know."

"I know."

"How about call me if you want to get coffee sometime."

"I will. Bye, Anna."

CHAPTER THIRTY-SEVEN

"Okay, Mr. Ferguson, let's start with some of the things you told the jury on direct. For example, you testified that you are an Air Force veteran. Do you remember that?"

"Of course."

"Would you like to change or amend that statement in any way?"

"No."

Mack took a deep breath. She had hoped that she could get him to concede some things at the start of his testimony, but apparently he was dead set on his story. She wondered if he had convinced himself that he actually *was* an Air Force veteran. Time for the narcissistic injury.

"Isn't it true, Mr. Ferguson, that you never actually completed basic training for the Air Force?"

"Well, I don't know if—"

"Sir, that was a yes or no question. If you don't remember, I can show you the relevant paperwork and we can go through it together."

"Show me the paperwork."

Mack turned to Judge McPhee. "Judge, may I approach with what's been marked as Exhibit 459?"

The judge nodded. Mack didn't want to test whether her bad mood had extended into a second day, and Diana hadn't been there to ask when she walked into court that morning.

"You'll see here, sir, that this is your discharge paperwork, finding you unfit for service. You were discharged in the second week of basic training, right?"

"I see that I was honorably discharged from the Air Force."

"After less than two weeks of basic training?"

"It looks that way, yes. But that's not how I remember it."

He wasn't losing his temper yet. Mack needed to raise the stakes.

"You often have issues with your memory, right?"

"No, not often."

"Well, let's talk about some of the issues with your memory just from this trial. For example, you don't remember killing Baby Henry, right?"

"I don't remember it, because that's not what happened."

"And you don't remember having sex with your underage daughter?"

"I don't remember that, no."

Mack made a note on a piece of paper. The jury couldn't see that she was scrawling gibberish, but she wanted them to remember his last answer. Not a denial, just a lack of memory.

"Let's talk about your struggles raising a daughter as a single dad, okay?"

"Sure, that's easy."

"Daisy never played sports, right?"

"Right."

"And didn't always go to school?"

"She went to school."

"And if I showed you enrollment records saying she was only going to school about half the time from second grade to eleventh grade, would that change your statement?"

"Those would be incomplete records."

"Okay, well, we'll get to those records in a little while. She wasn't in any clubs?"

"No."

"Girl Scouts?"

"No."

"So you weren't exactly driving her around town to activities."

"No. She was a homebody, just like I am."

Mack consulted her notes. He still wasn't giving her much to work with. "Mr. Ferguson, when did you decide that the used condom was the baby's father?"

"When the DNA results came in," Ferguson said, at the same time Colbey stood and said "Objection!"

Judge McPhee looked at the two standing lawyers, and at Ferguson, who was beginning to look annoyed—by the question or Colbey's interference, Mack wasn't sure.

"The answer will stand, but Ms. Wilson will move along."

Mack sipped water to cover her smile.

"Okay. You were interviewed by police, right?"

"Interrogated, yes."

"And you didn't say anything about how you were just protecting your daughter, right?"

"I don't remember."

"Want to check the transcript?"

Ferguson looked more angry now, his face reddening. He was breathing heavily, and Mack hoped he wasn't about to have a heart attack. She desperately wanted to avoid a mistrial. Daisy couldn't be put through this twice. "No."

"So you agree you didn't say anything about that?"

"I don't disagree."

"Excellent. So when *did* you decide to say that Daisy killed the baby?"

Silence.

"Mr. Ferguson? Do you need me to repeat the question?"

More silence. Mack glanced at Judge McPhee, who was watching Ferguson with interest.

"Sir," the judge said, "you need to answer the question."

Mack looked at the deputy. His hand was on his stun gun, and he was moving toward Ferguson. Whatever was about to happen, Mack wasn't the only one aware of it.

"Let me try rephrasing," she said. "Did you decide to say that Daisy killed the baby after the autopsy results were consistent with Henry having been shaken?"

"She killed my son!" Ferguson roared, leaping to his feet and lunging at Mack over the witness stand.

For a brief moment, pandemonium reigned. Mack stepped backward, trying to get to safety behind the prosecution table, dimly aware of Judge McPhee pounding her gavel. Wood stood and unstrapped the pistol she carried in an ankle holster.

The deputy must have activated Ferguson's shock belt— its crackling noise drowned out the other sounds in the courtroom—and Ferguson must have forgotten the locking leg brace. When he stood, he over-extended his leg, the brace locked, and he tumbled backward onto the floor.

Long moments passed before the jurors were able to return their attention to Judge McPhee. "We will break for the day," she said. "The jury is excused until tomorrow morning."

Mack and Wood remained standing as the jury filed out, Wood still loosely gripping her weapon. Three additional deputies rushed into the courtroom.

Judge McPhee stood and gestured them forward. "Is he awake? I want to address the parties, but he needs to be awake."

"Judge," Colbey said, "I know this is outside the normal role of advisory counsel, but I feel I must ask for a mistrial on behalf of Mr. Ferguson. The jury just became aware of his shock belt and leg brace, and there's no way they won't conclude that he's in custody. They can no longer be fair."

"The State strenuously objects to a mistrial," Mack said. "The defendant caused this kerfuffle by trying to attack me during trial. To reward him with a mistrial would be letting him win, Judge."

Judge McPhee hardly seemed to be listening. She was watching the deputies, who were giving Ferguson a rudimentary medical exam, checking his pupils and pulse.

Mack slumped into the prosecutor's chair and checked her own pulse. Elevated, as to be expected under the circumstances. She focused on taking deep breaths. Her hands were shaking.

A deputy looked up at Judge McPhee. "He needs to be checked out. We have to take him to medical."

She nodded mechanically. "The parties will reconvene here tomorrow morning at ten. We'll address the motion at that time."

Mack started packing her bag, already mentally inventorying her liquor supply. Anna had been right about the power of a narcissistic injury, after all, and Mack needed a stiff drink.

CHAPTER THIRTY-EIGHT

"You seem calmer this morning," Eric said.

Mack looked around the drab visitation room and yawned. "I guess I'm getting used to it here, unfortunately."

"I heard you had an interesting day yesterday."

Mack forced a smile. "That's one way to put it. I don't know what it is about me that attracts this kind of drama, but I'm starting to take it personally."

The door opened, and her father came in. He smiled when he saw Mack, but he seemed tired. The dark circles under his eyes were more prominent than they had been the last time she saw him.

"Hi, Mack. I wasn't sure you'd make it today. What happened with Ferguson is all anyone can talk about since he got back from medical."

Mack groaned. "Surely, *surely*, you can't be seriously talking about that like it was just a...whatever, a casual thing."

Marcus sobered. "It's not casual. He says he's going to finish what he started. You look out in court, okay?"

"Yeah." Mack knew she should report this secondhand threat to Judge McPhee but shelved the thought for later consideration.

Eric cleared his throat. "We don't have a ton of time this morning, so I want to discuss whether Mack is going to testify at trial."

"Absolutely not," Marcus said. "Right? I mean, you don't want that, do you?"

"I don't," Mack said. "But if Eric thinks it's necessary, I think we should hear him out."

"Here's the thing," Eric said. "As it stands, the jury is going to hear from Amanda's mom and some friends and other folks who will make her a real, vibrant person in their eyes. She's going to be humanized in a way that we need to make sure Marcus is, too. I'm not sure who else could give him that human touch, but I'm open to suggestions."

"No," Marcus said. "We're not arguing about this. She doesn't want to testify, she doesn't have to."

"Can I think about it?" Mack asked. "Maybe if I can just have some time to sit with it. I mean, I didn't even know before just now that it was an option. I was the prosecutor on the investigation—it never occurred to me that I could be called as a witness."

"You can think about it," Eric said. "I'm going to file a motion asking for a pretrial ruling, just so it's squared away if we decide you are going to testify. You're right that you having been on the case complicates things, so I want paper."

"There's nothing to decide," Marcus said. "You're worried about how it would look, right? For you to testify in my defense?"

Mack rubbed the back of her neck. The thought of testifying made her sick to her stomach. "File your motion," she told Eric. "We'll see what happens."

Wood was already in Judge McPhee's division when Mack walked in just before ten, but the courtroom was otherwise empty.

"You okay?" the detective asked.

Mack nodded. "Didn't sleep real well, but what else is new? Put the treadmill through its paces around midnight. I'm glad I don't have any adjoining walls."

"Yeah, I went to the gym after I left here. I normally lift heavy, but I set three new PRs from the adrenaline. I'm sorry I didn't shoot."

"I'm not. You know I had a case agent shoot a defendant during trial once? Back in the justice courts. It's not an experience I'm anxious to repeat."

"That was you? I heard about it, but I had no idea you were the prosecutor. Well, okay, then. I'm glad it played out the way it did."

The side door opened, and Ferguson shuffled in, dressed in civilian clothes but with his hands cuffed to a waist-chain.

"The black eye is new," Wood whispered.

Two deputies stood behind the defense table, but Mack was still on edge. If Ferguson was really motivated, he could get to her before they could stop him. She gripped a pen in her closed fist, ready to jab him in the face if he tried anything.

Colbey came in, looking disheveled. He smiled at Mack, who didn't respond. Until Judge McPhee denied his motion for mistrial, she had nothing to say to him.

Five minutes passed. Mack and Wood sat quietly, the detective on her phone and Mack staring vaguely into the middle distance. Ferguson and Colbey whispered furiously to each other. Mack tried hard not to listen.

When Judge McPhee finally took the bench, Mack searched for the outcome in her face. She didn't make eye contact with Mack or Ferguson, opting instead to look at her computer screen.

"Good morning," the judge said. "When we left off yesterday, Mr. Ferguson required some medical attention. I assume he has now received it?"

Ferguson nodded.

The assigned courtroom deputy stepped forward. "I have the paperwork, Judge. He was discharged with no lingering concerns." He handed a document across the bench.

"That leaves us with how to proceed. Mr. Colbey made a motion for mistrial, to which Ms. Wilson 'strenuously' objected."

Both lawyers nodded.

"I agree with Ms. Wilson that the defendant cannot buy his own mistrial. That's well established in case law."

Mack felt the tightness in her chest ease.

"But there are still issues to resolve. Ms. Wilson, did you have additional cross-examination?"

"I'm not sure, Judge. I think it depends on how we're proceeding."

"Under normal circumstances, I would say that the defendant has demonstrated that he does not want to behave appropriately and has therefore waived his right to be present in court. We would proceed in absentia. However, since Mr. Ferguson represents himself, that's an added wrinkle. What I'm inclined to do is take yesterday's outburst as an indication that Mr. Ferguson is not able to represent himself. I would then appoint Mr. Colbey as counsel to finish the trial. I'm willing to hear from the parties before I make my final decision."

"I don't have a problem with that," Mack said. "Although I would note for the record that we told the jury they would be done this week, so I would object to any continuance at this point."

"Understood. Mr. Colbey?"

"Judge, I anticipated that this might be your proposed solution, and I do object. Although advisory counsel often takes over after jury selection, or even after the first witness, at this point we are partway through the defendant's testimony. My understanding is that he has no further witnesses, so what remains to be done is the rest of his testimony and closing arguments. Mr. Ferguson tells me that he's been working on his closing argument since trial began, and if I am appointed to take over, he would expect me to give the closing he's prepared. As an attorney, though, I have certain ethical constraints that would prevent me from doing that. I think he needs to finish the trial, and if that requires a deputy to stand behind him for the rest of his testimony and his closing, so be it."

"So you would not be ethically on board with giving the closing argument he's prepared?"

"Correct, Judge. I can't get into the specifics, but suffice it to say we would have a breakdown in communications if I were to represent him at this time."

"And Mr. Ferguson, let's hear from you."

"I don't want him to represent me." From the sound of his voice, it was clear that the black eye wasn't the only injury Ferguson had sustained. Mack wondered if they were all from the scuffle on the floor, or if someone had gotten to him in the jail the previous night. "I want to continue to represent myself. I also want you, Judge, to direct the government not to be such an asshole to me."

"Sir," Judge McPhee said. "We've talked about your inappropriate use of language before. Ms. Wilson was asking relevant—if aggressive—questions based on your testimony on direct. I'm not going to tell her to change her approach on cross."

"Judge, I don't actually have anything else for cross. But I would ask you to strike all of the defendant's testimony, as a sanction for yesterday's outburst. I'd also ask for a curative instruction where you tell the jury exactly why you're striking the testimony."

Judge McPhee smiled. "I appreciate the ask, but that's a no. Is there redirect?"

Ferguson and Colbey leaned in close and spoke in low voices.

"I think it depends," Colbey said. "If you're appointing me, then no. If Mr. Ferguson continues to be permitted to represent himself, then yes."

The judge leaned back in her chair and closed her eyes.

"Let's bring in the jury. We will begin with redirect."

CHAPTER THIRTY-NINE

"So after all that, she let him keep representing himself?" Jess' shock was clear.

"She sure did."

"Meanwhile, if you'd dived at him across a table, there'd be a mistrial and you'd probably lose your bar license."

Mack swallowed the flavorless bite of salad she'd been chewing. "Is yours terrible? Mine is terrible."

Jess shook her head. "Pretty sure it's fine," she said, stabbing at Mack's lunch with her fork. "But we can trade if you want. I think you're just having a bad reaction right now."

"Maybe."

"Would you like to hear about the terrible date I went on last night, or do you need to focus on your closing?"

Mack pushed her salad away and looked for any sign that Jess was in distress. "I love hearing your terrible date stories, but given everything that's happened, is it okay for a bad date to be funny right now?"

"Yes. It's a gift from my heart to yours in your time of need. It's objectively funny." Jess folded her hands on the table. "So we meet for drinks—no place fancy, just that sushi place near my house. He rolls in a little late, so I have to tamp down the urge to leave or get mad, right?"

"Right. Too early to be a freak about lateness."

"He comes in, he's cute, he's tall—actually looks like his dating-profile photos were taken within the last six months. He's a pharmaceutical sales rep, which is not thrilling but is marginally interesting, and we have a nice enough time that two hours pass."

"So far, this doesn't seem bad."

"Just you wait, 'enry 'iggins. So Georgie—his name is Georgie, not George—says he has a buddy who's throwing a party, and he promised he'd be there, but he's having so much fun with me that would I be willing to go with him? And I think *gosh, that's weird,* but going somewhere with his friends is probably safe, right, because public?"

"Sure."

"So fine. I agree to go. I'll live a little. We get in his car—"

"Uh-oh."

"No, that was fine. He drives us out to Sabino Canyon, and we're having a nice time in the car, lots to talk about, blah blah blah. We pull up at this trailhead, and he says his friends are just like a hundred feet down the trail."

Mack cringed. "He sounds like a ki—" She closed her mouth before she could finish the word.

"No, I could see people from the trailhead. There were cars in the parking lot. I didn't think he was...he was like Adam. I had heels on, but they weren't that high, and the trail wasn't steep right out of the lot. So we join this group, and it turns out there are eight other people—four couples—and us. And the 'party' is that one of the guys has staged this as an opportunity to propose to his girlfriend. Georgie brought me, on our first date, to a proposal."

"Was he supposed to be there alone? Because that's awkward."

"No," Jess said, gesturing to the server for the check. "He was supposed to be there, I found out later from one of the women, with his wife. Who they are all friends with."

"Oh, no! He didn't tell them he and the wife are getting divorced?"

"Oh, he and his wife—Stephanie, apparently a lovely woman—weren't getting divorced. Maybe they are now, I'm not sure. But he didn't feel like going with Stephanie, so he started trawling dating sites, found me, and thought I would be the perfect chump. He didn't mention her in the several hours we spent together, or their two kids."

"Wait—when did you find *that* out?"

"Not until the after-party, which is at a restaurant out in that part of town. I was super uncomfortable, of course, but didn't want to cause a scene by getting an Uber from the trailhead, right? But when Georgie stands up to give a toast, he does a funny joke by getting on one knee and pretending to propose to me! Even he must have realized that everyone was mortified. I go to the bathroom to get a car—screw not causing a scene by that point, you know?—but two of the women follow me in and give me hell about the wife. I'm not sure they believed me about not knowing. So, anyway, they finally leave, and I get a server to show me out through the kitchen so I don't have to make things even worse by walking past their table."

Mack looked at her watch. "If you'd told me this over dinner, I would've ordered you a cocktail."

"If I'd told you this over dinner, I'd be three cocktails deep already."

"Sounds like the only reasonable thing under the circumstances."

"So that is why, when all is said and done, the evidence you have should leave you firmly convinced as to the defendant's guilt on all counts. I ask you to make the appropriate age findings, I ask you to compare Daisy's story with the defendant's story and see which one makes more common sense, which one is more reasonable." She clicked the button on her remote to advance to the final slide, which showed only the word GUILTY in large letters. "And I ask you to find the defendant guilty on all counts. Thank you."

Mack smiled at Jess, who was sitting in the gallery, as she sat down.

"Thank you, Ms. Wilson," Judge McPhee said. "Mr. Ferguson?"

"Yes, I have a presentation to show the jury, so I'm going to ask Mr. Colbey to help me."

Colbey approached the podium. He fiddled with the buttons for a moment, switching the input from Mack's laptop to the ELMO—the document projection system. He put the top sheet from a thick pile under the camera, and Mack moved her chair so she could see it clearly. For all intents and purposes, it was the cover slide of a PowerPoint presentation, except that it was handwritten in pencil on yellow notebook paper.

"Folks," Ferguson said, standing but leaning on the defense table and addressing the jury across the room. "I don't have access to the fancy presentation software that the government just used, so I've gone ahead and put this together to demonstrate to you why you should find me not guilty."

Mack considered objecting. The jury was not supposed to know that Ferguson was in custody, although in all likelihood that had been blown apart yesterday when he was shocked, leg locked, and piled on by deputies. She decided to let it go.

Ferguson nodded at Colbey, who put up the next sheet of paper. *Not guilty lives in the 1%*, it read.

"The government called their DNA analyst, and he's the only evidence they gave you that I was Baby Henry's father. But even their expert said he can only be ninety-nine percent sure. Why is that? Because the real father is in that one percent. And if one percent is enough to conceal the baby's true father, it's enough for you to acquit me."

The next slide read *What happened to Baby Henry?* Mack couldn't help but think of the old movie her mom had shown her when she was in her Bette Davis phase.

"The government talked a lot about what makes sense. Well, what makes sense about my grandson? Does it make more sense that I killed him, even though I raised another child successfully? Or does it make more sense that his mother killed him and then asked me to help cover it up? She was young, she was inexperienced, and you heard her on the stand—she couldn't even keep her story straight, even though she's had years to think about it. The truth is easy to remember. Lies are harder."

Mack forced herself to keep quiet. No lawyer would get away with saying that, but she knew Judge McPhee wouldn't shut Ferguson down. She jotted down some notes for her rebuttal close and shuffled papers as he droned on.

An hour passed. Colbey had put over forty pieces of paper on the ELMO. Most of them featured catchy little phrases, others had drawings, even cartoons. Ferguson had painstakingly drawn a diagram of Aunt Nancy's house, including the trash bag where he'd discarded the used condom. As he wound down, attacking specific word choices made by police officers, Daisy, and Mack herself, he started to lose steam.

"So that's why you should find me innocent on every count," he finished at last.

Colbey sat down, leaving the final sheet of paper—which just read *Innosent!*—on the ELMO, and Mack brushed past him to take it down.

"The defendant talked to you about what makes sense, ladies and gentlemen. Well, let's think about that." She tented her fingers in front of her face and made an exaggerated puzzled expression. "Does it make sense for him to say the real father is concealed in the level of confidence for the DNA evidence, but simultaneously say that he realized that Daisy had impregnated herself with his sperm by using a used condom—but he only realized it once the DNA results came in?"

She took a deep breath to slow herself down and glanced at the court reporter, who was shaking her head but not interrupting.

"I would suggest to you that there is only one story that makes sense here. One story that hangs together, that leaves no loopholes, that doesn't require you to suspend disbelief regarding what you know about human behavior..."

"So that's why, again, I am asking you to find the defendant guilty on all counts. Thank you."

Judge McPhee looked at the courtroom clock. "We have reached our stopping point for today," she said. "So you will all be excused, and you'll come back in the morning to start your deliberations. My clerk will select the alternates from this very fancy hat."

The clerk dug into the judge's Diamondbacks cap and pulled out two folded slips of paper. "Number Two," she read, "and Number Ten."

Mack scanned the jury, trying to remember who jurors Two and Ten might be. Two was an older man—a retired machinist—who Mack thought was probably pro-defense. He'd asked Daisy some of the most pointed questions. Good riddance. But Ten was a loss—a retired schoolteacher who seemed sympathetic and took copious notes during Mack's closing arguments.

"Now we wait," Jess said as she and Mack walked back to the office. Wood had left them in the courthouse, urging Mack to call her when the verdict came in.

"Hopefully it won't take them very long," Mack said. "Although they do have a lot of counts to deal with. We might not hear anything until tomorrow afternoon."

CHAPTER FORTY

They didn't hear anything the next afternoon, or the day after that, and then it was Friday, when juries don't deliberate, and then the weekend.

Mack spent her workdays catching up on other cases. She did laundry for the first time in weeks and stocked her fridge with fresh fruits and vegetables. She even threw away the accumulated leftovers from the takeout she'd been eating during trial.

During the sixth day of deliberations, Nick Diaz called to see if Mack had time for a quick lunch or coffee. Her heart sank. She still had no idea how to respond to his proposition. She could never defend Campbell. He was insufferable and a perfect example of how high a mediocre white man could soar, but at least he valued community safety. With O'Connor at the helm, the office would collapse under its own weight.

"I know you've got a jury out," he said. "So I promise it really will be quick. Melissa just asked me to circle back and see if you'd had time to think about it."

"Honestly, Nick, I'm going to pass on lunch or coffee. I haven't had time to think about Melissa's offer. Actually, I guess I haven't *taken* time to think about it. I do think I'm the wrong choice for this position. All I've ever wanted to be is a trial prosecutor. I don't want to be an administrator. There are plenty of people at the office who'd leap at the chance, but I'm not one of them."

"Is there anything I can do to change your mind?"

"I don't think so. I think, well, I think I'm sticking here. Taking my chances with Campbell."

"I'm sorry to hear that," Nick said. "And I really do think you're making a mistake, Mack. Melissa is the future. Campbell is stuck in the past."

"You might be right, but I don't agree. I don't see a future where we do away with cash bond and the community gets safer. Call me old-fashioned, I guess, but I just think the job of this office is incompatible with what Melissa stands for."

"Well, given your current situation, you've got to be on board with her plan to stop trying death cases, right?"

Mack inhaled sharply. "Excuse me?"

"You know, with your dad? You've got to be glad she's going to get rid of the death allegations, right?"

Mack's hands clenched, and she tilted her head side to side, enjoying the cracking noises. "Nick, I'm going to tell you politely one more time that I'm not interested, and then I'm going to stop being polite about it. Do you understand me?"

"That's pretty conclusive. I guess I'll let you go. I hope you'll consider staying on as a line attorney, at least, when Melissa wins?"

"We'll see what happens. No promises, either way."

On the ninth day of deliberations, Judge McPhee summoned the parties to court. Colbey and Ferguson were already there when Mack walked in. Colbey was on his phone, as far away from Ferguson as he could be while still at the defense table.

"Was there a jury question?" Mack asked the bailiff as she unpacked her bag.

"No, Ms. Wilson," Judge McPhee said, emerging from the corridor into the courtroom. She didn't have her robes on, and Mack was shocked that she would take the bench in capris and a peasant blouse. "No jury questions in nine days. No communication from them at all, except that they're diligently deliberating. Each afternoon, they tell us when they want to come back in the morning. My staff says they never hear raised voices coming from the jury room, and they seem in good spirits when they break for lunch and break for the day. They're just taking their time."

"They've long outrun their screening date," Mack said. "We're not in danger of losing anyone?"

"Not that we've heard. That's why I've brought you all in, though. To decide how we move forward from here. Ms. Wilson, if there is a conviction, do you intend to present aggravation?"

"No, Judge. Because there are so many life counts, the State will waive aggravation."

"Sounds good. What I'm weighing is calling in the foreperson and asking whether they're still deliberating and need more time, or whether they've reached an impasse and just haven't informed us of that fact. Thoughts from anyone?"

Mack shrugged. She didn't see the harm in the judge's suggestion but wasn't sure it would accomplish much of anything. Neither Colbey nor Ferguson seemed to have any input, either.

"Hearing no objections, bailiff, please bring the foreperson in."

A timid young woman came into the courtroom and sat in the jury box. Juror Three. Mack flipped through her voir dire notes. High-school graduate, worked at Amazon, not married, no kids. The other jurors had probably selected her—against her will, no doubt—to give her the positive civic experience of being a leader. They thought they were doing her a favor.

"Hi, Madam Foreperson," Judge McPhee said, smiling benevolently.

"Hi, Judge. Is everything okay?"

"Well, that's what we brought you in here to find out. You and your cohort have been out for a long time, and we just want to make sure everything's going well back there. Your schedule is up to you, of course, but if there's an issue, we want to do what we can to help resolve it."

Juror Three looked slightly less terrified. "No, everything is okay. We're just really taking our time with everything."

"Everyone getting along back there? No one refusing to participate?"

"No, Judge. Everyone's fine. We don't all agree—I mean, I think you probably know that already, right? Because of the time? But everyone's being polite."

"Do you think you will reach verdicts?"

"I think so. I don't see why we wouldn't."

Judge McPhee turned to Mack. "Anything?"

Mack shook her head. "Thank you."

"Mr. Ferguson?"

He whispered with Colbey, then shook his head.

Juror Three left the courtroom, and Ferguson immediately stood.

"I would request a mistrial, Judge. You just suggested to her that there's a way where this ends not with verdicts. You influenced them into hanging. That's a mistrial, right there."

"Denied. Anything else from anyone?"

Mack hid a smile. This was the Judge McPhee she was used to.

"Okay," the judge said, standing. "Then we continue to wait."

* * *

Mack went back to her office, where she found the same clean desk and neatly organized files she had left. She was caught up on all her cases and had even reached inbox zero. She continued down the hall to Jess' office and dropped morosely into the guest chair.

"How are the vibes?" Jess asked. "Rootin' and tootin'?"

"Vibes? Here? Why, the vibes haven't been rootin' or tootin' 'round here for twenty-five years."

Jess laughed and leaned back in her chair.

"Still deliberating," Mack said. "No news, except that I really do think this trial ate McPhee's brain for a while there. Maybe it was the four days of excruciating cross, I'm not sure, but she seemed back to her old self this morning."

"I'm over her. Did I tell you that, after that terrible pep talk last year, she sent me an email after the story about Adam broke?"

"No! Really?"

"Really. From her official government email to my official government email. Giving me her condolences for my fiancé turning out to be a serial killer."

"That is wild."

"Mm-hmm. Wild is about the best word for it, I agree. Hey, want to listen to episode two of the Petrou podcast? It just came out this morning, and I was getting ready to listen when you came in."

Mack shrugged. In fact, she couldn't think of anything she'd like to do less, except maybe call Nick back and let him talk about her father again.

"A resounding yes, if I've ever heard one. Away we go."

Mack swung the door closed as Petrou's voice filled the office. "Welcome back to *The Desert Murder*, a podcast brought to you by Tucson's very own KGUN. As both sides gear up for trial in the Marcus Wilson case, let's get to know his victim, Amanda Wagner, a little bit better."

"Wow," Mack said. "No presumption of innocence, huh? I'm surprised Campbell hasn't quashed this. It seems like a retrial waiting to happen. He just has to argue a tainted jury pool."

Jess didn't respond, and they listened to Petrou interview Amanda's mom.

"She wasn't seeing anyone, no," Lisa Linden said.

Mack snorted. "Nathan's going to love that that's on the record and ripe for impeachment."

A knock at the door startled them both, and Jess paused the podcast.

Sheila came into the room. "Oh, good," she said. "I hoped I'd find you here, Mackenzie. Let's go to your office."

Jess raised her eyebrows and tried to smile reassuringly at Mack's look of panic.

"Sorry, I know that sounded scary," Sheila said when they were settled. "You may well have been fine having this conversation in front of Jessica, but I wanted you to have some privacy."

"Thanks," Mack said reflexively. "Privacy is fine."

"I wanted to touch base about two cases. I suspect you know which two."

Mack did. She briefly recounted that morning's hearing in Ferguson.

"Excellent. Keep me posted. Now, as for Nathan's upcoming trial—"

"You can say it," Mack said. "My father's trial. You don't have to talk around it."

Sheila cleared her throat. "Mr. Campbell has decided that it would be best for you to have some paid time off during the upcoming proceedings. Best for everyone, really."

Mack sat back in her chair. Her mouth was dry, and her ears were ringing. "How…I mean, I don't understand. How would it best for everyone for me to hand off my caseload for, what, a month?"

"Nathan doesn't think it will take that long. The case is— well, the case is fairly clear, from an evidentiary perspective. So unless you have anything pressing during that time, I'm going to personally babysit your caseload. Then, when the trial is over, you can step right back in. You'll be compensated, of course."

"Of course. Paid administrative leave. I know it well."

"No," Sheila said. "This won't be administrative leave. This is—I suppose it's vacation time, but it won't be pulled from your accrued hours. But the admin-leave rules won't apply. You can spend time away from your home, you could even leave town— and you didn't hear this from me, but I recommend that you do. Travel, pursue a hobby, whatever you want to do with the time. It's yours."

"I don't suppose there's any room for debate? What if, say, my jury isn't back yet?"

"No, I wouldn't think there's any need to try debating. If your jury isn't back, I'll collect your verdict and let you know the outcome. You can also leave me any notes you think I'll need on other cases, and I can keep you apprised of things. This is a good thing, Mackenzie. The office recognizes the difficult position you've been put in and wants to do what it can to help ease the burden."

"So I guess I should thank you, then, right?"

Sheila stood and smiled wryly. "Let's not go overboard. Keep me posted about your jury. I know we're all eager to have resolution on that one."

CHAPTER FORTY-ONE

Election Day dawned with a beautiful electric-blue sky. Mack sat at her kitchen table, nursing her third cup of coffee and staring at her mail-in ballot. She'd missed the deadline to return it by mail, but she could drop it at a polling station on her way to work.

She had neatly filled in the ovals for every race except one—Tucson District Attorney. She'd been staring at the six words in two little rows for an hour:

Peter Campbell (Republican)

Melissa O'Connor (Democrat)

Every time she thought she'd made a decision, panic set in. She couldn't vote for Melissa, because she put the community at risk and—employment aside—Mack lived in the community. On the other hand, she couldn't vote for Campbell, because she'd worked for him for too long to trust him. Between his scrutiny of the Andersen case, her two brushes with administrative leave, and her pending involuntary vacation, she just couldn't do it.

She glanced at her watch and sighed. She couldn't take any more time with this. She folded up her ballot, district attorney race left blank, and sealed the envelope.

Voting complete, Mack slouched into her office. She'd passed a few prosecutors walking into the building, and tensions were high. The office had divided itself into pro-Campbell and anti-Campbell camps, and Mack figured she was the only one who was secretly rooting for an asteroid to smash into the Earth.

An hour later, Jess bustled into Mack's office, a box of donuts in one hand and a paper bag in the other. Her "I Voted!" sticker was prominently displayed.

"Election Day donuts? They're American-flag colored. I also brought you a bagel sandwich, if you'd rather skip the sugar."

Mack took the proffered bag. "I always forget you like to vote in person." She bit into the sandwich and hummed in appreciation. The everything bagels near Jess' house were the best in Tucson.

Jess shrugged and selected a donut topped with blue frosting and white sprinkles. "Call me old-fashioned, but I don't trust the early voting. I know I'm *much* older than you are, but I remember when in-person voting was the only way, and I guess I just developed a liking for it."

They ate their breakfasts in companionable silence.

"This donut is atrociously terrible," Jess said. "I should have stuck with an apple fritter."

Mack wordlessly offered her the remaining half of her sandwich.

"So who'd you wind up going with for district attorney?" Jess asked.

Mack chewed and swallowed, then took a long drink of her coffee. "I left that one blank, actually. I spent a long time over it, encouraged people to vote for Campbell. I just couldn't do it myself."

"I think that's okay, under the circumstances. No one could really expect you to be grateful to the guy. So, have you made plans for your vacay?"

Mack had thought about it, couldn't think about much else—except for her increasing fear that the pain in her stomach was an ulcer, and her permanent fear that Daisy Ferguson would kill herself if the jury acquitted her father, and her obsessive fear that if her father was a murderer it meant that she, Mack, might also have a genetic propensity for murder.

"Not really," she said. "I'd like to attend some of the trial, but Eric doesn't want me there. Says it'll distract my dad. I guess Nathan Moore filed a motion asking for special permission to call me as a witness, which is probably the actual reason why Campbell wants me to not be working. Easier to get me to be his performing monkey if I don't have a caseload to manage."

"Is Leyva going to go for it?"

Mack shrugged. "If Eric had filed it, I think it would be a no-brainer. Leyva definitely knows the law, though, and isn't afraid to be rigid when it hurts the State. The hearing is this afternoon. Eric asked me not to go, and Nathan didn't subpoena me—or even mention it to me."

"This is day eleven of the Ferguson deliberations?"

"Indeed it is. But they still haven't sent word that they need anything, so hopefully they're just doing their weird diligent work, and we'll hear something soon."

"What do you think they're up to in there? Restaging the whole trial?"

"Oh, how fun would that be!"

When the hearing started in Judge Leyva's division, Mack was in her office, drinking coffee and watching the livestream. She'd long ago sworn off coffee after lunch, but under the circumstances one cup couldn't hurt. She had lost track of how many cups she'd had that morning, so she'd just do an extra couple of miles on the treadmill that evening to work off the caffeine. It wasn't like she was sleeping much, anyway.

"We're here today," Judge Leyva said, "to address the State's motion to allow Ms. Mackenzie Wilson to testify, despite the fact that she was the assigned prosecutor on this case during the initial investigation. Mr. Flagler has opposed this motion. I have read the motion and the response. Does anyone have any evidence to present?"

The video angle showed the backs of the attorneys and Mack's dad. Judge Leyva was centered in the frame, facing the camera, and Mack assumed that wasn't coincidental.

Nathan Moore turned around, scanning the gallery. "No, Judge," he said. "I thought I might, but no."

Eric didn't bother looking around. "Nothing from defense except argument."

Mack smiled. She was sure Nathan had been looking for her. It would have been easy to subpoena her—just walk the damn thing down the hall and hand it over. It's not like she would have avoided service.

She watched Nathan make an impassioned argument in favor of breaking the rule that prosecutors can't be called as witnesses in their own cases. Mack hadn't been the prosecutor when anything substantive had happened. Her testimony was necessary to understand the police investigation and how they had found the defendant. She was even present when the DNA was seized. He didn't mention her connection to that defendant—or the fact that she was present because she was having breakfast with her father—but Mack knew that was coming at trial. It would be part of Nathan's theory of a grand cover-up. He was showing his cards early. If she had been in his shoes, Mack would have just called the witness and made defense deal with it on the fly. Nathan had a reputation as a meticulous prosecutor, and Mack had never seen anything to the contrary. This time, though, his by-the-book approach might come back to bite him.

It wasn't a bad argument, all things considered. Mack hadn't read the pleadings, so she wasn't sure how much he'd covered in writing, but his oral argument was clear, concise, and persuasive. If Mack was on the bench—and she fervently hoped that would never be the case—she'd be convinced.

When Eric stood to respond, Mack was struck by the contrast between the two attorneys. Nathan was short and slender, with a military haircut. He dressed impeccably, and his shoes were shined, even on casual Fridays. He had the credibility piece down pat. Eric, on the other hand, wasn't even wearing a suit, just low-slung slacks and a collared shirt with his tie loose. He hadn't cut the manbun. Mack wondered if she'd been wrong to forgo hiring Robert Miller but remembered her father's adamant refusal to postpone the trial and give him time to work.

"Judge, the key argument here is actually something that Mr. Moore didn't mention, which means that I, unfortunately, have to be the one to say it. The prosecutor in question has more involvement in this case than Mr. Moore would like to admit. She's the only child of my client, Marcus Wilson. When her father was identified as the main suspect, she was removed from the case and walled off. I don't want to impugn Mr. Moore, of course. I've worked with him before, and I respect him, but the real purpose of calling Ms. Wilson is clear. The State wants to imply—or maybe come right out and say, I guess I don't know how far they want to go—that my client used his daughter's employment to cover up his crime."

Mack was stunned. Despite her father's insistence on keeping their relationship out of the official record, Mack had assumed that it would come out sometime. But not like this. Not out of the mouth of his own lawyer in a public hearing. Petrou would have a field day. Her mother would be mortified.

"Now, there are two problems with that, aside from the rule, which I've laid out in my written response and won't belabor. The first problem is that there's no evidence to suggest that my client even knew what Ms. Wilson's job *was*. They were estranged for years before the events of this case. The second problem is that the only purpose for admitting evidence of their relationship would be to improperly prejudice, bias, or confuse the jury. Ms. Wilson has nothing to say about the early investigation that couldn't be said better and more efficiently— no offense to Ms. Wilson—by a police officer. Her personal feelings about the investigation are neither admissible nor relevant. The only possibility is that, again unfortunately, the State wants to win at any cost and are willing to sacrifice one of their own to do so."

Mack's office was cold, but a bead of sweat dripped down her forehead. There it was, the reality she hadn't allowed herself to consider. This was yet another attempt by Campbell, or Michael Brown and his cadre of homophobic cops, to get her out of the office—and this attempt wouldn't even give her the opportunity to appeal through the merit protection board. They were counting on her to quit rather than face the questions that would inevitably follow after Moore ripped her apart on the stand.

Mack turned off the livestream and sat quietly until the motion-sensing lights in her office turned themselves off.

Her computer dinged. The jury was back, and the verdicts would be read in thirty minutes.

CHAPTER FORTY-TWO

By the time Mack called Wood, emailed Jason, called Daisy, and tracked Jess down in Sheila's office, she had to jog to court.

She skidded into the courtroom. "How did you beat me here?" she whispered to Wood, quickly unpacking her tote bag.

"I've been working from the cafeteria, mostly. Cleaning up old cases, making calls. It hasn't been so bad, except my kids say I smell like pizza."

Mack laughed. She glanced at the defense table, where Ferguson and Colbey sat silently. Ferguson's hands were folded in front of him, and his head was bent. He looked like he was deep in prayer. Funny how the minutes before a verdict came in could convert even the most dedicated atheists.

A touch to Mack's shoulder made her turn around to find Jason and Daisy, whose red face and swollen eyes spoke for themselves. She ushered them into a side room.

"What does it mean?" Daisy asked. "They're letting him get away with it, right? They didn't believe me. I knew they wouldn't believe me—he told me no one would."

"It doesn't mean anything in particular." Mack patted her forearm, but she jerked away. "I've seen juries acquit after ten minutes and convict after six days. They were absolutely out a long time, but that's no reason to panic. We're going to go back inside and listen to the verdict. The important thing for you to remember is that you need to stay impassive when the clerk is reading."

Daisy looked confused.

"Whatever she says, you have to keep your face neutral," Jason said. "No crying, no laughing, no screaming. Okay?"

"Why?"

"Great question," Mack said. "And I don't have a good answer for you. I think really what it comes down to is that we don't want the jury to feel bad about their decision, whatever it is."

"But sometimes they should feel bad, right? Sometimes they get it wrong, and they should feel bad."

Mack didn't disagree, but this wasn't the time to debate the finer points of the criminal-justice system. They walked back into the courtroom, and Daisy and Jason made themselves as comfortable as possible on the wooden pews in the gallery. Judge McPhee had already taken the bench, and as soon as she saw Mack she whipped into action.

"Anything from anyone?"

No one responded.

"Let's bring them in, then."

Everyone stood for the jury, and Mack forced herself to remain still. Not that fidgeting would do any good at this point, but she wanted to appear strong as she looked at each juror in turn. None of them made eye contact with her, and Mack realized they were going to acquit him. Ferguson was going to get away with it, and Daisy would live the rest of her life afraid that he would come for her again.

The forewoman gave the red folder of verdict forms to the bailiff, who handed it to Judge McPhee. She glanced through it impassively before handing them to the clerk, who stood, cleared her throat, coughed, and started reading.

"We the jury, duly empaneled, do find the defendant as to Count One: Murder in the First Degree, not guilty."

Mack felt the chair drop out from under her and broke out in a cold sweat. It was happening. Her very first murder case without someone there beside her, and she'd bungled it. Judge McPhee caught her eye. Mack would have sworn the judge winked at her, but that didn't make any sense. She held her breath as the clerk shifted to the second piece of paper.

"We the jury, duly empaneled, do find the defendant as to Count Two: Sexual Conduct with a Minor, guilty. We further find that the victim was under age eleven, proven. We further find that the defendant was over age eighteen, proven."

Mack let out a shaky breath. Even without the murder count, Ferguson would spend the rest of his life in prison. As the clerk kept reading, Mack relaxed. They convicted on every other count, so Ferguson was looking at a minimum of seven consecutive life sentences plus fifty years.

She snuck a glance at the defense table. Colbey seemed no more interested than he would be listening to someone read the phone book. Ferguson, on the other hand, was chalk white and had a tight grip on the arms of his chair. The deputy stepped closer, but he made no move to rise.

"Members of the jury, we thank you for your time," Judge McPhee said. "You are now released from the admonition. You can speak to anyone you wish about this case. Lawyers are always interested in jury feedback, so if you want to talk to them, you can stick around in the jury room, and they'll come back shortly."

The parties stood one final time as the jury filed out of the room. Mack turned to Daisy, who was crying steadily but silently.

"We will order a presentence report and set a sentencing date about thirty days out," Judge McPhee said. "The defendant will be held nonbondable. Anything else from anyone?"

"I'd like to request a new trial," Ferguson said. His voice was firm and clear, no sign that the verdicts had taken any toll on him.

"Put it in writing. I won't hear any motions today."

After the deputy led a reluctant Ferguson out of the courtroom, Mack was surprised to receive a hug from Detective Wood. Normally, cops were angry at split verdicts, using them as evidence that the prosecutor hadn't worked hard enough.

Wood turned to Daisy and wrapped her in a bear hug. "Listen, I know you might be feeling like we lost, but we won. We won big. Don't worry about the one not guilty count. He'll be in prison on the sex charge, and he'll have an even worse time of it."

Daisy nodded and shyly offered Mack a hug of her own.

"You showed him," Mack whispered. "You could have just rolled over and let him win, but you were brave and strong, and you showed him he's not in charge anymore."

When they turned to leave, Colbey approached Mack and held out a bag of gummy bears. "Nicely done," he said.

Mack declined the candy. "You want to talk to them?"

He shook his head. "Honestly, I can't begin to care."

"Even if they say something that would help his appeal?"

"This is a perk of being advisory counsel." He shook a bear into his mouth. "I don't have to care about his appeal. To tell the truth, I think he's winding up exactly where he should be. I know all the research says he's a low risk to reoffend, but— pardon my French—fuck the research. He's a danger and a creep, and I hope, young lady, that you can piece the rest of your life together in such a way that you don't think of him ever again. As for me, I'll sleep just fine tonight."

He walked out of the courtroom without a care in the world.

Must be nice, Mack thought. She took off her jacket, aware suddenly that she'd been sweating since she'd heard the words "not guilty."

The bailiff came in from the hallway leading to the jury room. "You want to go back? Only one stayed, but she'd like to talk."

Mack followed her, steeling herself for her least favorite part of jury trials. She never felt better after hearing the true thoughts of the men and women who had just made the most important decision they'd probably ever make.

Only the timid forewoman had stayed. She was seated at the head of the jury table, hands clasped in front of her. When Mack came into the room, she stood, bumping her knee on the table. "Thank you for coming back," she said.

"I'm always happy to hear from jurors," Mack lied. "Just so you know, there are certain questions I can't answer, and our bailiff is going to stay, to make sure nothing inappropriate gets said."

The forewoman pulled the sleeves of her cardigan over her hands. "I wanted to apologize, actually, and I hope you'll pass it on to Daisy. I really wish we could have convicted on the murder, but there were a couple of people who just weren't sure. Like, the thing with the condom was obviously fake, but some of the older folks thought maybe he really hadn't been the one to kill the baby, that it made more sense that she'd done it. Not that anyone really blamed her, or anything. She was so young and clearly in a really bad situation."

"I can let Daisy know, sure," Mack said. "But there's no need for you to apologize. It's not your responsibility to come to any particular verdict. The evidence just wasn't strong enough on that count, and that's a thing that happens sometimes."

"Well," the juror said. "Well, the thing is, *I* believed her."

"Okay, thank you."

"No, I—I mean…" She sighed, frustrated. "I know where she's coming from."

Mack suddenly understood what the young woman was trying to say.

"Have you…Is this the first time you're telling anyone about this?" she asked gently.

The bailiff slipped out of the room and closed the door.

"I'd forgotten all about it. Then, when Daisy was testifying, I—I remembered."

Mack nodded. She'd heard this story before—from prosecutors, social workers, even defense attorneys. People could bury things deep, but once in a while they popped back up, unbidden and unwanted.

"I can give you a list of resources," Mack said. "There are people you can talk to. To discuss legal options, sure, but more importantly to make sure that you're okay. We don't want you walking out of here with a new load of trauma and nowhere to turn."

She sniffled. "I'd like that. Resources, I mean. I'd like someone I can talk to about it."

Mack wrote down the phone numbers of three organizations who worked with victims at low or no cost. She patted the juror on the back and returned to the courtroom, gathered her belongings, and left for her office.

CHAPTER FORTY-THREE

She should have been celebrating. No drink ever tasted better than the one that followed a guilty verdict—except maybe the one or two (or three) after that. Unfortunately, however, Mack found herself with no one to celebrate with. Anna was her usual celebration buddy, and she wasn't an option. Detective Wood had to get home to her kids. Jess had started her own trial and couldn't spare the time on a Tuesday. She'd suggested Friday as an alternative.

Mack scrolled through her phone and paused over Rocky Bailey's name. She'd been meaning for months to patch things up with the owner of Paradise, which had been her favorite bar. It had just never seemed like the right time to apologize, and Rocky had made it clear in their last conversation that Mack owed her a dozen years' worth of apologies.

"No time like the present," she said. She missed the easy friendship she had always had with Rocky, and maybe she could get it back.

The smell hit her even before she was through the door. Stale beer and Fabuloso and Mack didn't know what else, but it brought back memories of good times.

It was like coming home after the first semester of college. An uncomfortable return to a place that had once felt natural.

Mack stood at the bar and ordered an Angry Orchard from a cute young bartender. As the pint glass slid in front of her, she asked, "Is Rocky here?"

The girl shook her head. "She hasn't been coming in on Tuesdays. You want me to call her?"

Mack thanked her but declined. There were election results on the television hung above the bar, rather than the usual music videos. Campbell and O'Connor were neck and neck with forty percent reporting. They wouldn't have a result tonight. It would take days before the early ballots were all counted. Not that Mack was in a hurry. Best-case scenario…well, there wasn't a best-case scenario. Least-bad scenario, she'd have to choose whether or not to keep working for a man she didn't like or trust. Most-bad scenario, she'd have to choose whether or not to start working for a woman she didn't like or trust, and who knew that's how Mack felt about her.

She downed the last inch of her drink and gestured to the bartender for another. She felt depleted from the Ferguson trial. Numb. Not the way she'd ever felt after a guilty verdict before. She sensed, rather than saw, the person behind her and turned to find Beth.

"Pull up a stool?" Mack asked.

Beth kissed her on the cheek but didn't sit. "I can't." She turned to the bartender and ordered two vodka sodas.

"Ah. Here with someone?"

Beth nodded, looking guilty. Or maybe Mack was imagining that, seeing what she wanted to see.

"You look good," Mack said. She did, too, in a low-cut red shirt and tight black jeans. Her dark hair curled around her face, and Mack remembered what had initially drawn her to Beth.

"Thanks. You…well, you look awful, actually. But it's good to see you."

Mack laughed. "You tried for a compliment, I'll give you that."

"You could call me, Mack. It doesn't have to be like this. Things were good between us."

"Yeah, maybe."

Mack closed out her tab and summoned an Uber, avoiding looking at Beth and whoever she was there with. She knew she would never call.

On Monday, the city was still unsure who the duly elected district attorney was going to be, and jury selection started in the trial of State versus Marcus Wilson. Mack tried to ignore the trial and focus on her involuntary vacation. She and Jess had booked a trip to Vegas for the following weekend, her mom was planning a short visit for Thanksgiving, and Mack filled her time with books and movies she'd been meaning to catch up on.

Petrou had released two more episodes of his podcast, and Mack had grudgingly listened to them. Lots of factual errors, not much concern for the truth—typical for true-crime podcasts, in Mack's experience. It was trauma pornography of the worst kind, but at least no mention of her familial relationship to the case. Mack wondered if he was saving that bombshell for a later episode. Surely he knew about the hearing where it had all come out.

Judge Leyva had finally ruled by minute entry that Moore couldn't compel Mack to testify, and Eric had asked her not to come to trial. He texted her occasionally with updates, but never enough for her to feel like she was truly in the loop.

The doorbell rang, pulling Mack from her computer. She'd been looking at the public docket for her father's trial. They'd sworn the jury and started testimony, but that was all she could see. No hints as to how it was going. She was expecting Jess for dinner and a movie and didn't bother looking out the window before opening the door, so she was surprised to see Eric Flagler on her doorstep.

"Come on in," she said. "Is my address just freely available or something? People show up here, and I have no idea how they know where I live."

"I got it from your dad," he said.

"You could have called."

"I ran into Jess Lafayette today, and she made it sound like you could use some company. Plus, you're actually almost on my way home. So I figured it was worth taking a chance and seeing if you were in."

Mack showed him into her kitchen and offered him a beer. He accepted and waited as she opened one for each of them. He gestured at her computer.

"Things aren't looking good," Eric said. "I know that doesn't tell you much, but that's actually why I'm here. You need to be prepared for the verdict."

"Is it that bad?"

"It's not good."

"What'd Nathan say in his opening?"

"Nothing unexpected. Hammered the open-and-shut nature of the evidence. DNA and fingerprints, your father lied, there's a dead baby. The jury…well, how would you feel if you heard that story?"

Mack sipped her beer. She would feel like she could put the needle in herself. Like the death penalty wasn't harsh enough.

"We made the right call, having you stay away," Eric continued. "Petrou's been there every day and, well, I think if he saw you two in the same room, he'd put it together. The resemblance really is striking."

Mack forced a laugh. "My mom always called me his clone. Said we talked the same, looked the same, even walked the same, whatever that means."

They drank in silence for a while.

"Jury asking questions?"

"Unfortunately. It's just been basic witnesses so far—EMTs who treated her on scene, DNA people, a few cops. But the jury is real mad at me and your dad. One of them—we're pretty sure it's just one, based on the handwriting, at least—keeps asking why he didn't cop a plea. We aren't reading the inflammatory ones to the witnesses, of course, but I don't like where their heads are at. You see Petrou's column today?"

"No. I'm on vacation, and mostly when I'm on vacation I try not to consume garbage."

"He says it's all over but the shouting. The State could put on performing bears for the next week, and it'd still be death."

Mack looked at Eric across her kitchen bar. He was tired. The trial had aged him.

"Eric, do you like my dad? I don't mean do you think he did it. Do you like him?"

"What do you mean, like as a client?"

"No. Like, I don't know, just as a guy. If you were at Bob Dobbs and he sat down next to you, would you like him?"

Eric held his bottle up to the light, and they both saw that it was empty. She grabbed him a fresh one from the fridge.

"I don't know," he said. "I try not to think about them like that. He's braggadocious, overbearing, and I'm meeting him during the worst ordeal of his life. But, all that aside, yeah, I think I do. He's funny. He's got great stories to tell. He really seems to like his kid, even though it's taken him a while to wrap his head around who his kid actually is. I think under other circumstances, I'd like him a lot."

"I don't remember ever liking him. Don't get me wrong, I remember loving him. I remember missing him when he was gone. I even remember having fun with him sometimes. But I don't remember ever thinking, *Gee, I really like my dad.* Do you like your dad?"

"I did, yeah. I liked him a lot. Not all the time. But I bet he didn't like me all the time, either. I was a feral little gremlin when I was a kid."

Mack laughed. "I'd like to get to know him, I think. I hope it's not too late for me to have that chance."

The doorbell rang for the second time that evening, and Mack found Jess on the doorstep with a bag of takeout and a six-pack.

"Join us," she said, gesturing Jess into the kitchen. "We're being maudlin about father-child relationships and the limited nature of our time on Earth."

Jess waved at Eric, who was putting his bottles in Mack's recycling.

"I'll leave you guys to it," he said.

Mack walked him to the door.

"For what it's worth," he said. "Whatever the verdict is, you'll have a chance to get to know him. The question is where, and isn't that kind of irrelevant? I mean, I don't want to be a buzzkill or anything, but if I could have my dad back, even if he was on death row, I'd take that in a heartbeat."

CHAPTER FORTY-FOUR

The next night, Mack found herself alone and in need of distraction. She was too tired to run and too restless to go to bed. She took a long drink of Angry Orchard. She hadn't yet turned the heat on for the season, hating the smell of artificially warmed air, but it was cold enough that sweats and a blanket still left her shivering on the couch. She grabbed her phone, but her call to Jess went straight to voice mail. She texted instead: *If you are anywhere other than on a date, it's very rude not to answer. If you are on a date, it was very rude not to tell me about it. In any event, you're very rude.*

She thought about calling her mom, but talking about the trial or Petrou's podcast was the last thing she wanted to do. Instagram would have to suffice.

An hour later, Mack was deep into an online sphinx-cat community. As she scrolled through yet another hashtag, she considered, not for the first time, getting a pet.

The next picture caught her eye. It was location tagged in Tucson and showed a pretty young woman holding the ugliest naked cat Mack had ever seen. It was the ugliness of the cat that made her stop more than anything else. As she zoomed in on the cat's face, however, she realized that she recognized the woman holding it.

It was Amanda Wagner.

Mack sat up abruptly. What was Amanda doing on her Instagram feed? It wasn't Amanda's account, and the photo was dated two months before her death. She peered at the image. That wasn't Amanda's house. Of course it wasn't—Amanda hadn't owned a cat. She clicked on the username, a jumbled series of letters and numbers, and scrolled back in time to the photo she had just been looking at. There were more photos and videos of Amanda—posing flirtatiously on a barstool, one arm around a good-looking man in a pool, screaming along with the band at a concert. The photos stopped about two weeks before Amanda died. Then nothing—no posts at all—until six weeks later, when whoever owned the account started posting again. No mention of Amanda's death. Just the same mix of sphinx-cat pictures and the documentation of daily life.

The guy Amanda had her arm around in the pool showed up in pictures both before and after her death. He must be the owner of the account, Mack reasoned, because she didn't know any straight guys who so consistently featured other men in their photos. Blond hair, tall, tan—he looked a lot like Mack's dad, only thirty years younger. It seemed that Amanda had a type.

Mack scrolled to the beginning of the guy's feed. He had posted his first photo in 2013, the same year Mack joined Insta and the service really seemed to take off. Blurred, overly filtered photos of food and beaches just like the early posts of almost everyone Mack knew. But then, a picture so fortuitous that Mack couldn't believe it for a second. It had to be a joke. He had posted a shot of his diploma from Northern Arizona University.

William Bradley Cameron.

"Billy Bumble," Mack whispered. "Mother of all that is holy. I found him."

She wasn't sure what to do about it. She needed more. One last fact to tie everything together in a neat package, easily digestible by her father's jury.

She called Dave while booting up her computer, apologizing to Jess in her head all the while.

"Hi, Mack," Dave said. "Good to hear from you. Been a while."

"I know, and I'm sorry about that. It just seemed like—while the trial is going, at least—I probably shouldn't be coming over for dinner."

"Ricky misses you. Hell, me and Meredith miss you. But you're not calling this late at night just to catch up."

"No, I need you to run someone for me. I'm looking him up in our system, but that doesn't give me the NCIC data, and that's what I need."

Dave cleared his throat. "Do I want to ask who it is, or why you need the information right now?"

"That's up to you. I recommend asking those questions over dinner sometime. This call will end faster if you just look him up for me."

Mack gave Dave the name from the diploma. "Not sure on the exact age. Thirties somewhere, I think. White guy. My system—this is trash, I'm sure, because my system's only showing some drug stuff from about five years ago."

Mack heard typing from the other end of the line, followed by a long silence and then a low whistle.

"Guy's been busy. Mostly up in Phoenix, but some misdemeanor stuff in Yuma and even Vegas. Violent. No facts in NCIC, of course, but from the charges it looks like he likes to use a little meth and hit women."

"You got an address for him?"

Dave rattled off an address, and Mack entered it into Google Maps. It was less than a mile from her house.

"You're a peach, Dave. One more question. If I've got a phone number and a name, how can I figure out if they've ever been associated?"

"Like if the name ever used the phone number? You can't, not directly. The best way would probably be to throw a tracking warrant on the number. Then figure out where your name likes to spend time and see if they intersect."

Mack's heart fell. She knew that she could ask Dave to draft an affidavit and apply for a warrant in theory, but she didn't want to risk telling him what she was up to. He would have to report back to Nathan, and her surreptitious involvement in the case would be over before it even got started.

"Not the answer you were looking for? You could always try calling the number and seeing who picks up, but that leaves a lot more to chance."

"Thanks, Dave."

Tiredness gone, Mack thought about tracking warrants as she changed into leggings and a sports bra. She thought about tracking warrants as she pulled on expensive running shoes and tied them just a hair too tight. She thought about tracking warrants as her feet pounded the treadmill.

And then it hit her, so hard she tripped and barely kept herself from smashing her face on the handrail.

Her calls went to voice mail three times, but the fourth time was the charm. Eric answered, sounding groggy. Mack checked her watch.

"I'm so sorry," she said. "I didn't realize how late it was."

"That's okay," Eric croaked. "My wife loves midnight phone calls."

"Please apologize to her on my behalf, but I found Billy Bumble."

"Excuse me?"

She explained.

"What good does that do, if we can't prove this guy actually is the other boyfriend?"

"It's too late to request a tracking warrant now—we're already in trial—but I'm ninety percent sure the cops got one back when they were trying to ID Billy and Cesar, before they zeroed in on my dad and never looked back."

"Then what? Sorry, I feel like you expect me to see where you're going with this, and I don't."

"Then you provide the social media and the phone records showing that he was also dating Amanda, and you show that you've done the investigation the cops should have done. You provide a viable alternate suspect."

"We are three days into the State's case, Mack. It's too late for a viable alternate suspect."

"No judge in Arizona would keep this out. Not on a death case. Not if you can prove it's recently discovered. I—I'll testify. I'll explain exactly what happened. Leyva will have to let it in. It's the only way."

All Mack could hear was Eric's quiet breathing. She bent over, rubbing her thigh where it had hit the treadmill. She could already tell that the bruise would be nasty.

"Okay," he said. "Okay. I'll start digging through for the tracking warrant and data. Assuming they got one, and assuming they disclosed it, which are both big assumptions. I can get my investigator on it right away, and then I'll draft the motion when everything's in place."

"Why not send me the discovery, and I'll take care of it?"

"It's very late, Mack. Shouldn't you get some sleep?"

"There's no point. I won't be able to sleep with this hanging over me, and at least I'll feel like I'm doing something. Please, Eric, I want…I want to feel like I'm helping."

The email came through less than five minutes later—a link to a secured Dropbox account with, as far as Mack could tell, all the discovery in the case.

She started digging. After two hours, she located the tracking warrants, one for Cesar Chavez and one for Billy, but the warrant return—the tracking data, which was what Mack actually needed—was only there for Cesar.

That was a problem. Had they never gotten the data on Billy, or was it discarded as irrelevant?

Mack knew what she needed to do.

CHAPTER FORTY-FIVE

"You ought to consider varying your routine," Mack called. "If I can find you, anyone could."

She held out the coffee she'd picked up for him, hoping she remembered the way he took it. He sipped it warily, and a smile spread across his face. He gestured for Mack to follow him as he walked to his pickup truck and slung his messenger bag into the back seat.

"Not that this isn't a pleasant surprise, but what's up, Mack?"

"I know this will come as a shock, but I need a favor."

Dave grimaced. "It's five a.m., and this isn't a great time for me to be doing you any favors, anyway. What with me being the case agent in your dad's murder trial and all."

"Hey, what's a little conflict of interest among friends?" Mack waited for a laugh that didn't come. "I was going through the discovery, right, and found tracking warrants for both Cesar and Billy."

"Sure. That would have been SOP, but I didn't write them. It probably would be the tech guys."

"They issued. I don't remember who wrote them, but they issued. But there are only returns for Cesar. I assume because everybody figured Billy was irrelevant?"

"Probably. We were pretty firmly focused on Marcus by the time that stuff would have come in."

"Okay, here's the favor. Can I have the results for Billy?"

Dave flinched. "Absolutely not."

"Listen, I totally get why they wouldn't have been included in discovery, except I have a hunch there's some clearly exculpatory information in them. So there are two ways this can go. I can call Eric Flagler and tell him the State withheld exculpatory information. He'll file a motion, name you personally, and we all know what Leyva will do. Your case? Dead in the water, Dave. Or, you can slip me the results, and if I'm wrong you'll never hear about it again."

"What if you're right?"

Mack searched his face in the half light. She saw defensiveness, which was natural, but no sign of deception or fear. Dave was her friend. He had killed a man to save her life. She owed him honesty.

"At this point, he doesn't know they weren't disclosed. I offered to do the digging, and I can just tell him that I found them. You won't be the source of the records. If I'm right, Eric will cross-examine you about them. I might have to testify. He'll present Billy as a third-party defense and try to get my dad acquitted."

"Are you sure you know what you're doing, Mack?"

She laughed. "I have no idea what I'm doing. I feel like I'm doing ninety on city streets, gripping the wheel and screeching like a pterodactyl as I blow through red lights. But if someone else did it—if someone else killed Amanda Wagner, I mean— don't you want to know? Don't you want to get the right guy, not just the easy guy?"

Dave's head dropped. "Of course I do. And, to be clear, I believe that's what we've done. I think you're chasing something that isn't there."

"So give me the records. If you're right, we'll never talk about it again. Unless you want to do some kind of told-you-so dance or something. Which would be a weird flex, but I wouldn't object. Look, I'm going to go. I'm signed up for a yoga class this morning. People keep saying I need a hobby. Just—just think about it, okay?"

The tracking warrant return was in Mack's email by the time she got home. She didn't bother changing, just stood at her kitchen counter and started reading.

CHAPTER FORTY-SIX

Eric reluctantly agreed that Mack could come to court and watch his cross-examination of Dave firsthand. He would be the State's last witness. Eric still hadn't decided whether Mack would need to testify—that would depend on what Dave was willing to say—so she agonized over what to wear. She faced the rack of suits in her closet, dismissing each one in turn. Not the navy blue—it was too "rah rah America" for a defense witness. Not the black—too harsh. Not the red—too flashy. She finally settled on a cream summer-weight wool with navy buttons over a navy silk shell. With her hair in a bun, she decided she looked likable but still credible. She didn't look like a defendant's daughter. She looked like a prosecutor, charged with seeking justice wherever it could be found.

She sighed. However she looked, she felt tired and anxious.

Jess joined her at the coffee shop across from the court complex and eyed her critically. "You on the verge of a little menty-b, friend?"

"Is that what you youth are calling them now?"

Jess nodded. "Little grippy-sock vacay?"

Mack gently slapped her shoulder and Jess immediately sobered.

"Do you want me to go with you? Not that you need hand-holding, but it can't hurt to have someone in your corner, right?"

Mack appreciated the offer but declined. She was planning to sit on the defense side of the courtroom and didn't feel comfortable asking Jess to join her. They agreed, however, to meet for brunch on Sunday.

"How about Millie's?" Mack asked.

"Are you kidding?"

"They don't take *everyone's* DNA." Mack tried but failed to keep her voice lighthearted. "That was a special onetime thing."

Jess watched her, unsmiling.

"This is the same thing as you hiking Tanque Verde. It's just exposure therapy. And mine comes with bacon!"

"Okay," Jess said. "If you're sure. They really do have the best pancakes."

The courtroom was mostly empty when Mack walked in. Jess had told her that, the first couple days, there had been lines out the door, but apparently interest had quickly dropped off. The reality of a trial was never as sexy as the crime itself.

Dan Petrou was seated against the back wall on the State's side of the gallery, and he seemed surprised to see Mack. She looked the other way and sat in the far corner, buried in her phone. Luckily, more observers trickled in, and soon her view of Petrou was blocked.

Dave—according to the most recent episode of the podcast, which had dropped that morning—had been the State's most important witness. On direct, Nathan Moore had artfully woven together Dave's interview of the defendant, his investigation that disproved Marcus's alibi, and the disparate threads of the investigation. Things looked grim for Marcus Wilson as the State prepared to conclude its case.

Mack avoided Dave's eyes as he took the stand. Even though she'd told him what was coming, she felt guilty about how she'd handled it. It amounted, she knew, to emotional blackmail.

"Good morning, Sergeant Barton," Eric said. His usual easygoing manner was nowhere to be seen. He seemed tense. Mack knew he was uncomfortable with what he was about to do. That was the problem with playing by the rules. When the game changed, you weren't ready.

"I want to go through lots of what you said on direct on Thursday, but let's go ahead and start with something else, okay?"

Dave nodded.

"I'm approaching the witness with what's been marked as defense Exhibit 203."

Nathan stood. "I'm sorry, Judge, but what is that exhibit?"

Eric swallowed hard, his Adam's apple bobbing. "It's a copy of a tracking warrant return on the phone number referred to as Billy Bumble's number. And then I'm going to show him 204, which is the return on the phone number referred to as Cesar Chavez."

"Were these part of the State's discovery?" Judge Leyva asked, sounding uninterested.

"Yes, Judge," Eric said. "They were generated during the police investigation."

Close enough, thought Mack.

Judge Leyva granted his approval, and Eric handed two thick stacks of paper to Dave.

"You're familiar with these reports, right?"

Dave looked at the top sheets. "I've seen them, but I wouldn't necessarily say I'm familiar with them. They're pretty technical reports, generated by the phone companies."

"In very brief summary, these reports tell you where a cell phone was during a given time period, right?"

"Yes. Based off of which cell towers they accessed. It's not, like, a precise location, usually. It's an area."

"Perfect. I'm going to have you start with 203. That's Billy Bumble's phone, right?"

"Right."

"And based on that report, can you tell the general area where Billy's house probably was located?"

Nathan stood. "Objection, Judge, as to relevance. Also, I can't seem to find my own copy of the document defense is referencing."

Mack tensed. This was the moment when her plan could fall apart. She had to trust Judge Leyva to do what he liked to do best—screw the State.

"Overruled," the judge said, a pleasant smile on his face. "If it's a document generated by the State, I'm sure you have it somewhere. And if it was generated during this investigation, I'm willing to entertain the relevance."

Eric put a poster board showing a map of Tucson on the easel next to the witness stand. "Will you draw—a rough estimate is fine—the area where you would expect Billy's home to be, based on that tracking data?"

Dave looked at the records, looked at the map, and looked at the records again. Finally, he took the black marker Eric offered him, stood, and uncertainly drew a circle in the northeast part of town.

"Perfect," Eric said. "And if you could mark Amanda Wagner's house with a little X?"

At least one juror gasped as Dave drew an X within the circle. Mack hid a smile behind her hand. If they were impressed by that, they hadn't seen anything yet.

"Great. Next, I'm going to have you look at the Cesar records. Got them?" Eric waited for Dave to nod. The defense attorney's nerves were starting to dissipate. He seemed to realize at last what Mack had known all along—Leyva was going to give him as much rope as he wanted. "Okay, one of the compelling facts against my client is that the Cesar records—which you linked to him, no one is disputing that—show that he was in the area of Amanda's house the night she died, right?"

"Right," Dave said. "Between eight-thirty and ten, we have several pings that put him in the area, and his alibi is contradicted by those pings."

"Agreed. And what time was Billy in the area that night?"

Dave flipped back to the records for Billy. "Well, he was there consistently from six until seven thirty the next morning.

But since his house is in the area, that doesn't tell us much. He could have just been home."

"And you never identified Billy, right?"

"Right."

"Because you were focused on my client, who you were able to identify more quickly?"

"I suppose. We had better evidence—more evidence—against your client."

"Let's talk about that." Eric handed a stack of papers to Nathan, who flipped through them. "Judge, I'm showing the State what's been marked as defense Exhibits 205 to 235. I would expect that these have not been seen by the State, because they were only recently discovered by defense. Of course, if the State had conducted the kind of investigation this case warranted, everyone would have seen them a long time ago."

CHAPTER FORTY-SEVEN

Nathan's jaw dropped. Mack wasn't sure if he understood the significance of what he was looking at, but he certainly understood it was bad news. "Can we…let's…Judge, can we take a brief recess and discuss this outside the presence of the jury?"

Judge Leyva nodded and had his bailiff show the jury out of the room.

"What is this, Eric?" Nathan asked as soon as the door clicked behind the last juror. "We don't do trial by ambush. How could you possibly think producing these in the middle of my case would fly?"

Eric didn't respond and kept his eyes on Judge Leyva. Mack glanced at Petrou. He had his head down and was typing furiously on his laptop.

Judge Leyva cleared his throat. "Mr. Moore, please hand me the documents in question." He shuffled through the pack of pages. "Okay, Mr. Flagler, explain."

"I understand the State's frustration, Judge, but this came together very last minute. As you know, my client did not want to waive time. He wanted his day in court as soon as possible, because he has always maintained his innocence of these horrible charges. Despite his wish to let a jury decide the case in an expeditious manner, I had a duty to conduct the investigation that TPD failed to do on their own, namely, to discover the identity of Billy Bumble, who we believe was Ms. Wagner's actual killer. An…investigator working with my office recently uncovered the Instagram records you're now looking through. In combination with the tracking warrant return, they demonstrate Billy Bumble's identity and put him in the area of the murder at the time of the murder.

"The jury *must* receive this evidence—which, again, a thorough police investigation should have turned up. Without it, they're receiving a biased and incomplete picture of the evidence. The State wants to say that my client responded inappropriately to the death of his girlfriend? This guy uses Instagram every day and didn't acknowledge her death. The State wants to say their GPS data puts my client in the area at the time of death? This guy was there, too. These records mitigate every piece of circumstantial evidence the State has."

"But Judge," Nathan said. "No third-party defense was noticed. This is untimely. The rules exist for a reason. If they'd presented this to us in a timely manner, we could have responded to it, interviewed this William guy, ruled him out through fingerprints. By springing it on us midtrial, Mr. Flagler has effectively cut off our ability to further investigate."

Eric slammed his hand on the table, and everyone in the gallery jumped.

"That's the whole *point*, Judge! This is all stuff that the State should have investigated. They generated the tracking warrant. I didn't do that. This guy's Instagram account wasn't locked. If we could find it, they could have found it. The jury deserves to know that the police weren't interested in a fair and thorough examination of the available evidence. They decided that the guy they called Cesar did it, got enough evidence to figure out who Cesar was, and charged my client. They weren't interested in finding the truth of who killed Amanda Wagner and holding that person accountable. They were interested in presenting a neat little package to the jury that's full of confirmation bias and hoping no one looks at it too carefully."

Judge Leyva held up a hand. "I understand that passions are running high. I want to slow down. I'm going to give my gut reaction, and we'll go from there."

Eric and Nathan both sat, faces red. Mack kept her eyes on her father, who had showed no reaction to the whirlwind going on around him. She wondered if he even understood what was happening.

"Mr. Wilson did not notice a third-party defense before trial. However, it seems clear that this information was not known to him before trial. Mr. Flagler, proper procedure would have been to bring this to the State—and the Court—before ambushing the detective on the stand. Although I will say that the detective seems remarkably unruffled by your revelation. I wonder if, perhaps, he appreciated the importance of the tracking data before Mr. Moore did. My inclination is to offer the State its choice of ways to proceed. We can take a brief continuance and pick things up next Monday, when you've had time to do whatever follow-up you deem necessary. Or, I could also declare a mistrial, and the parties can come back and try again another time."

At that, Eric and Marcus leaned in close, whispering furiously.

"Judge," Eric said, rising.

"Not right now, thank you. I want to hear Mr. Moore's position."

Nathan stood, his shoulders slumped. "We can come back on Monday."

As Mack moved toward the courtroom doors, a hand touched her arm. She looked up. Sheila. The two women went into the hall together.

"An interesting development," Sheila said.

Mack nodded noncommittally.

"Mr. Flagler must have one heck of an investigator to come up with that Instagram account."

"I suppose so."

"I know that you're on vacation, Mackenzie, and what you do with your vacation time is certainly up to you, but I don't recommend that you come back next Monday. Someone— Petrou, Mr. Campbell—might start thinking too hard about what a millennial prosecutor sitting on the defense side of the room does in her spare time. I strongly encourage you to remember what I said about insubordination."

Mack whipped her head toward her boss, who was casually examining her manicure. "I—I'm not sure what you mean."

Sheila met her eyes. There was no hint of humor or compassion on her face, just the steely glint that defense attorneys had long feared. "You and Sergeant Barton are close, I know. I imagine that the trauma you shared last year solidified your bond. And, of course, your friendship with Ms. Lafayette is well known. Some people might even suggest that if you were implicated in questionable or even unethical behavior, it would be likely that they were involved, too. Stay home next Monday, Mackenzie. Stay home, or go to the Grand Canyon or Seattle or Brisbane. But don't come to this trial again. Are you sure what I mean now?"

Mack swallowed hard and nodded. An elevator dinged.

"You go ahead," Sheila said. "I'll wait for the next one."

CHAPTER FORTY-EIGHT

They called the district attorney race on Friday night, when all of the mail-in and provisional ballots had been counted and then recounted. Peter Campbell would remain district attorney. Melissa O'Connor had lost by less than a hundred votes. As she swayed gently in her backyard hammock, a beer in hand, Mack watched the newscaster call it on her phone.

She wondered what Melissa would do next, and if Nick would go back to being just some defense attorney.

She looked out toward the mountains, amazed as always by the vibrant red sunset. She couldn't imagine a more beautiful place.

When her phone rang early Saturday morning, she woke with a start from a nightmare in which she was chasing Anna through the desert. Heart pounding, she fumbled to accept the call without looking at the screen. A tinny prerecorded voice came through the speaker.

"This is a collect call from the Tucson City Jail. Inmate"— she heard her father's voice inserting his name—"is calling you.

Be aware that this call is recorded and monitored. Press one to accept the call. Press two to reject the call. Press three to block all future calls from this inmate."

Mack almost dropped the phone in shock. In the six months he'd been in custody, this was the first time he'd called her. She pressed one.

"Dad? Are you okay? What's going on?"

"Everything's fine, Mack. I just wanted to catch you before you started getting ready to come down here for our visit today. I don't think you should come. There's a lot—well, there's a lot going on. I have a lot of stuff I need to talk to Eric about before we go back to court on Monday. I think it'll be easier if you're not here, okay?"

Mack slumped back against her pillows. "Sure, if that's what you want. No problem. I'm going to come on Monday, though, okay? I don't think you saw me the other day."

"No, Mackenzie. I don't want you there on Monday. I want you to stay as far away from this as you can. This is being recorded, you know that, right?"

Of course she knew it. How many times had she used a defendant's jail call statements against them? How many times had a family member let something slip? She'd even charged a defendant's brother with witness tampering based mostly on his attempts to speak in code during a recorded call about threatening an assault victim into recanting.

"I know. I won't come. I'll be thinking about you, though, okay? Maybe I'll watch the livestream."

"I love you, Mack. I won't call you again. I'm almost out of time on this call as it is. Tell your mom, too, okay? I love her and you both, and I—"

The sound of crying filled Mack's ear, and she tried to remember the last time she'd heard her dad cry.

"I love you, too, Dad. Everything is going to be okay. Really. Eric—well, Eric's a good attorney. He's doing what he can do. Everything is going to work out."

Abruptly, the call ended.

She spent the rest of the day in bed. She couldn't sleep, but the idea of getting up, doing chores, or going for a run held no appeal. Jess called, but Mack sent it straight to voice mail. She didn't want to be the recipient of the same sort of platitudes or encouragement she had earlier offered her dad, didn't want to ignore the feelings until she'd exhausted herself. Didn't want to do anything.

Sunday, though, Mack woke up ready to take a step back into the world. She showered and dressed in jeans and a ratty Dartmouth crewneck sweatshirt. Fall had finally come to Tucson.

She beat Jess to Millie's, put her name on the waitlist, and scanned the restaurant for anyone she might know. Sitting alone at a four-top with a copy of the Sunday *Arizona Republic* was Sheila Erlich. Mack groaned.

"Good morning," Jess called as she walked into the lobby.

Sheila looked up and smiled. "Good morning, ladies. Why don't you join me?"

"Was this a setup?" Mack whispered to Jess.

"Not exactly."

When their coffees were delivered and breakfasts ordered, Mack decided that enough was enough. "What's this all about? It feels very *Spy vs. Spy.*"

Jess looked away guiltily.

"Jessica happened to mention that you were having breakfast this morning, and I thought I'd join you. I wanted to talk to you both about what the future holds for you."

"What do you mean?" Mack asked.

"You were approached by the O'Connor campaign, and Campbell knows that. Even though Jessica was not approached, she appears to be guilty by association."

"Well, if they know Nick talked to me, they should know I turned him down, right?"

The waitress appeared with their breakfasts.

"They should," Sheila continued. "But what I'm hearing is that the administration believes your choice was not motivated by loyalty. They think you're likely to act as some sort of mole, doing oppo research for Mr. Campbell's next opponent, be that Melissa or someone else."

"So, what? They asked you to talk to me? To get me to quit? And Jess, who seriously didn't do anything?"

"No. I very much want you both to stay. Increasingly punitive policies are coming. The legislature has signaled its intent to make the penalties for fentanyl possession and distribution harsher. The rate of violent crime, including murder, is creeping upward for the first time in decades. What I need—and, not to put too fine a point on it, what Tucson needs—is prosecutors who are dedicated to the fair administration of justice, not just the blind execution of Pirate Pete's orders."

Mack blushed. She hadn't realized Sheila knew their old nickname for the district attorney.

"I, for one, am staying," Jess said. "I've thought a lot about leaving, especially after everything that happened last year. But there's nothing else I can see myself doing. I can't go to the dark side, not after this long in prosecution. I'm not qualified for anything outside of Criminal. The only thing open to me, really, is to stay and fight."

Mack methodically cut her omelet into small pieces. "Is there a risk?" she asked Sheila. "If we stay, will Campbell be out to get us? Or Michael Brown, or whoever?"

Sheila shrugged. "They might. But that hasn't stopped you so far. I was on the hiring panel the year you and Michael interviewed. Do you remember that?"

"No, I'm sorry."

"That's okay. There's no reason you should remember me. But I remember you. We ask every candidate if there are crimes they don't think should be prosecuted. Our idea is that the candidate will say no, and that answer is designed to start a conversation about whether or not it should be illegal to steal bread to feed your starving child. Morality, ethics, the big questions. But not you. You jumped in with 'Personal possession of marijuana shouldn't be illegal.' Oh, the stir you caused. Three people voted against hiring you just based off that answer. But I saw something in you. You were a fighter then, Mackenzie, and you're a fighter now. Stay the course. Keep fighting."

"What'd Mikey say?" Jess asked.

Sheila laughed. "He said if a parent was willing to break the law to feed a starving child, then CPS should take the kid. To no one's surprise, he flew through the hiring process with flying colors."

Mack sipped her coffee. "Okay," she said. "I'll stay."

CHAPTER FORTY-NINE

Mack was awake before six on Monday, and she spent the morning puttering around her house. Despite the brilliant blue sky and brisk breeze, she didn't want to go for a run. She didn't want to clean, or watch TV, or read a book. She just wanted the clock to tick to ten thirty, when the livestream of her father's trial would begin.

Finally, she settled on the couch with her laptop and a cup of coffee. As she waited for the feed to connect, she wondered what her dad must be thinking. Was he afraid of being wrongfully convicted? Hoping to get away with murder? There was no way to know.

The video showed an empty courtroom. Strange—it was almost ten thirty-five, and Judge Leyva was known for being a stickler about starting on time. Long moments passed before Nathan and Eric emerged from the hallway leading to chambers. Her father was brought to the defense table, shock belt and leg brace hidden beneath his suit. Judge Leyva took the bench.

"I know that we're running behind schedule this morning, but let's go ahead and memorialize the conversation we just had in chambers. Then we can put the witness back on the stand and continue. Mr. Moore?"

"Thank you, Judge. I'm sure Mr. Flagler will correct me if I misstate anything. I informed the Court and defense that Sergeant Barton was able to access the Instagram account and verify its contents. I still take issue with the late discovery, but I understand that that's not compelling to Your Honor. Sergeant Barton submitted a warrant for the Instagram account's user information and confirmed that it belongs to William Bradley Cameron. To the extent possible, Sergeant Barton was able to verify that Mr. Cameron lives—or lived, at the time—less than a mile from the victim's home. Sergeant Barton tried to contact Mr. Cameron several times between our last session and this morning but was unsuccessful. He was, therefore, not interviewed. The Court asked me in chambers whether I was willing to dismiss the case against Mr. Wilson at this time. I am not. With the forensic evidence, the motive, and the lies that Mr. Wilson told police, I believe—and my office believes—that there is still a reasonable likelihood of conviction.

"Also in chambers, I asked if a longer continuance was possible to locate Mr. Cameron and have him interviewed. Three jurors reported, however, that if this trial goes beyond their original screening date, we will lose them to preplanned vacations or work commitments. That would cause us to end in a mistrial. I think, therefore, that the only thing to do is move forward. If I am able to have Mr. Cameron interviewed, I will inform the Court and Mr. Flagler promptly, and we will reassess. Obviously, the possible outcomes will be different, depending on what he might have say. I might want to call him as a witness. Mr. Flagler might want to do the same. He could, I suppose, need counsel appointed."

"Good," Judge Leyva said. "That matches my recollection of our conversation. Mr. Flagler?"

"Nothing to add, Judge."

Mack half watched the rest of Eric's cross-examination of Dave. Since she had been the one to write the questions and knew what Dave would say, it didn't seem important to pay close attention. The evidence she'd gathered about Billy Bumble was circumstantial. None of it meant that her father couldn't have killed or didn't kill Amanda Wagner.

But trials weren't about what had happened, they were about what the State could prove beyond a reasonable doubt. (And how many mothers had she said that to, as an apology for her inability to charge cases where their daughters had been abused or assaulted?) Billy Bumble provided reasonable doubt, and that's what mattered.

Eric finally sat down, his cross finished, his points made. It had been an excellent presentation. Nathan stood, ready to redirect Dave, but there wasn't much point. It was clear that the damage had been done. What could he do, other than reemphasize the forensic evidence? Point out the lies in Marcus's police interview a second time?

Redirect didn't take long, and Mack respected Nathan's restraint. In his shoes, she would have beaten the dead horse all afternoon.

The jury had no questions for Dave. Their minds were made up, and Mack just wished she could tell who they believed. Had Eric broken the case wide open, or did they think he was grasping at straws?

"The State rests at this time," Nathan said.

The jury was excused for an early afternoon break so that Eric could make his Rule 20 motion for a directed verdict of acquittal and Judge Leyva could deny it with a smile.

"Is your client going to testify, Mr. Flagler?"

Eric turned to Marcus, and Mack held her breath. They hadn't talked about this. She had no idea what he was going to say, and she'd been going around in circles about the wisdom of it for months.

"No, Judge. I will not testify." His voice was steady. He was sure.

They moved on to final jury instructions and scheduling, and Mack turned off her computer. It was all over but the shouting, and she needed to go for a long, fast run.

CHAPTER FIFTY

The jury was out for less than a day, and Mack was on the treadmill Thursday afternoon when Dave's call came.

"This conversation never happened," he began.

Mack panted and wiped the sweat from her forehead. "What conversation?"

Dave chuckled. "The verdict is in. You've got forty-five minutes to get to court."

She hung up and rushed to the shower.

Ten minutes later, her hands were shaking as she buttoned her blouse and brushed her hair. The dark circles under her eyes were worse than ever.

Despite what Sheila had said—even despite Eric's and her father's warnings—Mack knew she needed to be there to hear the jury's decision. If they convicted, it was the last time she would be in a room with her father without a pane of mesh-enforced glass separating them. If they acquitted without her there, only Eric would be there to congratulate him. Everyone else in the room would be focused on grieving Amanda and the lack of resolution.

Mack knew from other cases that an acquittal could be as emotionally difficult for a defendant as a conviction. There was no reintegration process in place, no assistance in dealing with the trauma of having been incarcerated and abruptly released. She had even heard of guys who immediately committed crimes just to get back behind bars, where they had learned to be comfortable. Even after an acquittal, her father would need to see her friendly face.

She found Jess waiting for her outside the courtroom door. "Come on. Let's get seats on the defense side before they're taken by the media."

Mack felt tears gathering behind her eyes. "You didn't have to be here."

"Oh yes, I did. Your dad doesn't need me, but you do."

Inside, Mack was shocked to find Anna, saving two seats with her suit jacket and briefcase. Mack took the seat beside her and held hands with Anna and Jess.

The jurors didn't look at anyone when they came into the room, and Mack didn't know whether that was good or bad, under the circumstances.

Judge Leyva reviewed the verdict forms and handed them to the clerk.

"We the jury, duly empaneled, do hereby find the defendant as to Count One: Murder in the First Degree, to wit Amanda Wagner, not guilty."

A murmur swept through the gallery. The clerk turned to the next page.

"We the jury, duly empaneled, do hereby find the defendant as to Count Two: Kidnapping, not guilty."

Lisa Linden was openly weeping.

"We the jury, duly empaneled, do hereby find the defendant as to Count Three: Burglary in the First Degree, not guilty."

Anna gave Mack a one-armed hug and stood, leaving the courtroom before the clerk could read the final verdict form.

"We the jury, duly empaneled, do hereby find the defendant as to Count Four: Murder in the First Degree, to wit unborn child, not guilty."

Mack exhaled shakily.

"Thank you to the members of our diligent jury," Judge Leyva said. "The justice system could not function without you, and I hope that you did not find this process too onerous. Your service is complete, and you are hereby released."

Once the jury was gone, the judge turned back to Marcus. Mack could see the relief on her father's face. "Mr. Wilson, you have been acquitted. In the absence of any other open cases, you will be taken back to the jail to be processed and released. I wish you good luck in the future, and I say sincerely that I hope to never see you again in my courtroom."

Mack tried to keep her emotions in check, tried to look like any other prosecutor observing a major verdict. She watched Nathan, who hadn't moved from his seat. His eyes were closed, and he gripped a pen in both hands.

"Let's go," Jess said, eyeing Dan Petrou across the courtroom. He was speaking into his phone in a low voice, no doubt recording the next episode of his podcast.

In the elevator, Mack's composure dissolved.

"Where are you headed this afternoon?" Jess asked.

"I'm not sure," Mack said, wiping her nose with the back of her hand. She'd forgotten tissues in her rush to get out of the house. "Either straight home to throw myself into the shower and stand there until I prune, or just driving until I run out of gas."

The elevator stopped. Sheila and Judge McPhee stepped in together. Mack straightened her back and did her best not to make any noise, ignoring that her red face and swollen eyes were dead giveaways of her emotional state.

"Ah, Mackenzie," Sheila said. "Nice to see you. I assume you'll be back at work in the morning? Let's meet at eight to go over the changes in your cases."

Mack nodded. Her mandatory vacation must be over.

"That's perfect," Judge McPhee said. "Because I was hoping you'd have time to discuss your trial advocacy and recent experience in my division. Say eleven, if Ms. Erlich will be done with you by then."

The four women rode quietly to the ground floor.

"Come on," Jess said. "I'll drive you home."

"What about my car?"

"Leave it. You can Uber in in the morning. You're in no condition to drive."

Mack also wasn't in any condition to argue, so she wordlessly followed Jess to her Infiniti and slumped against the cool leather.

Jess turned on the car and turned down her stereo, which had started blasting the Jonas Brothers.

"Really?" Mack asked.

"I like that one song. Just that one, though."

"It's catchy. I'll give you that."

Mack let her eyes drift closed and was surprised when she opened them to find that they were pulling into her driveway. She must have fallen asleep.

Jess grabbed a duffel bag out of her back seat and trailed Mack into the house. "I talked to Anna, and we thought maybe I should stay, if that's okay with you?"

Mack nodded and went straight into the kitchen, kicking off her heels. She pulled a bottle of Svedka from the freezer and set two glasses on the counter. She downed a first liberal pour without speaking, then refilled her glass.

"This feels like a stupid question under the circumstances," Jess said. "But how are you feeling?"

"I am choosing to believe they got it right," Mack said. "Because, really, I have two options. I can agonize over this for the rest of my life—did I help a murderer walk free, did I put the community at risk to serve my own interests, did I do the same thing we see countless women do when they believe the men in their lives over their own senses?—or I can believe I did the right thing. People *do* get wrongfully convicted. That really is a thing that happens. Imma choose to believe I prevented that from happening."

Jess sipped from her own glass but didn't respond.

"Why don't you order dinner?" Mack asked. "I'm going to get in the shower. Should I be expecting any more company this evening?"

Jess shook her head.

Mack wasn't ready to ask why Anna had been in court that day. After all the drama of the previous year, she wasn't sure she wanted to know if Anna and Jess were in cahoots. She couldn't decide which would be worse—if they'd formed an independent friendship, or if Jess had reached out to her for the special occasion of the verdict. Either way, fleeing the jurisdiction was looking like a better and better option.

* * *

Mack was on the couch, her hair wrapped in a towel, when the doorbell rang. She set down the water Jess had handed her after her shower and went to retrieve the Thai delivery, only to find her father on her doorstep.

"Like déjà vu all over again," she said, stepping outside to join him and pulling the door shut behind her. She wrapped her arms around herself, shivering in the cool evening air.

Marcus shoved his hands in the pockets of his jeans. "I came to say I'm leaving town, getting out of your hair."

Mack's eyes widened. "So soon?"

"Yeah, well, I'm a little soured on this place, all things considered. And I've caused you enough trouble for a lifetime, so it seems like the best thing for everyone. Don't you think?"

Mack sighed and sat on the bench beside her door. "I don't know what I think anymore. I have to ask you, I have to know—"

"Mack, despite everything, getting to spend time with you these last few months has been one of the best things I've ever gotten to do. I'm very proud of you, and who you've become."

"I—thanks, Dad. Thank you."

"Mack, look at me." He smiled. "I didn't kill her, honey. I swear it."

She remembered that smile. It was the smile he used to get women to do what he wanted. The smile he flashed at cops to get out of tickets...

She shook off the memories. Either she was going to trust him or not.

She made her decision.

"Where will you go?" she asked.

He shrugged uneasily and leaned against the wall. "I'm flying to Cleveland tomorrow morning. At least for a while. Your mom's picking me up at the airport. I'll spend some time with her, see some old friends. Then I'll go where the work takes me, like I always have."

The delivery guy walked up and paused, uncertain who to hand the bag to. Mack stood and accepted it. She hoped Jess had tipped when she ordered, because she didn't have any cash. She laughed. What a stupid thing to care about at that moment.

Marcus placed a hand on her shoulder and squeezed gently. "I love you, kiddo."

"I love you, too, Dad."

She watched him walk away. He didn't look back.

It wasn't until Mack had locked the door behind her that she realized her father's glib response hadn't actually answered her half-formed question. Was he intentionally deceiving her, or had their wires simply gotten crossed, as they had so many times before? She knew what her mother would say—she was reading too much into it, expecting too much from him. Was it true, this time? Had he been honest, despite her inability to believe him?

"You two were out there a while," Jess said. They'd divvied up the green curry shrimp and were sipping pumpkin porters at Mack's kitchen table. "You okay?"

Mack shook her head. "No. But I will be."

CHAPTER FIFTY-ONE

The meeting with Sheila was both less stressful and more stressful than Mack had anticipated. Not much had changed in her cases, so they'd wrapped up their official business in twenty minutes. Mack was aware, however, of a steady stream of prosecutors and staff members walking past Sheila's corner office, all "subtly" sneaking peeks at her.

"Everyone knows, huh?"

Sheila took off her glasses and put her hands behind her head. "Everyone knows you were out for a couple of weeks— while the case you were walled off from was tried—and now are back. That's always an exciting thing. If you're asking whether or not they know the reason you were walled off, I couldn't say. Rumors spread like wildfire around here, but my office seems to be oddly insulated. I never hear anything."

Mack stood and gathered her files.

"If you're asking my opinion, though, I'd suggest insulating your office in the same fashion. You've got the Brecht case set for trial in two weeks, so you certainly have more important things to focus on than idle chatter."

Mack was late to Judge McPhee's division. She'd gotten absorbed in trial prep and hadn't even found time to sort through the emails that had accumulated while she was out.

The judge waved aside her apologies and gestured at the leather couch she reserved for preferred visitors. "I hope you're not offended, but Sheila did tell me a little about your situation after we saw you yesterday afternoon. It's incredible that you had to balance all of that during the Ferguson trial. How are you doing?"

Mack smiled. "It was easy to put it aside and focus on the case." That wasn't true, really, but she didn't need to tell the judge that every day she had come closer to letting the spinning plates crash down around her.

"We can talk about your trial performance if you wish, but that's not really why I wanted to see you."

Mack waited, tense. Judge McPhee was known for these postmortems, but if she didn't want to critique Mack's trial skills, then what did she want?

"Do you think I was too hard on Daisy?"

Mack sat up straight. "What?"

"Daisy. Your victim. I let him cross-examine her for so long and I—I just…Should I have done more to protect her?"

Mack had no idea what to say. Yes, she did think Judge McPhee should have done more. She always thought the judge should do more. She also thought defense attorneys should be kind and criminals shouldn't crime in the first place. The world would be much nicer if Mack's thoughts had any power to cause change.

"I think…you did what you could to protect the appellate record, and that protects Daisy. If she had to go through a retrial, she'd be worse off."

"She seemed so tough, but after a while I wondered if that was just a front. Eventually I saw her as a scared little girl going up against her father. Her abuser, too, of course, but he's still her father."

"It was cathartic, I think. For her. She didn't believe she'd survive standing up to him, and now she knows she can."

Judge McPhee smiled. "She certainly showed him he can't boss her around anymore. I like that kid. She's a firecracker. Do you know what she plans to do from here?"

"I don't. She didn't really seem interested in confiding in me, and she doesn't view the system as a friendly force. I'll ask Detective Wood. Sometimes those bonds are stronger."

Judge McPhee had a faraway look in her eyes, and Mack saw herself out. She wondered what about Daisy had specifically resonated with the judge.

Mack couldn't take the whole day, and, after lunch with Jess at the deli down the street, she slipped home. She fell into bed and into a deep, dreamless sleep.

When the ringtone woke her, it was dark, and she struggled to find her phone in the sheets.

"Hi, Dave."

She could hear sirens and people talking in the background.

"Mack. There's been another murder. Same MO as Amanda Wagner."

Mack's heart stopped beating. "Do you have an estimated time of death?"

"About five this afternoon. Now that we're getting things situated, Detective Caldwell asked me to call."

"Craig?"

"Yeah, he's the case agent. Do you...do you know where your dad is?"

She hung up without responding. Of course Craig wanted the killer to be her father.

He had always had a grudge against her, and he was still out to get her. If he could demonstrate that her father was a killer, that would end her career.

But, personal animosity aside, could he be right? What if her father was a sadist, a killer, and he'd claimed another victim? Was she now responsible for the death of a second woman?

But her dad was in Cleveland. He'd taken a morning flight. Hadn't he?

Mack picked up her phone, not caring about the three-hour time difference, and called her mother.

The phone rang.

"Please," she said, not sure who she was asking and not really caring. "Please let her pick up."

The phone rang a second time.

She could feel panic rising. Her palms were sweaty, and her breathing was shallow and jagged.

A third time.

"*Please*," she said again, now fighting tears. "Let her be okay, and I'll never ask for anything again."

On the fourth ring, just as Mack was giving up hope, someone picked up the phone.

"Mack," her mother said, her voice thick with sleep. "Are you okay? Do you have any idea what time it is?"

"It's late, I know. But, Mom, it's important. Did you see Dad today? Did you pick him up from the airport?"

"He's right here, honey. Do you want to talk to him?"

Mack slumped back in her bed, relief flooding through her. "No, that's okay. I just saw him last night. Let him sleep. I love you, Mom."

"Love you too, baby," her mom said and ended the call.

Mack wasn't sure what to do. She wasn't on call, couldn't go to the scene even if she wanted to. Despite the fact that her father couldn't have committed this murder, the appearance of impropriety would keep her from participating in the investigation. It was too late to call Jess, who probably had her phone on Do Not Disturb since she was in trial.

Mack made a decision and placed a call. It went to voice mail, and she smiled in spite of herself as she listened to the familiar outgoing message.

"Hey," she said after the beep. "Anna, it's me. Does that coffee offer still stand? Call me back, okay?"

Acknowledgments

To the team at Bella Books, thank you doesn't even begin to cover it, especially Heather Flournoy, whose deft editorial touch makes this a breeze. You have all welcomed me with open arms and make writing feel like a treat instead of a chore.

To my wonderful and supportive readers, your willingness to embrace a flawed protagonist is a dream.

This book, like its author, has benefitted from the training and experience of innumerable police officers, attorneys, and judges I have known during my career, not to mention victim advocates, psychologists, and other criminal-justice professionals. There are too many of you to name, but I am much obliged to you all.

I want to recognize everyone who helped me get the science, law, and process right in this book. Any mistakes I've made are my own, and you probably tried to warn me. I am especially grateful to Stefanie Walesch, Eli Ditlevson (without whose patience and insight this book would not exist), Kyra Goddard, Erin Pedicone, Jenny Carper, Jordyn Raimondo, Ariel Serafin, and Drs. Tina Garby, Holly Salisbury, and Nicole Pondell. As always, it's not a criminal conspiracy if it's just research.

My parents remain incredible sources of support. Thank you to Victoria Jones for giving me the audacity to say "I think I want to write a book"—and then do it two more times. Thank you to Josh Pachter, editor extraordinaire, for introducing me to crime fiction, encouraging me to keep going, and always helping me keep my head above water.

The world-famous luchador El Resque, who is an amazingly dedicated prosecutor in the real world, is everything Mack wishes she could be when she grows up. Thank you for being such a good role model for both of us.

More Titles from Bella Books

Hunter's Revenge – Gerri Hill
978-1-64247-447-3 | 276 pgs | paperback: $18.95 | eBook: $9.99
Tori Hunter is back! Don't miss this final chapter in the acclaimed
Tori Hunter series.

Integrity – E. J. Noyes
978-1-64247-465-7 | 228 pgs | paperback: $19.95 | eBook: $9.99
It was supposed to be an ordinary workday...

The Order – TJ O'Shea
978-1-64247-378-0 | 396 pgs | paperback: $19.95 | eBook: $9.99
For two women the battle between new love and old loyalty may prove
more dangerous than the war they're trying to survive.

Under the Stars with You – Jaime Clevenger
978-1-64247-439-8 | 302 pgs | paperback: $19.95 | eBook: $9.99
Sometimes believing in love is the first step. And sometimes it's all
about trusting the stars.

The Missing Piece – Kat Jackson
978-1-64247-445-9 | 250 pgs | paperback: $18.95 | eBook: $9.99
Renee's world collides with possibility and the past, setting off a tidal
wave of changes she could have never predicted.

An Acquired Taste – Cheri Ritz
978-1-64247-462-6 | 206 pgs | paperback: $17.95 | eBook: $9.99
Can Elle and Ashley stand the heat in the *Celebrity Cook Off* kitchen?